LIVING WITHOUT

CAROLINE SPRINGS CHARTER

LILA ROSE

Second Edition 2019
ISBN: 978-0648483557

To MariaLisa deMora — Having your Rebels men helping out the Hawks has been a true honour. I adore you, my friend.

Thank you!

DISCLAIMER

Warning: This book contains explicit sexual situations, violence, disturbing sensitive and taboo subjects, offensive language, and very mature topics. Recommended for age 18 years and up

CHAPTER ONE

NARY

*a*t the age of twenty, some would think I would have known what I wanted with my life. I didn't. No, that wasn't right. I knew where I wanted my career to go at least. What my mind was up in the air about was my love life.

As I walked to my car, my thoughts wandered. It was only then I realised it was so late. The stars shone while the cool air held a scent of rain. I found myself glad my uni had enough lights around to spotlight the car park. I pulled my eyes down to my watch; I was late for my pizza date, and no doubt, Jerimiah would be worried. Especially when he found out I hadn't left the media room with a group of people like I'd told him I would. Regret formed low in my belly, churning it. I'd wanted time alone to work on my assignment, so it was my own stupid fault for lying and becoming paranoid someone was watching me.

Thinking of Jerimiah, a smile formed on my mouth and I couldn't help but picture the time I'd met him. He had been in my business class; it had been the only one we'd shared together, and throughout it, he'd kept glancing over at me. Of course I noticed out the corner of my eyes, who wouldn't, especially when the best-looking guy in there tried to catch my attention. As soon as I met his gaze, he'd smiled and waved. Then he'd actually blushed. I'd offered an attentive smile back and gazed back down to my work. It was the next class where I'd found the—usually free—seat next to me occupied by Jerimiah. My heart had skipped a beat and my stomach had started playing havoc, as if there was a stampede of tiny bulls running wild in there. As soon as I'd sat, he'd turned to me and introduced himself. From that day on, we'd become close, having coffee with each other, going to the movies, and spending hours studying together.

This was despite Jerimiah being a part of the Venom MC, a club that brought my family's MC club, the Hawks, nothing but trouble. I'd discovered about his membership two years earlier, but that hadn't stopped us forming a relationship.

It had been two weeks after Jerimiah and I had met and become friends—with a side of something else, something that warmed my belly—when I'd gone to the Hawks compound in search of either Josie or Low. I'd needed advice.

I open the front office door to the side mechanical business at the compound, only to find the office empty. With a frown, I walk to the door that opens into the garage. Stepping out, I see Muff, a biker brother to the Caroline Springs Hawks charter.

"Hey, Muff. Do you know if Low or Josie is here?"

"Nah, babe. I think Josie is at uni and Low's out with Dive somewhere."

"Nary," is bit out behind me. Straightaway, I know who it is. I know his voice, regardless of the tone, anywhere. Though with me, it's always growly, snappy, or short.

Turning, I face Saxon. He's the one man who takes my breath away, who stole my heart when I was sixteen, who is on my mind constantly. Even when he's a prick to me, my heart doesn't seem to care. Though my mind often tells me to forget about him.

"Saxon?"

"Office, now," he clips before he turns and steps back into the office.

Listening to my mind, which tells me to ignore his order and get out of there, isn't an option, especially when my heart beats faster in his presence. It has me following him silently.

Moving through the door, I stop just on the other side to find Saxon already near the front entrance with his arms crossed over his chest scowling at me. "Dodge wants to see you in his office out back."

My head jerks back. Why couldn't he have told me that in front of Muff?

When I realise that's all he wants to say, my shoulders sag in defeat. He holds nothing in his heart for me, and I have to stop holding out hope for him. Looking to the floor, I nod, turn, and walk back into the garage. Anger has me slapping my feet on the concrete floor harder than usual as I stomp towards Dodge's office. Another question slips into my mind. Why does Dodge want to see me in his office?

Ignoring it, I come to the door and swing it open. My eyes widen when I notice it isn't only Dodge in there, but other members fill the space and the room is thick with tension.

"Nary?" Dodge asks.

"Oh, um...." My eyes shift around the room, and a gasp falls from my lips. "You, you're... no," I whisper before turning and running back down the hall. Seeing Jerimiah standing in there, behind a man who looks like him wearing a Venom MC vest, slices hurt through me. Even in the two weeks I knew him, he could have said something.

He hadn't.

I bolt through the garage, as someone calls out to me, but I ignore him and keep running, right outside. My chest hurts with the breath I try to gulp in from the shock and adrenaline pounding through me. With fast movements, I make it to my car and unlock it. However, before I get in, I look back to the garage once, and I wish I hadn't.

Standing outside, leaning against the brick wall is Saxon and on his handsome face is a smirk.

That day I finally realised Saxon and I would never be anything to each other.

The knowledge had settled deep within my lower abdomen, causing it to churn with a hollowed sadness.

I'd always hoped, always believed he would have eventually seen what we could have been one day.

He'd known who I would see in the room that day. And he'd been happy my heart had hurt at the betrayal that had sliced through me from Jerimiah keeping something from me.

The whole scene had angered me, and yet my heart still cared for Saxon.

Honestly, I had started to consider my heart as a second person because my mind was on a different path to what my heart had felt. My mind was sick of my unrequited love for Saxon. Rejection stung. It wanted to move on, and it could with a guy like Jerimiah. Which was why I had been officially dating Jerimiah for the last four months. He'd come to my apartment two years ago, after that night I'd discovered he was a part of Venom and explained his whole situation of having a controlling father. He didn't want to be with Venom, and he'd told me as soon as he could, he'd make the move to leave. From the time I'd already spent with him, I'd felt as though I could trust him, and his words. So I continued being his friend, until twenty months later when he'd kissed me one night. The touch of his lips had sent my body into a wave of desire.

He was sweet, caring, rough, and just what I'd needed.

He showed me I was worth something. His time and feelings.

Even a part of my heart warmed to the idea of letting it all go to Jerimiah. He treated me right. He didn't ignore me or look at me with disgust in his eyes. He didn't think I was being a stupid girl with a small crush.

Saxon had been hurtful on so many occasions, so why

couldn't I let my whole heart fall for Jerimiah and let go of what I tried to cling to for Saxon? I should hate him. He wanted me to. He tried to get me to in so many ways.

Sighing, I unlocked my car door and tried to rid my thoughts of Saxon. Besides, I was heading home to meet with Jerimiah for a study date, which would probably end up in a make-out session. My boyfriend was sweet and very thoughtful. He was hot, as in smoking, and his smile always brought one of my own to my mouth.

"Nary." My name was yelled from across the yard. Looking up, I spotted Josie standing near the building, under the light, smiling wide and waving. I giggled to myself. Jerimiah had probably called her or one of her guys to make sure I made it to my car safely. Jerimiah had wanted to stay back with me, but I'd told him not to because I was safe at the always-bustling university, no matter the time of the day or night.

Everyone who had a connection to the Hawks MC was more cautious because of Baxter Davis. He had it out for all members of Hawks and wanted us to pay in one way or another. I wasn't sure why he had a vendetta against my Hawks family, but it was there, and until someone put a stop to him, we all had to be careful, making sure no one was alone.

Still, I thought no one would be stupid enough to try anything at the university. As I looked to Josie and offered a smile and wave back, I noticed all the people walking or rushing around, either coming from the cafeteria or going out for the night. Just behind Josie, my eyes landed on Billy.

He somehow saw my gaze and offered me a chin lift. What could have helped his view of me was the street lamp I'd purposefully parked under. My friend was one lucky woman having two men at her back. Two men who loved her so deeply, they were willing to share. She deserved happiness.

"I'll see you tomorrow," I yelled with another wave. I wanted to get in the car so I could get to my place and Jerimiah. My stomach growled at the thought of the delicious pizza. It also flipped at the thought of the man who would be waiting for me. Things were progressing well with Jerimiah and myself. We hadn't moved to the final stage of the relationship. Something was holding me back from sleeping with him. Yet, we still fooled around and a thrill bubbled up inside me each time, even when the learning process was sometimes embarrassing. Still, Jerimiah was patient, and he enjoyed teaching as much as I loved experiencing.

As I threw my bag across to the passenger seat and I was about to slide in myself, my name was screeched across the area. My gaze rose to see Josie running for me. Billy was on her heels and about to take over her as he reached into the back of his jeans and pulled a gun, pointed right at me.

My eyes widened. A scream built in my throat, but it never erupted from my mouth because a hand covered it.

My eyes connected with Josie's. Fear. All I could see was fear. My stomach dropped in panic. My body trembled in terror. People roared in alarm as a shot was fired. My captor, a man, something I could tell from the large body

7

behind me, cursed as I was roughly pulled down to the ground. A car's engine revved high near us. I craned my neck back to try to get my mouth free. I couldn't. Still, I screamed behind it. I kicked, grabbed hold of the arm holding me around the waist, and ripped into the skin with my fingernails. He swore and jolted me back and forth hard against him. "Stop," he warned.

Why wasn't anyone doing anything?

I heard more screams around me. People rushing our way. People running away. Another shot was fired. It pinged off the roof of the car just before I was pulled up and shoved inside. I yelled, kicking out at the man trying to get in after me. He grabbed my leg and bent it in a way that I cried out in pain.

He shoved harder, and I scooted back and tried the other door. Even though the lock wasn't in place, the door wouldn't open. I growled in frustration at my attempt. I banged my fists against the glass. I screamed, cried, while tears ran freely down my cheeks.

Nothing worked.

No one helped me in time.

The car sped away with me inside it.

Frantically, I climbed to my knees. My hands went to the back window. Billy was there, standing in the middle of the road, lights shinning down on him. I saw the gun pointed right at us. Though he didn't fire, no doubt worried it would hit me. His face crumpled in rage before he threw his hands up in the air and screamed. Josie ran onto the road and started for the car. I could no longer see her face clearly through my own tears and the darkness surrounding us, but I knew she would be feeling everything I was.

Pure horror.

My hair was grasped and my head tugged back. The man sitting next to me moved his face close to mine. He was in his early thirties, with a shaved head, a beard, and blue eyes that told me I was not in a nightmare. I was living one, and he would be happy to deliver some pain.

"Sit the fuck down," he bit out. "You'd better behave. I don't have to deliver you fully intact," he commented before he harshly pushed me back to my bottom in the corner of the car.

"D-do you know who I am?" I asked on a whisper. Glancing to the man in the front driving the car, who drove like a crazy person, I saw his gaze flick to me. Hard, dark green eyes stared back for a second before they went back to the road.

"Nope, and I don't give a fuck. I was told to keep an eye on you, grab you when I could, so I did." He eyed me up and down my body, a smirk spread across his face. "Boss Baxter knows when a good thing would pay and, honey, people will wanna pay big bucks for you." He studied my face and abruptly asked, "How'd you get the scar?"

"A gun shot."

"What happened to the person who gave it to you?"

"He's dead. Just like you will be if you don't let me go. My family will do anything to get me back."

He scoffed. "Yeah? And who's your family?"

Sitting up, I jutted my chin out in fake bravado and replied, "The Hawks MC."

His gaze went to the driver's in the rear-view mirror. The driver shrugged and my captor turned back to me. "Like I said, don't give a fuck. You'll be outta my hair and in my boss' soon enough, and then it becomes his problem."

Licking my dry lips, I laughed without humour. "If you think so. But I can tell you now, the men of Hawks harm everyone involved when taking what belongs to them. Everyone."

His jaw clenched. He shifted forward and pulled something from his back pocket. "You're annoying me. Time to go bye-bye." His arm shot out and I looked down as a taser was placed against my stomach. With one shock, I was out.

CHAPTER TWO

DODGE

*M*y woman sat on the edge of my desk in my office at the garage. We'd just come from my room in the compound next door, and fuck, she had an I-just-had-the-best-sex-of-my-life look on her gorgeous face. Of course it was true; I was all male in the bedroom.

"Handsome, I have to go get Texas and Rommy from Jason, so kiss me like it's our last breath."

Smiling up at her from my seat, I reached my hand up, until my fucking phone rang. "Hold that thought, little bird." One hand went to her thigh, while the other picked up the landline with a brisk, "What?"

"Fuck, fuck me, Dodge," Billy chanted into the phone.

Snorting, I quickly said, "You're not my type."

"She's been taken."

His words caused my body to stiffen. Low, sensing it, stood while I sank back in the chair and breathed out a growled, "Josie?"

"No, Nary."

Standing abruptly, I ordered, "Christ. Tell me how in the fuck it happened and when?"

"Uni, in the school car park just now. I wasn't fuckin' fast enough. I got my woman crying in my arms. I'm getting her to the compound."

"Baxter?" I asked.

"No one else is dumb enough to fuck with us. Has to be. Call everyone in, brother."

"On it," I barked and shut down the phone. My eyes went to my woman. Hers were wide with worry. "Take Knife and go get the kids. I need you to be strong for them, little bird."

"Who was taken, Trey?" she whispered; she must have heard Billy.

"Baby, the kids—"

"Who?" she demanded.

"Nary."

"No," she cried, tears pooling in her eyes. I moved and wrapped her in my arms. "Not Nary, she's... she..."

"Little bird, the kids."

She shook her head and looked up at me. "I'll ask Jason to have them overnight. They don't need to know anything, and they love hanging out with him."

"Low," I started.

"No. You will need me. *Josie* will need me. I'm here. I'm staying with you, Trey, and no one can move my arse."

My forehead pressed against hers. I closed my eyes for a second before I opened them again and met her determined ones. "Okay, baby. Call Jason and then come into the compound. Billy's bringing Josie there." I moved to the door.

"Where are you going?" she called.

My hand was on the doorknob, but I turned back and said, "I have to tell Saxon." Her gasp said it all. Shit was about to hit the fan. We needed to find Nary, and soon, or it wouldn't be only Saxon losing his shit. I'd have to call in Stoke, Nary's stepdad, from the Hawks Ballarat charter, and he'd come with vengeance on his mind.

Hell, not that it wasn't already on mine. No one touched a Hawks member, especially Nary, who was like our club princess. Blood would soon be spilt.

Stepping out the door, I called, "Beast, Dallas, with me, now." I kept walking, knowing Saxon was in the compound. I'd seen him when Low and I had walked from my room earlier.

"What's goin' on?" Dallas asked in a rough tone. He'd already sensed something was happening from my pinched lips and drawn brows. Beast would already know as well; he just wouldn't say anything.

"Nary's been taken, gonna inform Saxon."

"Fuckin' hell," Dallas clipped low.

SAXON

I stood at the bar with Handle and Gamer. I'd just taken another shot of whiskey when the door, which led into the garage, came open with a bang. All eyes went there, and I swear, the room filled with tension when our president, along with Dallas and Beast, walked in.

Something had happened. Something bad if I read their solemn expressions right. They scanned the room—brothers sat around just shooting the shit. But Dodge didn't focus on anyone, so I wondered if what he had to tell us was something regarding the fuckstick Baxter. He was a dick who wanted Hawks taken down. He'd had a hard-on for Hawks since Talon turned him down fucking years ago to become a member and since Dodge beat the hell out of him in a backyard brawl. Which was when Talon had approached Dodge to become Hawks.

Dodge stepped up to the bar and gestured to Muff behind the counter. Muff quickly poured him a shot. It was then I felt heat at my back, only I didn't look there because Dodge started talking, his gaze down on the bench.

"I need you to keep your cool, brother."

Looking to Handle, he shrugged. Who in the hell was Dodge talking to?

Then he raised his hard-as-fuck eyes to me.

My jaw clamped tight, my body stood tall, only to stiffen. The only reason he'd ask for my cool was if something had happened to... "Nary?" I whispered on a growl.

He nodded once. "She's been taken."

One second.

Two.

Three.

Rage hit me. I threw my head back and screamed through the pain slicing over and over my heart. My eyes narrowed, my voice stilled. I flung my arm out, taking all the drinks on the bar to the ground. I picked up a stool and threw it across the floor. Someone grabbed me. I spun, punching the person in the face. He went down.

Another brother wrapped their arms around my shoulders, drawing me back against them. I fought, my hands grabbing their arms to remove them. Even if I ripped them from their body, I didn't care. Only, the fucker was strong. I shifted my head forward and threw it back hard and collided with a nose.

The person cursed, his arms loosening, but before I could move, I was taken to the ground.

"Get the fuck off me," I clipped harshly. My heart pumped hard behind my ribs. My mind kept playing the words over and over. *She's been taken. She's been taken. She's been taken.*

"Saxon!" Dodge yelled, leaning over, his face in mine.

My vision cleared of red and I settled, blinking up at him. "Billy's coming in with the information. You need to get it under wraps, brother. We'll need you on this to find her."

She's been taken. She's been taken. She's been taken.

I narrowed my eyes. My head spun to the fucker holding me to the ground. Dallas.

"Fuck," Dodge bit out before he stood. "He's gone again. Get him to calm down. He's useless otherwise." Dodge sighed.

Dallas shifted and that was all I needed. I scrambled up to my knees from under him and made a move to run for the door.

"Take him down," Dodge demanded.

Brothers came at me. I managed to knock two to the ground before I was grabbed and dragged from the room. Still, I didn't let up. I struggled and fought.

"I'm gonna kill him. Fuckin' gut him," I roared.

"Who?" Dodge asked from somewhere.

"Fang. He was supposed to watch her. He goddamn swore he'd take care of her. I'll kill him. Shoot him between the eyes."

The door before me opened and I was thrown in, landing on my hands and knees.

"Take a moment," Dallas ordered. "We'll find him and get answers. She'll need you, Vicious. She'll need you to be fully aware to help find her."

"And then I kill?"

"Then you kill, with us at your back," he promised.

The door was slammed shut behind me and locked, but still I didn't move. I didn't move because I was bleeding. Only no one could see the blood. It was on the inside.

Red.

Rage.

One second.

Two.

Three.

I was up and destroying the room. My mind wild, my heart bleeding, and my soul shattering. She'd been taken. Not Nary. Anyone but her.

Fuck.

Christ.

TWO HOURS LATER

STOKE

It wasn't too late at night when my phone rang on the bedside table. We'd gone to bed early, because I'd worked my arse off at the construction site. My woman was sitting up before I'd even moved. Rolling, I snapped the phone up and answered, "Yo?"

"Stoke. Dodge. You need to come to Caroline Springs, brother."

I was sitting before the movement registered with my brain. Fuck. Something had happened. His voice... Dodge's voice was rough with fear.

Shifting so I was sitting on the side of the bed, my feet planted on the floor. I barked into the phone, "Brother?"

"Just get here, bring Mally and Josh."

Hell. My gut dropped. My heart pounded.

Nary.

Something had happened to our girl.

"On it." I hung up the phone. Standing, I turned to my woman who was also ready and standing on the other side of the bed. Her brows were drawn low in worry, her mouth pinched tight in fear. "Get Josh, pack what you can, but hurry, love."

"Declan?" Her hand went to her throat.

"I don't know, love. He didn't say anything. Let's just get going, yeah?"

With a nod, she raced from the room to wake Josh. I wished to Christ my feet could move, but panic overrode my senses and I was frozen to the spot.

Something had happened to our girl.

Christ.

Blood will spill.

Shaking off my fear, I pulled a bag from under the bed to pack some shit. I also reminded myself to grab the bag filled with weapons from the garage before we left.

In no matter of time, I was out the front door and heading to the car with my woman and our eighteen-year-old son. All of us remained silent, in our own concerned thoughts. All I knew was I was about to break a few speeding laws to get to the Hawks compound in Caroline Springs.

A door behind us banged. Just before we all climbed into the car, we looked over and saw Mrs Cliff heading our way.

"Mrs Cliff?" Mally called.

Only, the old bat's eyes were on me, and she ordered,

"Get the fuck in and drive, but I'm coming with you lot and no one will stop me."

Not in the mood to argue, I did what she said, sending her a chin lift and getting into the car.

Once we were on the road, Josh asked, "How'd you know something was happening?"

Looking through the rear-view mirror, I saw her shrug. Then a smirk came onto her face and she said, "I have your phones tapped."

Josh paled and whispered, "What?"

She barked a laugh and shoved him. "Just kidding, son. I don't want to hear all your phone-sex calls with your girlies."

I smirked and looked to my woman to see she was smiling also. Mrs Cliff always knew how to ease the tension. Though, we all knew it wouldn't leave.

And yet, it only worsened when a roar of Harleys pulled onto the road behind us as we hit the highway.

My brothers had my back.

Dodge had called them in. That meant whatever we were about to find out was going to break us all.

Fuck.

Forcing one hand from gripping the steering wheel to take my woman's hand, I rested them on her thigh. The car filled with silence once again. We all knew. We all prepared ourselves in our own way. But I'd make fucking sure we'd be there for one another.

Even if my heart was in my throat, I was ready to hurt any motherfucker, if they'd hurt my girl.

ONE HOUR LATER

SAXON

Fucked if I knew how long I'd been in the room. What I did know was that my mind wouldn't stop. As I sat on the small cot in the corner of the room, I gripped my hair and tugged. Still, the pain wouldn't take away my panic for Nary. Nothing could. Lowering my hands, I looked to my scraped knuckles. No matter how much I punched the walls over and over, my mind kept running through the scenarios of what they'd be doing to her.

Fuck.

Jesus.

Stop, stop, stop.

She'll be safe. We'll make her safe.

My body stilled. I raced to the door. Had it been? Yes, another scream hit the building, followed by, "No, not my daughter. No!"

Closing my eyes, I rested my forehead against the door. I envisioned Stoke's woman, Nary's mum, clinging to her man after finding out her daughter was taken. Her heart would be fracturing in fear like mine had.

More yelling started. A few thumps, like some things were being thrown and then muffled talking. They weren't quiet, yet with the hall and all doors closed, I couldn't hear what was being said.

I wanted to be out there. I needed all the information so I could hunt for Nary.

So they couldn't touch her.

Taint her mind.

"Fuck," I bit out low.

Be strong, angel. I'm coming.

Christ, it was killing me being locked up, knowing she was in the hands of a fucked-up man. I needed my head. I needed to show them I *sort of* had my head. Though, it was too soon to say I'd keep it once I got my hands on a few people. Jerimiah for one.

My ears pricked up at the sound of the hall door being whacked open and hitting the wall. Loud pounding foot-steps approached the room. They'd better be there to let me the hell out.

I took a few steps away from the door and waited.

The door was unlocked and flung open. In it stood Stoke, the man I looked up to the most.

Clenching my jaw, I stood tall as he strode into the room tagged the front of my tee, and pulled me close so our faces near touched. Then he growled out the words, "They've taken her. What are we gonna do?"

"Find her."

"They touched her. What are we gonna do?"

"Make them pay."

"They hurt her. *What* are we gonna do?"

"Kill them," I snarled.

"Fuck yes," he hissed. "Now get the fuck out there with your head together. We find my daughter and we do it together. You hear me?"

"Yes," I clipped. Adrenaline pumped hard over and over in my veins. He studied my face, probably to make certain I had my head together. Then he nodded once, let go of my tee, and stalked from the room, while I followed.

In the main room, he walked right up to Nary's mum, who sat on the couch surrounded by Low, Josie, and Mrs Cliff. They weren't the only ones around. Talon, Griz, and Killer were there from the Ballarat charter. Josh, Nary's brother, was with Handle, as he talked quietly to the kid. A lot of brothers from our charter weren't there, and I knew why; they were already out hunting.

Stoke bent low, taking the back of his woman's head in his hand. He pulled her gently forward. Their eyes met. Stoke's jaw clenched and he clipped out, "My hands are gonna get dirty, love."

Her hand reached up and curled around the side of his neck. "Do what you have to do to get her back."

He touched her lips with his once, stood tall, and turned to the room. "Let's roll." He started for the door outside. I was close behind when he said to me over his shoulder, "You're with me. I'll fill you in on the way to some places about what's been going on while you... caught your breath."

I didn't reply. He'd known I'd lost it when I'd found out she'd been taken. Everyone knew I fuckin' loved her. Only no one knew why I fought that love and kept her far from me. And if I had my way, it'd stay that way forever.

Until the moment I'd discovered she was taken. Things would change because *when* we got her back, she wasn't leaving my side.

I'd have to tell her everything.

Would she hate me in the end?

Possibly.

But it was a risk I had to take.

CHAPTER THREE

NARY

*W*hen I woke, it was to a dark and cold room. As I dragged my hands around me, I realised I lay on a mattress on the floor. My heart sped in panic and my hands shook as I sat, frantically patting myself down to make sure I had all of my clothes on. I did. My jeans were still buttoned and my tee was still on, with my cardigan over the top. The only thing missing were my shoes. Touching the space around me, I discovered a wall to the right of the mattress and a gritty floor to the left. Whatever else was in the room, I had no clue.

Fear was present, turning my stomach over and over. Instinctively, I wrapped my arms around my bent legs and leaned against the wall.

What were they going to do to me? I'd been stupid, absolutely stupid to go into the car park alone. Apparently bad guys didn't care if there was a crowd; they still took what they wanted. I guessed when it came to money, they got desperate. I banged my head back against the wall angry with myself and my foolish move. I should have walked out with people. I should have had Jerimiah there with me. Josie even. I should have gone to her late class and waited for her so we could have walked together. At least Billy would have crowded us, and everyone knew not to screw with him.

I should have. I should have. I should have.

There were so many and yet I got nowhere wishing for a different outcome. I was still taken, tasered, and stuck in a dark room.

Closing my eyes, I took a deep breath. "They'll come. My family will come."

"T-they won't find you."

My body stilled at the small, shaky feminine voice. "Who and where are you?"

Shuffling started in front of me, and then a hand lay over my arm. When I jumped from surprise, it was removed.

"S-sorry… I'm… my name is Kelsey."

With my heart in my throat, I said, "My name's Nary, Kelsey. How long have you been in here?"

She snorted. Her movements scraped on the floor, and then I felt the mattress sink beside me. "Can I sit here?"

"Yes."

"The floor, it's cold, and when they came in, they placed you on the only mattress in here."

Was she avoiding my question? I blindly reached out and

found her close, next to me. I moved my hand down her arm to her hand and took hold of it in mine. "Kelsey, please, how long have you been in here?"

She cleared her throat. Her cold hand felt so small and it shook in mine. "I-I don't know. I was taken on the 16th of January. I remember the day because it was just after my birthday."

I gasped. Eight months ago. "How old had you turned?"

"Thirty."

"Kelsey... that was eight months ago."

Her hand squeezed mine. "It feels longer."

"But, I thought they sold people." I was confused and sick to the belly with concern, not just for myself, but Kelsey. What would be her state of mind? Living in the dark for eight months... and yet, she seemed okay.

"T-they do. They have. Many women get thrown in here and then leave a few days later. B-but me. He won't sell me."

"Why?" I whispered.

"I'm his... plaything. The only one he's kept for himself."

My nose crinkled and lip curled in disgust. He kept his woman caged like an animal. I gripped her hand tighter and promised, "When my family comes, I'll get you out. He'll pay for what he's done."

Her voice was low, in hope maybe. "What makes you so sure your family will come?"

"I just know. They're fierce in everything they do, love, protect... hunt and kill. They'll come, and when they do, hell will rain down on everyone who's involved in this sick business."

"I-I hope so, for your sake."

A thought occurred to me. "How many women have you seen come through, Kelsey?"

I felt her body move. Her shoulder brushed against me when she shrugged. "Over five, I think." She sighed. "I should have kept count, took names and dates... but I don't have a good memory on those sort of things. And I-I'm not allowed pens anymore, not when I stabbed one in one of his people's eye."

A laugh escaped me. "Good for you."

"No," she whispered. "It wasn't good. I was beaten, Nary, and then he lent me out to h-his men. Fighting back isn't an option here. Please remember that."

The problem was, I wasn't bred like that. Stoke was my dad. I was taught to fight back. I was Hawks. No one had the right to mess with me. However, from the tremor in Kelsey's body, I knew I would have to pick my battles with whatever came next.

"I'll try not to fight back," I offered. "Is this room secured?"

"Yes. It's locked and even if it wasn't, there're men on the outside."

Shit.

"Okay." I sighed. "I guess I'll have to wait and see what happens next." And pray my family found me before anything damaging occurred.

"I saw when they brought you in how pretty you are. It won't take long to sell you, at least you want to hope." She snorted. "I know it sounds messed up, but s-staying around here isn't something anyone would want. They're mean, Nary, and creative. Let's hope your owner isn't like them."

My stomach rolled.

My owner.

"The whole situation is crazy, Kelsey. How can people get away with this type of thing?"

"I honestly don't know," she whispered. "But—" She broke off when we heard footsteps outside the door and then the jangle of keys. Kelsey shifted, her tremors worsened. "Do whatever they want, Nary, and they won't hurt you...."

"Too much" was left off the end of her sentence. My whole body chilled and started to shake. The door flung wide, and I squinted at the sudden light shining in. For the first time, I saw Kelsey clearly and what I saw brought tears to my eyes. She was small in height, her body littered in bruises, and all she wore on her thin form was a silk nightshirt. Black hair sat in a messy knot on her head. Her pale blue eyes were wide in fear, only it wasn't for herself. As she looked at me, she mouthed, "Don't fight."

A bulky man entered first with a smile upon his pocked face. Behind him, two others entered and those two were just as large as the first, and just as menacing. They held their bodies tight, their heads high, and the glint in their eyes told me they were ready for anything to happen. They wanted me to fight, to run, because they'd like a chance to chase, to hurt.

I wouldn't give them the opportunity.

Kelsey was right. I couldn't fight, not all three of them. One maybe, but not three their size.

"So this is the piece of fluff the Hawks want back. You disappearin' is really stirring the pot, babe." He laughed. "It's good to see. Wanted to fuck with them for a long time. Nothing else I do seems to work, except now." He waited for me to say something. I didn't. "That the way it's gonna be, silent treatment? Fine, I'll see if I can get you singing." He looked over his shoulder to the man with long blond hair and then gestured him towards us.

As the man stalked our way, Kelsey cringed back against my shoulder. I did nothing but stare up at him with a glare. The man reached down and gripped Kelsey by the hair. She cried out. I went to reach for her, until she yelled, "No, don't."

The man yanked her from the bed. Stumbling, she tripped as he dragged her to the other side of the small room. There he placed her back to his front, so she faced me. He pinned her to his body with an arm around her waist and chest. Tears ran down her grimy cheeks.

She knew what was about to happen, and it wasn't going to be good.

Shit.

"Baxter, please, don't do this. Please," Kelsey suddenly begged. Her eyes pleaded with the man at the door who I'd already guessed was Baxter.

Looking to him, I watched him chuckle. He rolled his eyes and said, "When have I ever listened to you, honey?" With a flick of his hand in my direction, the other man came towards me. I made sure to sit still and appear unfazed, when on the inside I screamed in panic and fear.

When he reached me, he sat on the mattress next to me and then roughly pulled me from my seated position to plant my butt on his lap. He then spread his legs, and I was shifted to sit between them. His arms went around my chest and waist, much like how Kelsey was being held.

My eyes darted to Baxter when he huffed and said, "Still nothing. This is gonna be fun." He stalked towards us, only to stop right above us. Leaning over he said, "Let's see what we have. She's a looker for sure. Don't you think, boys?"

The man behind me grunted before he ground his erection up against my butt. I flinched in disgust and bit down on my bottom lip to remain silent. The other man holding Kelsey said, "Sure is, even with that scar."

Baxter chuckled. He then straddled my thighs. I closed my eyes and breathed deeply, fighting the urge to struggle. I jumped when his hand touched my cheek. "Yes, very pretty." His hand slid down my neck, over my chest, and gripped a breast, hard. I whimpered, but then cut it off and closed my eyes tighter. He hummed and said, "Nice handful."

Think of something else.

Anything else.

Jerimiah's smile just before he kisses me, how he...

Baxter's hand slid lower again. "Flat, firm stomach." They slid to my sides. "Love handles to grab onto. Men are gonna love you."

Jerimiah and the way he talks sweet...

The button of my jeans was popped open. Turning my

head to the side, another whimper escaped me. I thinned my lips as tears pooled behind my shut eyelids.

Jerimiah and...

The zipper was slid down and next I felt the weight leave my thighs, but my whole body jerked up as my jeans and panties were ripped down my body. Cool air touched my skin; my body shook from it and dread filled my stomach. Hands at my thighs roughly spread my legs wide.

Jerimiah, the way his hands caressed my body, the way...

"Fuck, she looks tight," Baxter said. "Stan, grab that leg." One arm left my waist, but one still held my chest against his body tightly.

Two fingers were forced inside of me. I winced and whimpered again, biting my lips between my teeth as tears ran down my cheeks.

It hurt. It burned.

He forced them deeper still.

"Hell, I think we have a virgin on our hands, fellas. She's so tight."

Stop, stop, stop. Please, I silently begged.

"Fuck, man. That looks hot. Can I wet my tip in your woman?" the man over the other side called.

"No," Baxter bit out. "I'm gonna need her after this. Such a tight little body. Jesus, I can't stop pumping my fingers in her hole. Feels so good."

Each pump was like a shard of glass being stabbed up inside of me. I wanted it to stop. I wanted to fight.

God, I wanted to fight.

My chest heaved; bile filled my mouth.

"She's gonna chuck," Stan, the other man holding me, called out.

"Don't let her," Baxter barked.

A hand covered my mouth. My ragged breath fought its way out of my nose.

Saxon. The smile I've seen from a distance. The warm eyes I've seen when he looks at the younger kids.

Saxon. Even his hard gaze did something to me...

"Fuck, you pumping her pussy is making her rub against me. I'm gonna blow my load."

"I don't care," Baxter said. "I'm going in for a taste." His fingers left me and then... *No, no, no...*

Saxon. His beautiful green eyes. His black hair. The way he cared, but wouldn't show it.

When I was sixteen and tackled him to the ground.

He looks up at me with humour showing in his eyes for the first time.

"You wanna get off me, Viper?"

"Do I want to get off on you?"

I hadn't understood the question because I had been currently on top of Saxon Black trying to save him from Malcolm, my stalker, who had shown up at Mrs Cliff's to harm us. Still, it was a moment I replayed over and over in my mind. It was a moment where I thought there could have been something between us.

The man behind me shuddered and grunted. "Fuck. Yes."

My body shook with the sobs raking it.

"Christ, she tastes sweet," Baxter said. Slowly, I opened my eyes to see him lean back on his knees and then stand.

"She's gonna be a big pay up being a virgin and all. Tell the men no one touches her... except me. Wanna taste that pussy while I fuck my woman one night." He rubbed his hand over his hardness behind his jeans. Looking over his shoulder, he ordered, "Get her to my room. I need a fuck and now." Glancing back to me, he smiled. "I'll be back tomorrow for the photo time. Get you all pretty for our buyers."

I glared up at him. He chuckled, turned, and left the room with a sobbing Kelsey. My eyes met hers just before she was pulled out of the room. I softened my look. She smiled. Of course, it didn't reach her eyes.

The man behind me tried to slide a hand between my legs. I clamped them shut. He laughed. "Don't matter, I already got off." He shoved me hard to my side. I scampered up and in the corner to watch Stan climb to his feet and face me. The wet patch on his light blue jeans was ever-present. Bile rose once again.

Dirty.

I felt so dirty.

My breath caught on a sob. I wiped at my eyes with the back of my hand.

"See you soon, sweetness." He smiled down at me before he walked from the room, shutting the door behind him.

Leaving me in the dark.

When I heard it being locked, I madly moved to search for my jeans. I fumbled with them so they were in the right way and quickly pulled them up my legs without my underwear on. It helped a little, but still, I couldn't help but sense the darkness had somehow snuck into my chest and had started to take hold of my heart and soul.

"Please, please, please hurry," I begged aloud in the silent room for my family. I wasn't sure I would still be myself if it took them forever to find me.

Leaning my head against the wall, I closed my eyes and thought of the one person who could take me away from the situation I was in. The one person who kept my mind busy from when they touched me.

Saxon.

CHAPTER FOUR

SAXON

*A*s we drove, Stoke told me about the plates Billy got off the car that took Nary. He'd passed them onto Lan to see what he'd get off them. There'd better be some good news soon from them. I was going crazy on the inside. My hands fisted on the seat, my jaw clenched in frustration as I stared out the passenger window.

Stoke also mentioned why Fang hadn't been around his woman at the time. Bloody Nary had sent him off, saying she was safe and would leave with a group of people. Still, I didn't give a flying fuck. It was a stupid move on his part, and I'd be having a word with him when I saw him. I was fucking furious when Stoke told me because Fang and I had an understanding. He was to take care of our girl, give her the world, and I'd leave them be. But he'd fucked up big time, so he had to pay.

My chest hurt and it hadn't stopped since I'd found out Nary was stolen. Absently, I rubbed at it.

Stoke looked over. "We'll find her."

I sent him a chin lift. I wasn't in the mood to talk. Hell, when was I? Looking back out the window, I glanced at the brothers on their rides surrounding us. Being a part of Hawks... fuck, it changed my life for the better. If Stoke hadn't taken me under his wing and offered a chance to get out of my hellhole, I'd be screwed.

Stoke caught my attention when he asked, "When we get her home, you gonna step up?"

My upper lip raised. "Yes," I snarled. I was. I had to claim my woman.

He snorted. "'Bout time."

"Thought you wouldn't want me for her."

"Shit, brother. The way you watch her, I know she'd be the safest in your hands." He sighed. "You're a good kid, Saxon. No matter what your dad cemented in your head about your mum." I stiffened. "Yeah, I know, and I reckon it's all bullshit, you were pro—"

"Do not fuckin' talk about it."

He shook his head. "Don't let it consume you. Don't let it dictate your life. When we get Nary back, she's gotta know all of you. My girl should get the best, and I'll make sure you give it to her."

"Why would you let me be with her if you know—"

"You're a good kid." My jaw hardened at the second time

he'd called me a kid. He ignored it and went on. "My girl has had it bad for you for four fuckin' years. She deserves what she wants, and what she wants has always been you. So don't fuck this up."

Moving my gaze to the side window, I couldn't help but think if Nary knew everything, I'd fuck us up in the end anyway.

As if reading my thoughts, Stoke said, "She won't care. One day we'll get all the details, and when we do, I know my girl. She'll stick by you no matter."

A change of subject was needed, so I asked, "Where we goin' anyway?"

A smirk touched his lips for a second before a frown came back. "We're gonna visit the Venom MC."

"They aren't gonna say shit we haven't already asked."

His smirk was deadly. "They will when we bring force."

"We goin' in hard and fast?"

"Fuck yeah. Someone in there has answers, and we're gonna get them even if we hav'ta take the whole lot out. Fang and Parker are gettin' us nothin'. So it's time to bring it up a step."

"We'd better find somethin'," I muttered.

"Yeah, brother. We'd better. But, if we don't, I still need you with your head screwed on. You can let loose when we get her back. Let loose on those who have touched her."

As we closed in on the Venom compound, I sent Stoke a chin lift. I wasn't sure if Stoke knew what sort of payback I could deliver. Though, he had seen my work on Malcolm, the dick who'd thought Nary was his. After his attempt to kidnap her, we'd taken him to a holding cell at the Hawks compound in Ballarat. There I proceeded to take my fury out on breaking five of his fingers and giving him a split lip after punching the hell out of him. I was sure I even broke a couple of ribs, along with fracturing his skull.

Even back then, when Nary was only sixteen and I was just about eighteen, I'd had my eyes on her. Who wouldn't? She was a beauty. My cock hardened every time she stepped into the same room as me. But Christ, I couldn't go there. She was everything I wasn't... Though, I had to set everything aside. Shit had to stop happening to her. She didn't deserve it, and I couldn't stay back and watch from afar any longer, not when she'd made it perfectly clear she'd wanted me.

Hell. *She* wanted me.

Had since she was sixteen.

I wasn't anything special. Sure, I took care of her, but I treated her like shit. Shaking my head, I ran a hand over my face because thinking of the way I was with her, it chiselled a piece of me away. It fucking hurt like hell when her eyes would dim, when her smile would fade, and yet... she still wanted me.

I'd planned for her never to know what she meant to me. How much I loved her, and had loved her since she fell on me, taking *me* to the ground to "protect" me from Malcolm. Hell, to be honest with myself, I'd fallen for her even before then. When I'd first laid my eyes on her.

Never would she know... until now. Until the day I got her back.

I had a lot to make up for, and if she was willing to accept me, flaws and all, I'd start cherishing the ground she walked on. Though, it wasn't like I didn't already; she just didn't know it.

Christ. I was a fool. A fucking idiot to her. So many times.

"Saxon?"

I turn to find Nary, my angel, standing before me and yet even when I want to smile back at her hesitant one, I don't. My eyes narrow into a glare, and my upper lip rises in a snarl. "What?" I clip out.

We'd been at Dodge's party at the compound when she'd approached me. I'd clamped my hands into a tight fist whenever I was around her. To Nary, it would look like anger, but it was so I didn't reach out to claim her, to touch her. So I didn't drag her close and kiss her sweet lips. She'd moved to Caroline Springs not that long ago and enrolled in uni. Why she'd moved, I had no clue. But I couldn't think it was because I'd moved there. I wouldn't let myself contemplate it since I was still doing everything I could to keep her at arm's length.

"I just wanted to see how you've been doing in a new town."

Smirking, I stupidly reply with, "Good, all new pussy to screw. Been a man's dream."

Her shoulders sag, only she quickly stands tall and juts her chin out, glaring at me with her own. "You don't have to be a dick. I was hoping since we're in the same town, we could be civilised with each other. I guess I was wrong."

"You'd be right."

She let out a sigh and then in a whiplash voice, she says, "Why are you mean to me, Saxon?"

"Name's Vicious. Use it." Ignoring her question, I walk around her and quickly out of the room.

She didn't understand I had to be mean. I had to keep her away because I was poison. A man had to be, if he was the one to kill his own mum.

"You ready?" Stoke asked, bringing me from my thoughts.

"Yep," I replied curtly. The street the compound was on bustled with vehicles. Someone was having a party. When the gates came into view, our brothers pulled back to let us through first. The yard around the compound held a shit-load of people, which explained who was having the party.

They were about to get a nice surprise.

Stoke revved the engine before he laid his foot down on the pedal. We hit the curb and crashed through the gates. They burst free and people scattered everywhere. Men stayed and pulled their weapons free, though they didn't fire. Stoke stopped the car inches from Blackie, who was still seated in his chair around the fire pit, I stepped out as our brothers pulled up behind us and climbed off their rides.

Stoke met me at the front of the car, and we walked the few steps to Blackie. He raised a brow, but leaned back in his seat, making himself more comfortable.

"To what do we owe the pleasure of your sudden visit?"

"Call all your boys in. We want a word with every one of them," Stoke ordered.

Blackie's eyes looked to my side. Out the corner of my eye, I saw Talon and Dodge step up. He asked, "Talon, you gonna let your brother speak for you now?"

"I do when it concerns his daughter being taken."

Blackie's jaw clenched and finally he stood. Crossing his arms over his chest, he said, "First we've heard of it, so you gotta know we have nothin' to do with it."

I took a step forward. "Don't matter. We want a word with all your members. Someone in here is a rat to Baxter. We find out who, we find Nary, and peace between us all will be set once again."

Blackie scanned me from head to toe. He snorted. "Who in the fuck are you to talk, kid?"

"He's her man," was called from behind me. Fucking Fang stepped up and even if I wanted to take him to the ground, I didn't. It was just goddamn lucky he'd said *I* was Nary's man.

Blackie raised a brow to his member and asked, "Funny, I thought you were."

Wanting to know the answer myself, I looked to Fang next to me. His eyes held pain, a pain I knew well. "I was. I failed to take care of what was mine, so I lost the chance I had with her. Vicious wouldn't have made a stupid move like I had." Regret. His voice was full of it. Though he was right, even if Nary yelled at me to leave her alone, I wouldn't have listened. Not when there was a threat to everyone in Hawks. We travelled together. No one was alone so Baxter couldn't knock us down when we were unprotected.

"I don't give two flying fucks who she belongs to. What I do care about is you fuckers crashing our party to bring this bullshit to *our* doorstep when I'd gotten *my* brothers out of it in the first place."

Through a clenched jaw, I bit out, "Not all of us are pussies and dodge the drama from Baxter. You either fuckin' help us now, or we start doing a body count." Behind me, guns were cocked and pointed. Slowly, I took out my own, but kept it lowered and at my side.

Blackie scoffed. "You think you can just come in here and start shootin' shit up? What kinda prez would I be if I let you?"

"A smart one," Talon said. "Think about it, Blackie. What would you do if it was one of your kids taken and you knew someone from our club had information on their whereabouts?"

Blackie stiffened. "You threatenin' my kids?"

"Fuck no. I'm saying, put your goddamn feet in our shoes. All we ask is for some time with your men. You give this to us, we owe you one," Talon offered. Hawks owing another club was something huge.

Blackie looked to the sky and then back again, a smirk playing on his lips. "And if I don't go with this?"

"A blood bath," Dodge said.

"Not all my members would be hit, you do get this? We'd take some of yours down with us."

"It's a risk we take," Stoke replied.

"She must be important to you all."

"She's our princess," Dodge said. A princess in the club

meant everything. She was precious and no one should touch her.

"Fuck," Blackie clipped and then sighed. "All my members are here tonight." He turned to his brothers and yelled, "I want a show of who's on board with speakin' to the Hawks." Most offered a chin lift or a raised hand; about ten didn't. With a nod, he looked back to us and said, "Take the ones who didn't agree. That's all I'm offering."

"Spread out," Stoke yelled. Hawks members flew into action grabbing the ones who weren't down with a few questions before they could take flight. Some fights broke out, but soon enough, we had them down to the ground.

"Good play," Talon said beside me to Blackie.

He snorted and replied, "You didn't leave me much of a choice. Maybe next time instead of gate crashing, we could sit down with a nice cup of tea."

Talon threw his head back and roared with laughter. "Jesus, Blackie, it's a wonder you're prez."

Blackie's smile was devious. "I have my ways to make sure people follow the line." He moved his gaze to Fang. "You got somethin' you wanna say?"

"I want out."

"Known it for a while, kid. You gonna be Hawks?"

Fang looked to Dodge, who nodded. "Yep."

"Good." Blackie grunted and then called over his shoulder, "Cuff."

Parker in his Venom club get-up stalked forward.

Blackie, with his fist, clipped Parker in the shoulder

before he turned to Dodge. "Wanna take your pig with you?"

Everyone tensed.

Blackie laughed. "I ain't stupid. I let you have your play and have Fang and Cuff stay in my club to show I was clean of all things Baxter. Ain't my fault I have members who are stupid."

"There's always someone," Dodge said.

"True that. Now get the fuck off my property so we can resume our party." We started for our rides as Dallas pulled in with a van to take the Venom members we'd tagged back to our compound. "Yo," Blackie called. We turned. "Hope you find her real soon. No one touches a princess."

He was right, because if they did, their lives would be ours, and I was ready to end some lives.

CHAPTER FIVE

NARY

The footsteps in the hall caused my body to quiver. The hairs on the back of my neck rose and had me wrapping my arms around my knees tightly as I brought them to my chest, closing my eyes. If only I had Dorothy's magic red shoes and I could wish myself home. Instead, when I opened my eyes again as the door was pushed in, I realised wishing would get me nowhere.

Kelsey was thrown to the floor and before they managed to close the door, leaving us in the dark, I saw red staining her lip and nightshirt.

My heart broke for her. She'd been going through it all for eight months on her own.

Eight months, yet there I was having been taken for a few hours, and already I wanted to break down.

Going to my knees, I quickly felt my way over the filthy floor to where they'd dumped Kelsey. My hand bumped into her arm first. She squealed and tried to shift back.

"It's okay. It's Nary."

She settled somewhat, though like my body, the shivering never stopped.

"Come on, let's get you to the mattress." I stood, knowing there weren't any obstacles in our way. I helped her up and guided her slowly over to the mattress. As soon as my foot touched the edge, I turned her and shifted her enough to sit. Once I was next to Kelsey, I wrapped my arms around her and brought her in close. Her body never settled as it continuously shook. Her breath caught and she let out a loud keening, before she turned into me and sobbed.

Tears formed in my eyes and overflowed, spilling down my cheeks. "They'll pay. They will."

I felt her nod. She didn't say anything, and really, there wasn't anything to say. All I could do was offer her comfort. I bit my bottom lip as my stomach pivoted to the bottom. I hurt for her. However, the pain she'd suffered for the past eight months was nowhere near anything I'd felt before. Even after being shot and the recovery, it wouldn't be anything compared to eight months of hell.

As I pulled her back with me to lean us against the wall, all the time holding her, I couldn't help but think of the days I lay in hospital after Cameron, Josie's stalker, had shot me when I'd tried to shout for help. At the time, I'd thought those were my worst days, the agony I'd been in. I couldn't eat, drink, or brush my teeth without it hurting. On occasion, especially when I saw myself in the mirror, I was stupid enough to wonder what it would have been like, if he'd just taken my life that day.

However, realising what was probably to come to me in the next few days, weeks, months, I knew the agony I felt back then, the despair, would be nothing to what I was about to live through.

Mum sits at the side of my hospital bed. Her attention is on her phone in her hands and a frown tugs her lips down.

Picking up the pen on the pull-away table in front of me, I write, "What's wrong?" and then shake it at her.

When she sees the paper, a small smile lights her face, and then she reads it. She bites her bottom lip. A sigh falls from her mouth. "It was Stoke. He asked me not to say anything to you, but, honey... you have to know. Saxon"—my heart skips a beat at the mention of his name. I had been told he'd held me with a fierce protective streak until an ambulance arrived. The way people told me about how he was with me that day, makes it hard to believe he doesn't want anything to do with me. Though what makes me believe they're wrong is the fact I haven't seen him since—"he hasn't been staying away, honey," Mum whispers. My eyes grow wide. "He's been here waiting to hear how you are. He was here when you went into surgery, and he was here only moments ago when your dad left. I don't understand why he's keeping himself away from you. None of it makes sense. However, he has his reasons... I just need you to know he does care, but I think, for the best, it would be good not to push him on anything."

Tears tingle my eyes. I swallow hard and breathe deeply

through my nose. With shaky hands, I pick up the pen and write Mum another note. When she reads it, tears fill her eyes. She nods. "Yeah, it could be time to let him go even if he is your dream." She takes my hand and squeezes it. "Not all dreams are meant to be, but it doesn't mean someone out there won't build another dream for you."

Kelsey shifted in my arms, taking me away from my thoughts of Saxon. She pulled away to sit up, her grasp telling me it hurt her to move.

"Do they bring anything for you for pain?"

"No." She whispered. "Nary, I'm so sorry you had to go through that."

"Don't, please. You've been living in hell for eight months, Kelsey. I'm sure I can put up with it until I'm... until I'm sold." My bottom lip quivered so I bit down on it.

"D-do you really think your family will come?"

Clearing my throat, I answer, "Yes. I don't know when, but I do know they're out there searching for me. I know they will do anything to get the answers they need to find me."

"That must feel nice."

"Your family hasn't...?"

"No, I grew up in foster care. No one would be looking for me."

"Coworkers? Boyfriend?"

She let out a huff. "No, I was in between jobs, and the man I did like… he didn't know I was alive."

"Do you know what he meant about a photo tomorrow?"

Her hand touched the top of mine. I turned it and took

hold of hers. "All women who come through here get some provocative photos done to entice buyers. I'm sorry."

My stomach dropped. I closed my eyes. The already present dread intensified, sending a tremor through my body.

"Maybe if you do what you're told again, it won't be s-so bad," she suggested.

"Bad? He raped me, Kelsey. He touched me without my permission," I yelled.

"I-I know, I'm sorry," she whispered.

Gulping back a sob, I pulled her close, my arm around her shoulders. My voice quivered when I said, "No, I'm sorry. I shouldn't yell at you." I shouldn't be there. I shouldn't have had anyone force himself on me.

Oh, God. Please hurry. Please.

"Maybe we should get some sleep. The pain might s-settle after some sleep."

"Kelsey, will they give you anything for it?"

"I doubt it. I've asked in the past, and they've just laughed at me. I'll be okay though. He was a little rough down there that's all."

"Kelsey," I whispered, my heart hurting for her.

"I'll be okay."

"You have the will of a saint, Kelsey, but I'm glad I'm here now because it means when my family gets here, we can get you out. Help you live again."

She sniffed. "I'm not sure if living is what I would call it."

"Oh, honey, you will, and I'll be there to help, I promise."

"It's terrible to s-say, but I'm glad you're here also, Nary.

The confidence you have in your family makes me want to believe."

"You can. Hold on to it and keep it in your mind when something bad happens. They will come, and the men out there will pay with their lives."

She shuddered. "That is something I will also hope for."

"Good." I nodded. "Before we sleep, ah, Kelsey, where do we go to the toilet?"

She snorted. "In the corner of the room, there's a bucket." She lifted my hand and pointed in the direction of it. "But, um, for number t-twos they take us to a bathroom. We get a shower once a week. Though I'm sure you'll get one before they take your photo tomorrow."

"And food, water?"

"You m-missed today's. We get some at lunch every day."

My jaw clenched, tears falling once more. "They're animals," I bit out.

"They are," she whispered.

MY BODY JOLTED awake when a door crashed open. For a blissful moment, I forgot where I was, until Kelsey woke with a scream as two figures came towards us. The light from the hall was minimal so I couldn't see who it was. Not that it mattered. They were all evil.

Sliding up quickly to a sitting position on the mattress, I pulled Kelsey with me. I'd made sure she was the closest to the wall and got all my body heat because her small frame wouldn't stop shaking. I wasn't sure when we'd both fallen asleep, but it seemed not that long ago.

"Shower, now," a man barked from where he stood beside our mattress.

He started to reach down, until I yelled, "Wait, please. I'll do anything you say. I won't fight, but can you please give Kelsey something to eat with some pain meds?"

The man laughed and the other joined in. "Like you're in a position to ask for things. Get the fuck up."

He grabbed my arm, but I jerked it free. "All I'm asking for is a small amount of food and one Panadol. Please."

His hand gripped my hair, pulling my head up. I climbed to my knees to try to stop the stabbing pain. Kelsey screamed, pleaded, and tried to grab his hand. I pushed her back into the corner, and I bit down on my tongue to stop from screaming. "It's too bad I can't bruise you before the photo, but it doesn't mean I can't after. Learn to keep your trap shut and don't ask for things you'll never get." He abruptly let go, and I fell back. "You two lick each other out last night, and now you got a taste of her pussy, you want to protect her?" He laughed. "You can't, bitch, remember it. Now get the fuck up and follow me out."

"Go," Kelsey whispered. "P-please, don't worry about me."

What I wanted to do was kick the man in front of me in the nuts, take the other one down, and grab Kelsey to run. My hand went to my hollowed stomach because I knew I couldn't. There were more men out there, and we wouldn't be able to get away from all of them on our own.

Instead, I patted Kelsey's hand and stood. Both men turned and made their way out. As I got closer to the door, the light, even dim, hurt my eyes. I wasn't used to staying in the dark for so long. My hand came up to shield my eyes, but it was tugged roughly down, and I was jerked out of the room to walk swiftly down the hall. The second man stayed and stood outside our door.

As my eyes adjusted, I realised Kelsey had been right. Men stood around everywhere. I counted about ten in the rooms we passed down the hall. Some were eating, talking, or watching TV. All dismissive of what was going on. How could so many men want to be involved with selling women? With treating us as if we were nothing? Insignificant.

The man, who seemed in his late forties, pushed the door at the end of the long hall open. My eyes went wide when he pulled me in to a communal bathroom. Showers were set up along one wall and toilets along the other. Though that wasn't what had my eyes widening; it was the five men standing around. They all turned when we entered.

God, no.

What were they going to do?

My body shook and my shoulders slumped. I sucked in a breath through my nose and bit my bottom lip to try to stop the panic rising. Instead of crying like I wanted to, the dread brought bile to my mouth and turned my stomach.

With the hand around my wrist, I was jerked forward again. "Strip and shower," the man ordered me.

Again, I looked around at the other men. One I recognised as Stan, the man who'd held me down, and there was the other who had been holding Kelsey. The other three I didn't know, but all had a wicked glint in their eyes as they looked at me hungrily. Stan even licked his lips and palmed his dick behind his jeans.

More bile. I coughed, choking it back and whispered, "W-what's going on?"

"Strip, woman. Now!" When I didn't move fast enough, two men stepped up, and my tee was ripped from my body. Even as I tried to push them away, one of them undid my jeans and jerked them down my legs, leaving me naked.

Hands ran over my body, touching me everywhere.

"Stop," I begged. "Please."

"Shut up," was snarled in my face, from who I didn't know. I had my eyes closed. My bottom lip quivered and my hand went to my stomach, but I knew it wouldn't settle. Not when I felt so sick, disgusted.

Suddenly, I was shoved forward. Having my jeans still around my ankles, I fell to my hands and knees.

"Fuck, too bad she's a virgin and we can't use her because it's like her pussy is calling to me."

Glancing over my shoulder, I watched as they all took their dicks out of their pants and started palming them.

"Shower, now," was yelled by the man who'd dragged me into the room.

Kicking off my jeans, I moved to the showers with my heart in my throat. What calmed me a little was the fact they couldn't... rape me. Still, what they were doing, the way they touched me was enough to kill some more of me inside.

As I showered, they looked on, palming themselves. I closed my eyes and Saxon took my mind away from what was happening in that room. Saxon and his frown, his bark, and his hard gaze. Saxon beating up Malcolm, wanting to comfort me when I'd witnessed my mum being taken to the hospital. I conjured up a picture my own mind had made up of Saxon holding me after I was shot.

Lastly, before I was dragged back to reality from the gasps and grunts of them coming over me... Saxon and the looks I sometimes caught when he thought I wouldn't. They were sad, full of longing, and sweet.

CHAPTER SIX

SAXON

*B*ack at the compound, my fists met with Fang's face one last time before my brothers pulled me away. I left him with one last message: If he ever got in my space, I'd take him down forever. My brothers and I then spent all night questioning the men we had. After a few threats, broken bones, and bruises, we still had nothing. Eight men we let walk free. Two we kept because one had stupidly let slip he wouldn't tell us anything, which told us he knew something.

Even though I was about to get dirty, I'd gone for a quick shower to clear away the blood coating my hands and clothes from the first round.

When I walked out of my room at the compound, Billy caught me in the hall. "Vicious, meeting room, now."

"I've got work to do."

"He'll still be there when you get done with the meeting."

Fuck. I offered a chin lift and followed him down the hall, out into the common room, where the women were busy talking care of the men who came in for breaks from searching for Nary. I didn't want to stop. In my eyes, no one should until she was found.

We continued down another hall to where church was held in the large room. Billy opened the door, and I followed him in, spotting Talon, Dodge, Pick, Dive, Stoke, and Griz.

"Do I really need to sit in for some bullshit when I could be getting answers?"

Stoke stood. "We've sent Killer and Dallas in there instead. They'll get what we need—"

"What the fuck?" I snarled.

"Calm, kid. You do a fuckin' good job, but you need a break," Dodge said.

"This is bullshit. I don't need anything but to find her. The more time she has with them, the more time we let them do God knows what to her."

"I fuckin' know that!" Stoke bellowed, his fist coming down on the table.

"Vicious," Griz called. My glare turned to him. "If you don't get rest when you can and let your brothers help you out when we can, then you'll be outta fuel when the time comes to fight hard."

Shit. Trust the old dude to make sense.

"You beat the hell outta most men we had. Time to let

Killer and Dallas do what they do best," Dive said. It surprised the hell out of me he'd come back. Though anyone would do anything for Nary. He'd even brought his woman and kid, which meant he was staying for the long haul. What I'd also heard was that Dodge had called him in case Stoke, like I had, lost it. Only he hadn't. Fuck, Stoke had thrown some things around, but he'd got himself together before coming to the room to get me.

Talon stood. "We've spoken to her school. Told them Nary has a family matter to attend to. Malinda even backed it up, but after all the reports they received yesterday, they're still suspicious, even though Lan has also spoken to them."

"What did you tell them when people reported her being... when she was—"

"We said it was a prank gone wrong," Talon offered. "Another reason they're still suspicious. And when we don't have Nary for them to talk to, they're gonna cause us problems, and there's only so much Lan and Parker can do with the cops. Apparently, detectives aren't respected as much as they want to be."

Dodge added, "We're gonna get Josie to pretend to be Nary and make a call to the school. Though we're all worried about her and her state of mind." He glanced to Pick and Billy, Josie's men. They nodded. "Too much has happened to her, but we're sure she can pull it off. I'd ask my woman, but we all know she has no patience to deal with fuckheads. She'd end up telling them to mind their own business—"

"Mena could do it. Save askin' Josie," Dive interrupted.

The men all looked to each other. Pick said, "Josie would do it, but we want her to keep busy with the kids. It takes her mind off everything for a while, and if we asked her to call them, we're not sure she won't crack under the pressure."

Christ, I had to remember the shit Josie had been through as well. It was lucky she had two men who had her back. The strength they had in their relationship would be enough to help her through yet another fucked-up situation.

Wished I was with Nary so I could help her through hers.

Hell. We're coming, angel.

Talon nodded to Dive and ordered, "Do it. Go grab her now." Dive stood and left. Talon then looked to me and said, "Go and get somethin' to eat and drink. Take a goddamn nap. I don't give a shit if it's for five minutes. Just trust we have shit covered while you do this. We'll get her back to you, Vicious, but while we search, lean on us as well. You and Stoke need to know we have your backs. No matter how ugly things need to get."

My jaw clenched. This was what family was supposed to be about.

With a nod, I walked from the room just as Dive, with his woman, was coming back down the hall.

"Hi," Mena offered shyly.

"Yo," I mumbled and kept walking past them.

When I reached the common room, I didn't have a

fuckin' clue what to do. I stood there and looked around. Only a few brothers were present and they were eating, talking. Women of the brothers were fluttering around, checking on everyone. Hell, even the kids were quietly playing.

Everyone held a solemn look upon their face.

They were feeling it.

Feeling what I was. The loss, the pain.

Nary meant a hell of a lot to all of us.

I look to the car pulling up to Dive's place in Halls Gap. I can clearly see Pick and Billy in the front with their sunglasses on. Josie is the first to get out, and then fuck me, Nary. Turning to Dive, I say, "Headin' in. Got some beer, brother?"

Dive searches my face, a smirk on his lips. "Yeah, in the Esky out back."

I quickly move around the house to the backyard.

Shit. It had hurt seeing her and knowing she was taken, more than when I knew she was available. She had come to me a few months earlier than that day asking what I thought if she took up the offer of dating Jerimiah, or as I called him, dickface Fang. Wished I had yelled at her and said it was a fucking stupid idea because I wanted her for myself. But I hadn't.

I raise my upper lip at her and say, "What in the fuck are you asking me for? I don't give a shit what you do in your life, and I wish you'd stop thinking I do." Then I'd walked off.

Fucking hell, I was a cunt.

Back then, I thought she was better off with him anyway. He wasn't fucked up.

It was impossible to be around her because every time she laughed, spoke, Christ, or blinked, I wanted her.

I wanted her to be mine, and I wanted to kill Jerimiah for ever meeting her.

Only a dude could tell where my true feelings lay, and as soon as Jeri-fucking-miah saw me around Nary, he knew my act was a front. In fact, he'd approached me before he made it certain Nary was off the market and asked me if I was going to be a problem.

I sat in a coffee shop near Nary's uni, wanting to make sure she got home safe, when Jerimiah, who I've seen sniffing around Nary for some time, walks in. He spots me and stalks over. I lean back in my chair and bring a smirk to my lips. He glares, pulls out the chair opposite to me, and sits.

"I'm asking Nary to be mine," he states.

Slowly, I lean forward and bring my arms to the table. He stiffens. I smile. "What makes you think I care?"

He snorts. "Nary's blind to it because you're a prick to her, but I'm not. I want to know, Vicious, are you going to be a problem when I claim her?"

I clench my jaw because what I want to do is to punch the dickhead flat to the floor. He wants her. He makes her smile and laugh. I've never done it before.

I have no right to her, which kills me.

But she's better off with someone normal.

I'm not normal.

I never will be because I see my mum's dead body on the kitchen floor every night I close my eyes. Then I see my bloody hands holding the knife that killed her. Then I see my dad come home, see Mum on the floor bleeding out, and he raises a brow before strolling over to the kettle to boil it. I stand there in shock, in fear at the age of fourteen. I stand there doing nothing as he picks up the kettle and throws the boiling water at my chest and stomach. "Self-defence." Dad smiles and then calls the police and ambulance.

I meet Fang's hard eyes and say, "Have at her. But you have to swear you'll protect her with your life. If you don't, you step down."

"Done," he clips before leaving.

My hand absently rubs my stomach, over the puckered scars my dad had left me. Apparently he'd known Mum had been physically and mentally abusing me for years. However, he'd done nothing about it because he'd known one day I would snap. He was looking forward to the payout he'd receive after she died. And then he became my new tormenter, holding the fact I'd killed my own mother over me. Threatening if I didn't do as I was told, he would call the police and tell them the truth.

Thank fuck Stoke scared him enough to leave me the fuck alone. He'd heard bad things about Hawks; that once they took you under their wing, you were forever protected. My dad wasn't stupid; he couldn't fight a club for me. Since the day Stoke got me from that house, I'd never looked back. Still, it didn't stop the thoughts, the dreams, and how unhinged I was regarding it all.

She was my mother, and I'd taken her life.

There could have been other ways to deal with it, but I

chose not to go with any of them; instead, I'd taken a knife to my own mother.

Right to her chest.

Her blood was still on my hands.

Her blood was still fresh on my mind.

Nary deserved clean. She deserved untainted. She deserved the world.

But it was time to take a chance. It was time to lay it all out for my woman to see what she could take, and if she couldn't take the truth, the scars, the nightmares, then I'd walk away. For her sake, I had to. Didn't mean I wouldn't and couldn't protect her from afar. What I did know was that I would never trust another to keep her safe, never trust another with my angel.

I would always be there for her.

"Hey, you," was yelled across the room. I looked up to see Mrs Cliff's eyes on me. "Get your cute arse over here and eat."

Jesus. They just had to bring her. The lady was crazy.

Silently, I walked over to her as she stood in front of the table of food. She picked up a plate and shoved it at me. If I hadn't quickly grabbed it, I would have been winded from the force. Next, she took my arm, and as we made our way around the table, she piled food on the plate.

After she was satisfied with the amount of food she'd served up, she turned to me and said, "You need to keep your strength up to beat the fuckers who took our girl." When I nodded, she smiled. "Good. You know, if I were many years younger, Nary wouldn't stand a chance. I would snap you up in seconds. You may not walk for a few days after, but the tricks I could show you would blow your mind. Why just the other day I had—"

"Mrs Cliff," Malinda cried as she walked our way. "Please don't finish that sentence."

If I wasn't in a foul mood, the old bat would have had a smile out of me. Instead, I took my escape and went to sit down. They were right about one thing. I needed to keep my strength up.

Handle, a brother who'd lost his woman to Baxter because of his flesh-and-blood brother, sauntered up and sat next to me. "How you doin'?"

He was the one I'd gotten somewhat close to. We hung out, we drank, we talked, only it was about nothing important. Though, he was the only one who'd noticed I'd been flirting with the club whores but not fucking them. He'd asked me about it, and I'd told him I wasn't interested. Then Nary had walked into the room. My eyes went straight to her, like every time, and then he'd chuckled and said, "Yeah, I can see why you're not interested." Still, it didn't stop me from dragging a whore from the room, leaving Nary to think I was screwing her.

Shit, I was messed up.

Glancing to Handle, I swallowed the lump in my throat along with the food, and growled, "Fine."

"She won't end up like my missus," he declared.

Stiffening, I looked to him.

"She won't. We'll find them, take them out, and get her back."

"We will," I bit out.

"Yeah, we will." He slapped his hand to my back and said, "Always here, brother."

Before he walked off, I offered, "Goes both ways, man." I wasn't much of a talker, but for him. The way he'd been with me, his silent support, I'd open up.

He smirked. "One day I will. For now, let's concentrate on gettin' your woman back."

"Deal." I nodded.

CHAPTER SEVEN

NARY

*a*s soon as they'd had enough of me in the shower, I was ordered out by one man while another threw a towel at me. After I quickly dried, my stomach churning from all of the eyes on me, a silky white slip was placed in my hands. I threw it on, sick of the eyes on my body. What I would have loved was jeans, a skivvy, boots, and even a beanie. Tears threatened. How had Kelsey put up with it all for eight months? I wanted to stab them all in the eyes as they kept their unwanted gazes on me. The slip did nothing to hide my body.

An ache in my chest started. I wasn't beyond throwing myself to the floor and crying. Even though the room was cold, sweat pooled at the back of my neck, and the hairs on my arms raised. My body didn't know what it wanted to do.

"Over to the sink. Do some make-up," Stan ordered. With slumped shoulders, I silently made my way over. I hadn't noticed when we'd come in, but the last sink was covered in all sorts of make-up. "Hurry up with it," Stan added.

I sat at the chair available there and looked at myself in the mirror. I had bags under my eyes, and my tanned skin had already paled. Without too much thought, I picked up the foundation and started to apply it. Even if I couldn't take my body away from the situation, I could at least take my mind, so I pretended. I let my mind think of myself getting ready for a date, and even though I wanted it to be Jerimiah I was getting ready for, it wasn't. Saxon's face and form was always the first on my mind.

Was I self-harming thinking of Saxon? Probably. He'd never been the gentle, sweet man I knew Jerimiah was. He was harsh and brutal to the point it hurt my heart. Yet, I still couldn't let go, even after having four months of a perfect relationship with Jerimiah. Saxon would always hold a piece of my heart.

Did it make me pathetic? Yes.

Did I think of him as my knight in shining armour? Yes. He'd saved me in so many situations, how could I think of him as anything less?

If he'd just let go of whatever was holding him back, holding him away from me, I knew we'd be happy.

God, unless he really didn't want me.

Tears touched my eyes. I closed them and took a deep breath. No, I had to believe there was something holding

Saxon away from me. The looks I had received when he thought I couldn't see told me he had feelings and those feelings ran strong. Why else would he want to protect me?

"Hurry the fuck up," was snarled, causing me to jump and open my eyes to see the man, who had dragged me into the bathroom, standing there.

"What's your name?" I asked as I applied some eyeshadow.

"Malcolm. What's it to you?"

A laugh escaped me. His name was fitting since it was shared by another monster who'd tried to rape and kidnap me when I was sixteen.

"What you laughing for?" he asked with a growl.

Shrugging, I said, "Nothing."

"Why you want to know my name then?"

Meeting his gaze in the mirror, I told him, "Because when my family comes, I need to tell them I want you killed second."

He chuckled. "Yeah, okay, sweetheart. Who's first then?"

"Baxter," I whispered.

He stepped forward and fisted my hair at the back, forcing my head his way so he was leaning over my face. His other hand went to my neck. "You're dreaming. No one is coming for you, and if you keep giving me shit, I'll make you pay. Baxter will even give me permission." With that, he pushed my head forward. My hands landed on the sink, make-up flying everywhere. "Pick that shit up and finish."

My hands shook as I reached to the floor to grab the

fallen items. When I sat back up, I picked up the eyeshadow again and went back to pretending.

THE ROOM MALCOLM led me to was what I imagined a porn set would look like. It was a bedroom. The double bed was covered in red silk sheets, the walls covered in black, the carpet a plush white. My stomach rolled when I spotted a man dressed in a coffee-stained shirt and black slacks. His feet were bare, which I found strange. Then again, everything there was strange, painful, and sick.

He stood in the corner with a smile on his face, holding a camera. "You look amazing," he cooed at me, then licked his lips. My stomach rolled. I hunched my shoulders and quickly averted my gaze. The guy freaked me out. Actually, that was stupid, because he wasn't the only one. All of them did.

I jumped as the door to the room opened. I hadn't even realised Malcolm had closed it. Baxter and another man I hadn't seen before strode in. "Let's get this done. I want her sold quickly. I know men. They'll snap this virgin bitch up in a few days."

The thought of being sold ran a cold shiver over my body. God, I hoped my family would come before then.

Dread filled my mind.

They'd been searching for Baxter for so long...

Was my hope useless?

I placed my hand over my unsettled stomach. Tears

pooled in my eyes and my bottom lip trembled. Hope left me, leaving me icy inside.

"Bitch, get on the fuckin' bed," Baxter ordered. When I didn't move straight away, Malcolm gave me a shove towards it. I stumbled over, my hands landing on the bed as my knees hit the edge. "Make this look good, and then you and Kelsey can have lunch, dinner, *and* breakfast. Fight me on it, you both get nothing for four days."

I met his hard eyes, then looked to the ground. Kelsey needed the extra food. Nodding, I climbed onto the bed and faced the camera. Leaning back on my knees, I gripped the hem of my slip. With a deep breath, I pulled my gaze up to the camera and smiled.

"Perfect," the cameraman said. "Now pull up the dress a little more and bite your bottom lip. Yes, brilliant." He snapped picture after picture. I wanted to cringe away from the bright flash, but didn't. It would be over soon, and then at least Kelsey would get some much-needed food in her stomach. Mine wasn't faring well either. Something I hadn't had before. Hunger.

Even though Josh and I had a shit dad in our lives before Stoke came along, Mum had always made sure we were taken care of. She'd protected us from many things, made sure we did our homework, were fed and warm. After our dad died from doing stupid shit, and Stoke came into our lives, Mum was finally happy. Stoke was more of a father to Josh and me than our real dad had been. He brought us safety, rules, and taught us the wrongs and rights of life.

Another reason I knew my family would be trying

everything they could to find me. Stoke, my dad, protected what was his. When I became his daughter, actually even before that, when he started dating Mum, I knew he would fight his way through anything to keep us safe.

My thoughts immediately led me to Saxon. Would he be looking for me?

With everything I'd seen, the way he guarded me, even if he thought I didn't know, I could honestly say he would be right there with Dad looking for me.

The heat in my chest caused a nest of humming birds to flutter in my belly.

The knowledge of Saxon's determination made my heart beat in a frantic pleasant patter.

He was an arse. He was cruel sometimes. He was even a prick.

But he'd always been mine.

He pushed me away for a reason, and if I ever got out of the situation I was in, I would find out for once what was holding him back. I would demand to know, and if he didn't tell me, I would kick his arse. If he still didn't tell me... I would let him go. I would walk away, but not before I told him I loved him. Not before I swore, no matter how many days passed, years even, he would hold a part of my heart. Even if he kept being a dick, he would always have a place in my mind.

My body jolted. My mind came back into the room when Baxter yelled, "Stop, I'm sure that's enough photos."

I watched as the photographer nodded and smiled down at his camera. "Oh, these are good. They'll love her."

"Good. Money's with the man outside the door. Now get."

He smiled and said, "Always a pleasure working with you." He sent me a wink before he walked to the door and exited the room, shutting it again.

My eyes flicked to Baxter. He smiled and pulled something from his back pocket, handing it to Malcolm. Then Baxter started for me. Eyes wide, I scuttled back. Swallowing hard, repeatedly, fear bombarded my senses. My back hit the wall as he grabbed my wrist and jerked me from the bed. Before I stumbled to the floor, his hands went to my waist. He lifted me and placed me on my feet in front of him.

"Now it's time for a new photo." Looking over my shoulder, I saw him lift his chin to Malcolm. I glanced there to see Malcolm raise an instant camera.

"W-what's this for?" I asked.

"Stand still and be good," he ordered. One hand—oh God —one hand slid down and cupped my mound. He ground one finger in hard against my opening. My hands twitched to fight back, to push him away. His other hand gripped my breast.

"Why are you taking this?" I whispered.

"Just a picture to send home to your people."

I sucked in a hard breath and cried, "No!" Quickly, so he didn't expect it, which he didn't, I pushed my body back, he stumbled a little, and I gained room to move away from him. My knees hit the bed before I swiftly moved over it to stand on the other side.

"You can't do that to them, please. Please don't send them anything."

It will kill them.

I couldn't let it happen. I couldn't have my family see me like that.

Tears filled my eyes. *I'm so sorry, Kelsey.*

"Last chance. Get over here now."

Shaking my head, I said, "I won't."

His smile was sinister, only lifting up one corner of his mouth, his eyes narrowing on me. He jumped up on the bed. I was ashamed at my scream as I ran for the door. I didn't make it. Malcolm grabbed my arm and twisted it painfully behind me. My back hit his chest as he faced me towards Baxter, who was already stalking our way. I grunted through the agony.

"Stupid move, sweetheart," Baxter snapped, spittle landing on my face.

"It will break them. Please, please don't do this."

He threw his head back and laughed. When it died off, he looked back to me and said, "I want them to break. I want them to hurt."

"Why?" I whispered. I needed to understand his torture. How and why he'd become the way he was.

"Many reasons really. Many. Hawks has fucked with my life too many times and finally. Finally," he roared, "I get to pay them back in a way that will slice them open. In a way they'll remember forever."

"Just because Talon refused you to be a member? Because Dodge beat you in a fight?"

He grinned. "That was a start. But it didn't throw me over the edge."

"What then?" I screamed in his face. "What did they do that was so terrible to fuck you up? Because you are fucked up, all of you are. What you do, it's sick. You aren't right in the head. None of you are."

The punch to the cheek was expected. The slap to the other side of my face was too. With his fist in my hair, he ripped me away from Malcolm and turned me in his arms. He gripped the top of my slip with one hand and roughly pulled it down so one breast was naked. He squeezed it so hard I couldn't help the cry slipping past my lips.

"You fight this, you get worse. Though I'll make sure you heal before I sell you. At least a bit of blood on your lips and a red patch on your cheek will add to the photo. So thank you for fighting."

"Why are you doing this?" I pleaded.

"They screwed with my family."

"Who?"

"Cameron Peterson was my cousin."

My eyes widened. Cameron was the man who stalked Josie. He was going to kidnap her. He'd shot me trying to help her.

A snort left me. "He deserved what he got."

Baxter chuckled behind me. His hand once again cupped my mound. I bit my bottom lip when he forced a finger inside of me, making sure his nails dug into my skin everywhere they touched.

"So do the Hawks and so do you," he said. "Now smile for the camera."

I tipped my head down. There was no way I could get out of the photo, but at least I could show my refusal in some way. I looked up and narrowed my eyes, clenching my jaw despite the pain. I had to show my family I wasn't broken. I could only hope they'd see it in my eyes.

CHAPTER EIGHT

THREE DAYS LATER

SAXON

*N*early a week had passed and nothing. No leads. Nothing. After Lan had run the plates, he'd told us they were fake. Christ. Coming up empty played me hard. The thought of what Nary was going through tormented me. I couldn't sleep, and if I wasn't forced to eat, I wouldn't. We'd discovered, from the two men we had left from interrogations, one of them had been the driver of the car that took Nary. When he'd told us he'd handed her over at a destination, there was still no lead. He was killed by my hands. It didn't take much though. Killer and Dallas had worked him over for days.

I was a wreck. I bit heads off when the fury hit, hit things when the frustration got too much, or simply sat on my ride in a darkened street at night, staring up at the sky when the sorrow took over.

People should have known to steer clear of me. Only they never took the hint—strangers, yes, but my brothers and their families, no. Mrs Cliff and Malinda were like hovering mother hens, questioning me if I'd showered, slept, or eaten. They didn't care if I yelled and threatened; they ignored it and went on to get a brother to force me into my room to rest and shower, or force a plateful of food on me. At least that was the case when I came back into the compound to see if anything new had been discovered.

Three days seemed like a lifetime.

Whenever the sun rose on a new day, I cursed it. It meant we'd failed to find her once again.

My attention went to Dodge as he walked into the common room. He had some mail in his hands, already opening them. I flicked a gaze to my food and used my fork to push it around. Really, I needed to toss it aside and get back out on the road.

My chest ached. I didn't know where to go for answers. I'd been everywhere and got goddamn nothing.

"Fuck," was snarled. My head jerked up to see Dodge grip something in his hands. "Low, Josie, Malinda. Get the kids out, now." I could see Low wanting to argue, but after a stiff shake of her man's head, she did as he'd asked. All three women paled as they rounded up the kids and left. Dodge's eyes flashed to Josh, Nary's brother. "You also, kid."

He stood from the couch and shook his head, his jaw tight. "No."

"Josh," Stoke warned.

Josh spun to his step-dad and glared. "You already said I couldn't do the first ride out. I'm not missin' out on anything else."

Stoke went to him, his hands landing on Josh's shoulders. "You've just turned eighteen. When you're fully a part of Hawks, you get to know all. But if it's something Dodge doesn't think you should see, then you leave."

"Jesus," Josh clipped out. "She's my sister." He spun to Dodge. "Is it about her?"

My stomach dropped to my feet. My hands fisted before I picked up the plate and threw it to the table. Dodge wouldn't want Josh out if it wasn't about Nary.

Christ.

Fuck.

"Out, Josh," Talon ordered.

"But—"

"Out!" Talon barked. "As your president, you either listen now or you're no longer a prospect. Hear me?"

Josh mumbled a few things under his breath but quickly stalked out the door. What I should have been doing, instead of watching Josh, was keeping an eye on Dodge. I felt heat at my back. I looked over my shoulder to find Beast and Dallas there. My eyes went to Stoke to see he had Killer and Griz with him.

Shit. Fuck me, it was bad.

Bad enough Dodge got our brothers to be close when we'd lose it.

Motherfuckin' hell.

Quickly, I stood and bolted for Dodge.

"Wait," he ordered loudly. With the paper still in his hand, he pointed it up in the air and away from me. With a quick, hard tap to his stomach, he hunched over and I grabbed the paper.

My eyes went to it.

I stumbled back. "No," I bit off harshly. My free hand went to my hair and ripped at it. "Fuck!" I slammed my eyes shut, my head going back, eyes then opening to the ceiling. "Fuck!"

Behind me, I heard Stoke arguing with Killer and Griz to let him go. Then everything faded. My knees hit the floor. I crumpled the photo in my hand before my hands slapped to the ground. There, I dry-heaved.

They'd touched her.

Put their hands on her.

Her eyes... Christ, her eyes, scared and yet fierce with anger.

Someone landed beside me and snatched the photo from my hand. "What. The. Fuck!" was snarled. "No, fuck me. Not my girl. Not Nary. Jesus. Fuck!" Stoke rambled. I glanced up to see tears in his eyes. Killer was next to him, taking the photo away. The whole room soon erupted in cursing, complaints, and threats.

My eyes went back to the floor.

Rage.

Red.

One second.

Two…

A hand gripped the back of my neck tightly, a body got close, then a voice, Stoke's. He whispered harshly into my ear, "They're all dead. They'll pay. But we do it slow. They need to know no one fucks with us. No one touches our girl. We make sure they pay. Death. Slowly."

I nodded once.

Someone asked, "That Baxter in the… in—"

"Yes," Dodge grunted.

Loud footsteps were fast approaching down the hall. Stoke stood first, his hand held out to me. I took it, my body weak all of a sudden. He helped me gain my footing as the door burst open and Julian ran in.

"Julian, not now," Talon ordered on a sigh.

No one was in the mood for Julian's shit. Though, as he strode Talon's way, I saw no smile, no humour. What I did see was weariness, dark bags under his eyes and untidy, crinkled clothes— and Julian always took pride in the way he looked.

He stopped in front of Talon and said, "I found a friend who can help find Nary. She's good, really good. Even if she can't find her she knows many people who would know how to get into the buying system."

Talon's head jerked back. "What the fuck you talkin' about?"

Everyone stilled and went silent.

"Since I heard sweet Nary was taken, I started looking

for my friend. I hadn't heard from her in a long time, which worried me. She's really good at finding things for people." He leaned in and whispered, "Even the wrong type of people. She confessed this on a drunken night we had a long time ago. I'm not even sure she remembers telling me. But I thought, as a just in case my burly men aren't having luck, I should reach out to her, and I did. It took me days, but she finally got back to me. She should be here any second. She caught a plane over. She'd do anything for me. We're like siblings. We—"

"Julian," Stoke barked. Julian swung his eyes to him. They warmed with sorrow as he looked at Stoke and then me. Stoke shook his head. "You can't bring in a stranger to this when we'll be the ones to deal with the people who took her, get me?"

He nodded. "Oh, I get you, strong man." His hand lifted and he glided his finger across his neck and then gurgled, his head dropping to the side. *Jesus.* "She'll understand, like we all do."

"Julian, I don't think—"

"No!" he cried, his hands up in front of him. "Please, please give her a chance. You have nothing to lose, and besides she'll be here—"

"Boss," Jason called from the door.

Both Talon and Dodge answered with a "Yeah?" They looked at each other and rolled their eyes. Dodge made his way to the door. After he spoke with Jason, Blue's brother, who nodded and took off back down the hall, Dodge turned to us and announced, "She's here."

Julian let out a squeal, then clapped his hands. "Promise, she's kosher. You'll love her."

"Fuck, Julian." Talon sighed. "You should have run this over with me first. She's an outsider—"

"And a woman," Dallas called, his upper lip raised. "They cry too much. She ain't gonna be down with us killin'."

"She's not like that," Julian started, only to stop when Jason walked in. He was smiling, though—he was always smiling—then he moved aside, and a woman in her thirties stepped in, dragging a suitcase behind her. Her dark brown glare softened when it landed on Julian, and a smile lit her face.

"J-man," she screamed excitedly before letting go of the handle. Her bag dropped to the floor, so she could make a run for Julian. He held his arms wide, and she jumped into them. Jumped was the right word because the woman was short.

Even though it was good to see long lost friends united, it pissed me the fuck off. Anger still boiled low in my stomach. My hands ached to shoot something.

As they talked animated to themselves with hands flying everywhere, I dipped my head down, touching my chin to my chest. Clenching my jaw, I pulled in a deep breath through my nose.

They'd touched her.

That photo. Fuck, it killed something inside of me.

We needed to find her.

Looking up, my eyes landed on the new chick. If she, in

some way, could help us, I was willing to put up with anything.

"Can we get this show on the road?" I demanded. Crossing my arms over my chest.

The room quieted.

For the first time, the woman took in her surroundings. She leaned closer to Julian and said out the corner of her mouth, "You said you were good in bed, but to land one of these hotties... wow."

"Woman," Dallas barked. Her eyes went to him and narrowed. "This is men's business. We don't need your help. You need to fu—"

Her hand came up, cutting Dallas off. "Oh, no, Viking dude. You did not just go there." She turned her whole body to face him and took a few steps his way. "Actually, I probably got more balls than all of you put together. My J-man told me what was going down. I can help, so I'm here and I'm staying. In fact, I think I might just take over your bedroom to piss you off even more."

Dallas leaned in and snarled, "You mind yourself with me, tiny woman."

"Name's Melissa. Remember it, Viking man." She turned her back on him, dismissing him altogether. If I was in the mood, I would have laughed when Dallas's jaw dropped open and his eyes widened. "Now, I've heard talk about this selling women business. Usually they stick to homeless women, but I guess they're stepping up. Being a woman myself"—she looked over her shoulder to meet Dallas's glare with her own—"I can't get an in. *But,* I know someone who can. If you let me, I'll ring him and explain what's going down. He's a good guy. I've known him a long time, even before Julian, and he'll hate what's going on. He'll help, and even though he owes me one, you'll still owe him in return. The debt he owes me will be to get one of his people over here. The rest will be all yours if you agree."

"Who?" Dodge asked.

"Davis Mason from the Rebel Wayfarers MC in America."

CHAPTER NINE

DAVIS MASON

(This part is written by MariaLisa deMora)

*M*ason leaned one shoulder into the door frame and scanned the crowded room. It had been a family barbecue at the Fort Wayne clubhouse, and his Rebels had kicked into high gear for the much rowdier and not-so-family-friendly party following.

Davis Mason, national president of the Rebel Wayfarers MC, was at home in any of his club's houses, but probably most so in the Fort, as locals called it. A beautiful brunette caught his eye from the other side of the pool tables, crooking her finger at him from across the room. He grinned as he shook his head. His old lady, Willa, struck a pose and pouted, tipping her chin down as she crooked her finger at him again. "Not happenin', babe," he called, and she laughed. She'd already known he wouldn't be summoned like that.

She whirled and bent at the waist, reaching back and smoothing her jeans over her ass. "Now that is something worth crossing a desert for," he shouted and started in her direction. A ringing from the office behind him caught his attention, and he twisted to look back. His cell was on the desk in the darkened room, the screen lit up. With his position, every call had the potential to be critical, so he turned, yelling over his shoulder, "Hold that pose, sweetheart," grinning broadly as he heard Willa's belling laughter at his back.

Picking up the phone, he saw a name he hadn't expected. A name he hadn't seen in years, but one that caused the corners of his lips to tip up in a smile. Engaging the call, he didn't wait for a greeting, just gave his own. "Iss. Damn, woman, been way too long. What's shakin', girl?"

Silence met him, and he was surprised because Melissa Stevenson wasn't known for her lack of manners. "Iss, everything all right?"

Her whisper cut through him. Melissa wasn't a whisperer, either. "No, Mason, it's not. Nothing's right." He froze in place at her next words. "You owe me, and the debt's come due. I hope it's still good because I'm callin' it, Mason."

He did owe her. Had told her more than once, "Whatever you need, Iss. No expire date."

She sucked in a breath, and that sound told him so much. Whatever this was it would be big. And whatever this was, it mattered to her in a way that struck deep. With a shaking voice, she tried to joke, "Good to know, Mason. But stop calling me Iss. You know I hate that nickname." When she forced a laugh, the sound broke in the middle, and she cut it off abruptly. "Thank you. I knew I could count on you."

He reached behind him and grabbed the door handle, easing it closed, feeling the click as the lock settled into place in the frame. With the noise of the party muted, he walked around the desk to the window and looked out at the sea of motorcycles covering the clubhouse lot. Then he tipped his head to the side, and told her, "Tell me."

Ten minutes later, he reopened the door and again, stood in the doorway. Two members had taken up station against the wall, having moved there when he shut the door, signalling club business was going on inside. "Deke," he spoke to one of the men. "Find Gypsy. Let him know I wanna have a chat." He hesitated a moment, then added, "PDQ, brother. Need him five minutes ago. Also, I want Myron, now."

"On it," Deke responded, disappearing into the mass of bodies.

Mason knew his tech wizard would be able to find any kind of footprint the sick fuckers had left behind. Would get what they needed to help save the girl. Those bastards wouldn't be able to hide from Myron. He'd find them eventually, faster than Gypsy could get in the air, probably. From what Iss had told him, they could use all the leverage they could bring to bear. Mason tipped his chin down, studying his boots. Selling women like property. *Not happening when I can make a difference.* He thought of the Rebel old ladies, the daughters of his men. Thought of the picture Iss had texted him. Stomach lurching, he vowed, *Not happening.* When it came to it, Mason would be happy to make the deal to buy the woman, and then his brother would be there to take the entire fucked-up operation down.

He felt Willa's eyes on him and found her in the crowd. She stared, locking gazes with him, her face alert, no longer laughing and joking as she tried to read whatever was troubling him. Mason held out one hand, and she left her friends immediately, swiftly coming to him and letting him pull her into his arms. They'd been together for only a couple of years, but the way she knew and understood him made it seem a lifetime. Tipping her head back, she stared up at him, and he marvelled at all the beauty she gave him. "Got a little business to tend to, sweetheart. Nothing bad, just business." In a different time, he would have been the one taking this assignment. Knowing what he had in his bed made him glad he could send another in his place.

"Prez," he heard from beyond Willa, and Mason looked up to see Gypsy standing with Deke.

Mason bent his neck, brushing his lips across Willa's, whispering, "Back in a few," before he turned and stalked into the office, followed closely by Gypsy.

Looking at the man, Mason again ran over what he knew of Gypsy, hoping like hell he'd made the right choice for this particular project. He owed Melissa, and the need was dire. *Can't get it wrong,* he thought. *No choice but to get it right.*

Gypsy had been in the Rebels for years and ran one of their local businesses, Marie's. A restaurant with a thriving bar, as well as a fledgling musical venue side of things. The music had been Gypsy's idea and proven to be lucrative for the club. However, his business acumen wasn't the reason Mason had selected him for this project. Those reasons were much farther in Gypsy's past.

Douglas Tatum had been a cop, once, working under a crooked chief in a Chicago suburb. Tatum hated the look-the-other-way mentality required by the dishonesty and hadn't liked having his hands tied when it came to setting wrongs to right. He'd eventually had enough of both and resigned his position.

Without much of a plan, he had set about a one-man campaign of retribution against the crooked cops. Over time, Tatum had managed the impossible, finding a way to work both within and outside the law to bring the corruption to a halt. It had taken years, but eventually, Tatum had been satisfied with his efforts. That was when Mason snapped him up, easing him into the life gradually, wanting him to see that while not everything the Rebels did was a Robin Hood act, there was room for honor and rightness in the club.

Now, Gypsy was his go-to guy when there was an injustice that needed investigating, because once he sank his teeth into a problem, he didn't let go until it was solved. Exactly what Iss needed.

"Brother, you got a passport?" Gypsy's head jerked back, but he nodded, silent even as his eyes brightened. He was interested. *That's good*, Mason thought, *since I'm about to throw him to the wolves.* "Who can handle Marie's if I need you to take a run?"

Tipping his head to one side, Gypsy reached up and rubbed across his jaw. "Tequila's done it for me before. DeeDee can step in, too." He mentioned another full-patch member, as well as a woman who'd been with the Rebels nearly since the club was chartered. Both were good choices for a temporary replacement. "They've each done a few days here and there as I needed. What's up, Prez?"

"You think between them they could handle a few weeks?" Might as well set the expectations early, in case it took that long.

"Probably," Gypsy said immediately, tipping his head to the other side. "Where am I headed?"

"Australia."

MELISSA

Walking from the room, where I'd asked to have some privacy while I talked to Mason, my heart pounded in my chest. The Hawks men had shown me the photo of Nary. My teeth ground together just thinking of it. She had a swollen redness to her cheekbone, a cut to her lips, and wore a silk nighty. The man who stood behind her had an evil look in his eyes and a smirk on his face. He had one hand on her bare breast, the other cupping her sex. Bile had threatened to come up. Nary was living a nightmare my mother had, in a roundabout way. And even though I didn't know Nary, I knew my decision was right. Hell, even before I'd seen the photo, to when Julian called me, I knew I couldn't turn my back on her. Nary meant a lot to everyone there. So I was glad Mason had come through for me. Though, I knew he would. Not only because he was a good man when it came down to it, but because he knew I hated any of that sort of shit, like he did. Women being treated badly, hurt my heart, and burned my belly. I was brought up with a mum who took beating after beating to protect me from my father. She was also *taken* when she hadn't wanted it.

Before Myron, Mason's tech guy, came into his crew, Mason had found me. My name had got out, even over to America. I was a computer whiz, but also a thief who could steal anything from anywhere. It was my only way to make easy money while I'd finished schooling. Davis Mason had used my skills once and said I could either take his money or call in a debt anytime I wanted.

My debt was called in.

Looking up as I entered the main room, I schooled my features and said, "He's gonna get his man onto it, so he can buy her. Then he's sending one of his crew here to make the exchange."

"Shit, Talon. You sure we wanna owe Rebel Wayfarers?" Dallas asked. Before the call, I'd been introduced to them all, and Dallas was the one who'd got my panties in a twist right off the bat. I wasn't sure yet if it was a good or bad twist. He'd also been the only one to know who Mason and his club were. Had heard about them from his time in the army.

"We're doing it," Saxon bit out. Poor Saxon would do anything to find his woman. The feral glint in his eyes told me that.

"I agree," Julian piped in. "If my girl trusts these men, we can trust her judgement."

My heart flew. Julian had always had my back. God how I'd missed him being my neighbour. Not that I lived in the same place and hadn't for a long time. Back in the day, Julian had a knack to always make me smile, laugh, and enjoy life. I was so happy for him when he'd found Matthew and got rid of his poisonous parents from his life. Because if he hadn't, I would have done something eventually. I had the means to. Hell, some days I wished I hadn't listened to him when he'd asked me to leave it alone. Didn't matter though; he was finally happy and living the life he should have always been.

"If they can find her faster, then we chance owing Mason," Talon said. He stood in the middle of the room with his arms crossed over his chest, a vibe from his tense body, which said no one should question him.

"When does his guy arrive?" Stoke asked. He was the father to Nary and I could see the sorrow behind his eyes. Vengeance was also there burning bright in not only his eyes, but most of those around me.

"In a couple of days. I've never met him, but he's cool if he's a part of Rebels. He'll probably get here before Mason's tech guy can get the information for Mason to make the call."

"How we gonna pull off an American guy buying Nary and then makin' out he's somehow magically gonna get her back to the US without her fighting him?" Dodge questioned.

"She'd do it willingly if the guy pretended to threaten her family," Griz suggested.

"When Mason sets the deal or if his guy… Do you know his name?" Killer asked me.

"Mason said it was Gypsy."

"Get either of them to tell Baxter he'll have his mate make up a fake passport."

A phone rang and we all looked to Dodge. He pulled it out the back of his jeans pocket and answered, "Yo. What? Fucking hell." He pulled the phone away from his ear and said to Talon, "Two of our strip joints are on fire."

"Decoy, something to keep us busy," Saxon clipped.

"Let's deal with this. Then we still do what we gotta do to find Nary. No one stops looking even if Mason can come through," Talon ordered and started for the door.

Leaning over, I grabbed the handle of my suitcase and turned to Julian as men scattered around us. With a wink, I asked, "Which one is Dallas's room?"

He smiled, even giggled, but it didn't reach his eyes.

I'm praying all this works.

CHAPTER TEN

THE FOLLOWING DAY

NARY

*T*he sun rose and fell on four days. Four days without food or a shower. We got water only two times a day, and I ended up giving half of mine to Kelsey. I was so worried about her. She slept more and more throughout the day and night, and when she did, her thin frame wouldn't stop shaking, no matter how much I hugged her close and made sure she had most of the thin blankets. I was also concerned for myself. Every noise made me jump; every shadow had me cringing away.

The place was starting to wear me down. The men and

their lingering gazes, their brush of hands and their sickening smiles were getting to me more and more.

I was weak, so weak, and it made me angry.

Four days and I was feeling broken on the inside.

Fragile.

Afraid.

Scared.

As I wiped at my eyes, my mind drifted to my family. Josh would be going out of his mind. My brother, my sweet brother, didn't deserve the pain, the worry. None of them did. Stoke, Mum, Saxon, Jerimiah... God, he would be taking all of the blame onto himself. It hurt to think about it; it also hurt to think I'd betrayed him when Saxon was the one to consume my mind.

Jerimiah would be hurt more when... no, *if* I was rescued because he would see how strong my feelings were for another man. Hurting people was something I never wished to do. Mum had felt enough devastation when she was with my real father. I never wanted to experience or inflict that pain on another person.

In a way, I wished they'd killed me instead of the hell we were going through because I wasn't the only one it was happening to. My family would be feeling it as well, and thinking of it wounded my heart more.

My hand went over my stomach as it growled in complaint. Kelsey shifted beside me. It had only been a short time since she'd come back from Baxter's room.

When the door had opened and they'd thrown her in, I saw fresh blood soaking her lip and ear.

While she went through her hell, I went through my own.

My eyes closed as I leaned my head back against the wall, my jaw clenching so I could stop the sob wanting to escape. I didn't want to wake Kelsey.

After he'd taken her, his men had come in to our cell. They'd touched, they'd licked, and they'd made me...

Bile threatened.

My chest heaved up and down as I tried to control it.

I could still taste them in my mouth.

I was weak.

Broken and scared.

"Nary," Kelsey whispered beside me.

Sniffing, I ran my hand down her arm to let her know I was listening. My mouth couldn't form words just yet. I needed to get my emotions under control.

Her voice broke when she rasped, "I want to die."

"Kel—"

"N-no, I thought I could take it. I-I thought things would get better. They haven't. They won't. I can... I can only take so much." Her tremors worsened as tears overtook.

I gripped her tighter to me. "I promise we will get out of this. I promise." My own voice caught with emotion.

She shook her head. "I-I can't...."

My body stilled. "You can't what, Kelsey?"

She shook her head and kept shaking it.

No, no, no, no. She wouldn't. She couldn't.

"Shh," I demanded. "You listen to me, Kelsey Rye. Do not do anything stupid, please. I'm begging you. Hold on with me for a little while longer... If they don't come, we fight together. We try our best to get out of here, and if it fails... if we don't make it, we go *together*. Do you understand me? *Together*, Kelsey. You are not alone."

She would not die alone. She'd never feel alone again.

It was her main fear. Despite her isolation, she hated being alone, and when the other women came through that door, they never wanted anything to do with her. Afraid they'd be the next Kelsey and be kept for the men's plaything.

I wouldn't let her be alone again.

We had to stick together in every way.

If we didn't get out of there soon, if my family didn't find me, then we'd fight...

We'd fight until they took our lives.

THE FOLLOWING DAY

SAXON

My head thumped. My eyes felt like they had dirt in them, and my body was starting to fail me. I hadn't slept in forty-eight hours. Hell, it was probably more than that actually, but the previous day was spent organising shit for our American visitor, and then with the fires at the strip clubs, everyone was running low on everything.

As I stood in the baggage claim area, leaning my head back against the pole with my eyes closed, I also tried to tune out the two idiots next to me. Dallas and Melissa.

"What do you mean I wouldn't understand?" Melissa snapped.

"You're a woman. You don't get men's business."

"Riding a Harley is men's business? You're a dickwad. You know that, right? All I asked is why you enjoy riding so much. You could have just answered normally instead of saying, 'Women don't get men's business.' God, have you even got laid lately with that attitude?"

"Yes."

Melissa grunted. "Yeah, I'm sure you have." A pause—Dallas probably raised a brow at her. She growled. "Do you even know how to have a conversation with the opposite sex?"

"Don't need to."

"You don't need to? What about when you're with a woman? Do you talk to them, treat them nice, or do you give off this I-don't-give-a-fuck attitude?"

"All they want is my cock. They don't care if I talk or not."

"Oh. My. God. What about when you want to settle down with one woman, have kids? Would you really treat your woman like this? Like, women are lower than me?" I snorted when her voice dipped low to take on Dallas's. "They cry, they bleed out of their vaginas, which makes them weak. They don't get what men want."

"Simple, I'll never settle down."

She let out a frustrated hiss. "I really want to beat you upside the head right now."

"Why?" Dallas asked, the confusion clear in his voice.

"Why? Why? You annoy the fuck out of me. *Women* are not weaker than *men*."

Dallas grunted. "If you say so."

"You stupid, arrogant mother... Holy crap, he is way better in person than the photo Mason sent me."

Opening my eyes, I searched to where Melissa was looking and landed on a dude who was huge. His bulk told me he worked out. His loose tee told me he wasn't one to flaunt that shit, but women still took notice like Melissa was.

As he strode towards us, he sent a chin lift to acknowledge he knew we were the ones to meet up with him. Instead of hanging onto his bag, he flung it over his shoulder so he could grip his long hair in both hands and tie it up in a bun. Glancing out the corner of my eyes, I noticed Dallas had stepped up behind Melissa and crossed his arms over his chest. A sure sign of claiming a woman. If I was in the right mood, I would have smiled. I didn't. Instead, I straightened and held out my hand for Gypsy.

"Vicious," I offered. He took it and shook my hand.

"Be better to meet under different circumstances," he said, his voice deep.

I heard Melissa sigh next to me. "Hi, I'm Melissa."

Gypsy let go of my hand and smirked down at Melissa. "Mason's Iss, right?"

Before Melissa could say anything, Dallas clipped, "Dallas." Then he reached around Melissa, who looked up at him and glared, to shake Gypsy's hand.

"Right, got some news from Mason when I was stopped over in LA. Need to have church."

"Got any more bags?" I asked.

"Nah, man. This is all I need." His fingers tapped the green duffle bag on his shoulder.

"Let's jet," Dallas bit out.

At the car, there was an argument about who was sitting up front. It was Dallas's four-wheel drive and on the way, I had sat up the front, so Melissa was finding it strange Dallas was set she would be up the front with him.

"Why?" she cried, her arms raised in the air in frustration. "You make no sense. You said men sit up front and now you want me up there?"

"Darlin'." Gypsy caught her attention. "He wants you up there so you don't sit next to me."

Dallas coughed on his own breath and snarled, "That's bullshit. Fine, you sit up the front."

Gypsy shrugged and climbed in the passenger side while Dallas stalked around to the driver side grumbling. Melissa was still standing dumbfounded at the side of the car.

"Melissa?" I called roughly. All I wanted was to get this guy back to the compound to see what his president knew. "Get in."

She shook her head, and after she got in the back, she said, "You guys can call me, Lissa." I offered her a chin lift. Dallas grunted and Gypsy nodded.

"Can you tell us what your prez said?" I asked as Dallas drove off.

Gypsy turned in his seat to look back at me. He quickly scanned and asked, "You close to the woman taken?"

"She's mine."

His eyes lowered and when they came back to me, they were heavy with sorrow. "Sorry, brother."

"Nothin' to be sorry for. You're here to help get her back. That's all that matters."

"Hearin' you. But I'd prefer to tell everyone together, saves repeating myself. How far away is the compound?"

"In this traffic, 'bout twenty," Dallas said.

"Not long, yeah?" he said straight to me. Meaning I didn't have to wait long, didn't mean I didn't still want to hear it. I gave him a chin lift and looked out the window.

The car filled with silence, until Melissa sucked in a breath, and I knew she was about to give Dallas more shit before she said, "So you like me, Viking man?"

"Fuck," Dallas said with a groan. "No, tiny woman, I don't."

"I call bullshit," she sang. "You like me, you want to bump and grind me."

Dallas sighed. "No wonder you and Julian are friends. You're both annoying as fuck. Now shut the hell up."

My eyes moved to Gypsy as he turned again in the seat. He raised a brow to me. I nodded and said, "Always like this. Though, Melissa is new."

Dallas guffawed. "Wait 'til you meet Julian. Thank fuck Wildcat and her pussy posse didn't come our way."

Gypsy snorted. "Interestin'."

Dallas chuckled. "Yeah, you could say that about our crew."

Ten minutes later, we parked out the front of the mechanical garage that was off the compound. Melissa got out and skipped to Dallas's side. "Do you want to hold my hand as we walk in?"

He glared down at her, and she smiled wide. He gnashed his teeth and snapped, "I will break you, tiny woman."

She winked. "In a good way, right?"

He groaned, rolled his head back to look at the sky, and then he glared back down and said, "No, right now I'm thinkin' of wrappin' my hands around your neck 'til you don't breathe. Leave me the hell alone."

"Sure, my Viking man." The crazy woman then slapped him on the arse and ran for the door, yelling over her shoulder, "We'll try that dirty move later."

Shaking my head, I also walked towards the door with an annoyed Dallas, who was grumbling once again, and a chuckling Gypsy.

CHAPTER ELEVEN

SAXON

*T*hank fuck all the women and Julian were out when we got in. Melissa disappeared somewhere, so I gathered the brothers there and called for church. With a quick introduction, the meeting was called to order by Dodge, with Talon standing at his back.

"Right," Gypsy started and stood from his chair opposite me at the table. "Spoke to Mason. Our computer guy found the site." The room tensed. "Bad news, they were only sellin' women to Australians so they didn't get caught havin' clients trying to get them through border security."

"Fuck," Stoke cursed, his fist hitting the table. My fists clenched in my lap. The door then opened, and we all looked there to see Jerimiah walk in.

I stood and yelled, "What in the fuck you doin' in here?"

His jaw clenched, but he still bit out, "I'm helpin'."

"Like fuck. I don't want to see your face." I started for him, but Stoke was suddenly grabbing me.

He hissed low in my ear, "Leave it. He's one of us now. He's a brother."

Shrugging Stoke off, I turned to him. Stabbing my finger in Fang's way. "He's the one who didn't have Nary's back. He's why she was taken."

Stoke shook his head. "He ain't at fault."

"She said she'd leave with a group," Fang said, his voice hard.

Spinning to him, I glared. "You still don't fuckin' leave her."

"Enough," Talon boomed. "This pussy fight ain't gettin' us anywhere. Fang regrets what happened more than anyone. That's on his back and will be for a while, but playin' the blame game ain't gettin' us Nary back. Fang's Hawks now, Vicious. Get used to him being around."

Fuck!

Motherfuckin' hell.

I had to look at that fucker nearly every day since he was Hawks. My gut dropped. I swore if the dick tried to go near my woman, no one could hold me back from takin' him down.

Before I sat, I demanded, "Stay the fuck away from me and Nary when she comes back."

The room went back to silence. I flicked my gaze to Gypsy, and he gave me a nod. "Right, as I was sayin', they usually sell their women to Aussies. But Mason made a call to them, spoke to the main man Baxter. Reassured the dick we could get the woman to the US and not have anything fall back on him."

"How's that?" Dodge asked.

"We know a person with a private plane. Not that it'd come to it because your woman will be coming here. Mason also told Baxter he wants the woman because he has an issue with Hawks. He said we'd threaten Nary with the lives of her family if she doesn't follow through. Baxter liked the idea. We'd need a fake passport for her, just to show him."

"Like I said, she'd do anything for her family." Griz nodded.

"I could do up a fake passport," Gamer offered. "Just need a photo of her."

"Malinda will have one. See if she's back yet," Stoke said. Gamer stood and left.

"When's the deal being made?" Dodge asked.

"I'm gonna go down tomorrow night and I'll need five hundred thousand to show this fucker."

"We'll get the money," Talon assured.

"Where's it going down?" I asked.

"The dick wanted to make it a public place, didn't trust Mason." Gypsy smirked. "Didn't work though. Mason got on his high horse and said if he's trusting them with his man on their territory, he wants it where the woman is in case she makes a run for it. After some arguing he agreed."

"Where?" I barked.

"Ferntree Gully."

"Goddamn," Killer growled low. "How did we not find that shit out?"

"They're well hidden," Gypsy said. "Out in the country."

I leaned forward. "Why wait then? We can go there now and get her back."

"Too much to risk. We need a man on the inside, and Gypsy is gonna be that man," Talon ordered. "Handle, get some fuckin' Google Maps up. We need a detailed plan." Handle nodded and started for the door. Talon added, "Want some satellite images of the surrounding areas also."

"Hold up," Gypsy called, taking his phone out of his pocket. "Myron sent through what he found on the place. I'll email it to you guys. Just need an address." Handle rattled one off and then went out to grab the laptop.

"How we gonna know when it's time for us to crash the party?" Knife asked.

"A wire?" Griz suggested.

"They'll test for that shit, and then everythin' will be fucked." Gypsy glared.

"Not with the ones Beast makes," Knife said. "No one can detect his shit."

Gypsy's eyes went to the silent man Knife was pointing to. Beast nodded. Gypsy replied, "Wanna see it first."

The doors opened and Jason came in carrying a tray. "Thought people could use a drink." He handed them out with a smile on his face. As he dropped one in front of me, he patted my shoulder. "Gonna get more."

"Prospect, we'll be out soon. Don't worry about it,"

Memphis ordered. Then he raised his beer and pointed it to Gypsy. "To new brothers." People cheered around us.

Finally. Fucking finally, we were getting my angel back. All I had to do was wait twenty-four goddamn hours. I tipped my beer up and drank long and hard.

A thought crossed my mind. My brothers would hate it, but waiting more time when I knew Nary was going through hell was killing me. I could possibly stake out the place, see what I could do, maybe even get in there instead of sitting on my arse.

"Get Lan and Parker. We need to know they have our backs to cover us in the cop department. No one can hear of what's gonna go down," Talon ordered. Killer rose and left.

"You got cops on your payroll?" Gypsy asked.

"Nope. They're detectives, and they're Hawks in a way. They got our backs when rough shit happens. When we need to take the law into our own hands to protect our family."

Gypsy said nothing.

"How 'bout some more drinks?" Dallas asked. "Beast can show you his gadgets."

"Sounds good." Gypsy nodded and left with all the brothers, except Talon, Dodge, and Stoke.

As soon as the doors closed, I turned to Dodge and waited. He smirked. "You know what I'm gonna say?"

"Don't do anything stupid?" I guessed.

"That and you need rest—"

"I can't fuckin' rest when—"

Dodge's hand came up. "I know, which is why Jase put some sleepin' pills in your beer."

"What the fuck?" I yelled and stood, only my feet swayed. I gripped the table.

Stoke said from beside me, "You need sleep, kid, and then we hunt for our girl."

Nary.

I shook my head, my thoughts confused.

My angel.

Hunt for her.

"He's goin' down," Talon called.

"I got him," was the last thing I heard.

NARY

"Wake up!" The yell came with a rough hand shaking my shoulder. Blinking my tired eyes open was hard. Then reality crashed in, and I scooted up to press my back against the wall. Stan was leaning over us. Kelsey was on her back next to me with lowered, scared eyes.

"You." He pointed to me. "Baxter wants you showered." He stood and looked behind him. Two men stepped up and dropped two trays to the floor. "Eat. I'll be back in five to get you for a shower." The men walked to the door, only they left it open and stood on our side, leaning against the wall. At least we were able to see what we were eating. I looked down to the trays. They held bread, a stew of some sort, and pudding. Kelsey slowly sat up. Both our hands shook as we pulled the trays towards us.

"Eat slowly or it'll come back up," she warned.

Nodding, I took a bite of bread and nearly moaned as it slid down, dropping into my very empty stomach.

"Why would they want to feed us now?" I asked on a whisper.

She smiled sadly at me. "T-they found a buyer for you."

My stomach churned, and I felt the second spoonful of stew threatening to come back up. Tears pooled in my eyes, and as I looked to Kelsey, she cried silently as she nibbled on her bread.

"I won't leave you," I told her, my hand taking her free one.

"You have to, Nary."

"No. We're in this together."

"I-if he's good, a good owner maybe somehow… I don't know, get him to find me some help. I can, I think I can hold out for a little longer."

"Kelsey—"

"No, p-please, Nary. For your sake, go along with it. Please."

"What are you two whispering about?" one of the men barked from the door.

"Nothing," Kelsey replied. She squeezed my hand before letting go and went back to eating.

I wasn't sure I had it in me to go along with everything knowing I was leaving Kelsey behind. It hurt too much to think about it.

My eyes flicked to the door as Stan stood there; it hadn't even been five minutes. "Seeing Baxter first then shower. Now."

Meeting Kelsey's eyes, I watched her nod. It sucked. Everything sucked. I got to my feet, my body trembling and weak, and made my way to the door. The bright light had me narrowing my eyes. I rubbed at them and blinked a few times. Without looking back, I followed Stan down the hall, opposite to the bathrooms. The place was huge. I didn't know what lay behind most doors, and I really didn't care. When we reached the end of the hall, Stan opened the door, which led to another freaking hallway. We walked down it, my feet dragging on the floor. I had no energy, even though I'd just eaten something. Having nothing for four days had taken its toll. My body felt disgusting and grimy. I was actually grateful to be having a shower later, but I wished I had the guts to ask if Kelsey could also have one. Our bodies were caked in grime, our hair a tangled mess, and I smelt. With every breath I took, I cringed.

At the end of the hallway, Stan stopped at the door and knocked. Baxter called from the other side to enter. Stan opened the door, stepped in and to the side, and I slowly entered. It was an office. There were file cabinets, cupboards, and two chairs that sat in front of Baxter's desk. I looked to him as he sat behind his desk, and he gestured for me to sit. I did.

Baxter leaned forward, placing his hands on the desk, then moved them to the stack of folders where he tapped his fingers on the top. "Had a lot of interest on you. Finally narrowed it down to one man."

My stomach churned. The precious food I'd eaten threatened its way up.

Licking my dry, cracked lips, I asked, "Who?"

"Doesn't matter who. You just need to know he'll be here tomorrow to collect." He shifted in his seat, leaning back. "You also need to know if you cause any shit, well, the man who's taking you knows who your family is. You don't do as you're told, he'll kill the lot of them." He smiled. "I also want to add, you fuck this deal up at any time, even after you're gone, I'll make sure Kelsey pays for your stuff-ups." He winked. "I'm sure you know what I mean by that." He stood and came around, kneeling in front of me. "You gonna be a good girl?"

Closing my eyes, I jumped and opened them again with tears brimming when his hands landed on my thighs. "I'll do as I'm told," I said.

He hummed under his breath. "Good." He stood once again, only to lean over me. His hands spread my legs where he cupped my mound. "Would have loved a have had a go at your pussy. Would have fucked it good and proper, but they want you in working order for when the guy's man comes to get you." He straightened. "You do well making yourself pretty, shower, eat some more, and tomorrow you'll get another shower where you need to make yourself all pretty, and I promise I'll be gentle... well, gentler on Kelsey later."

God.

"I'll do all that if you leave her be for the night?"

He threw his head back and laughed. Shaking it, he brought it down to look at me. "Can't do that, sweetheart. You've made me all hard." He went to pass, only to grip my hair and rip my head back, startling a cry from me. "You don't make demands here. You do as you're told, bitch." His hold left me. Slowly, I pulled my head forward. "Get her out of here to shower and then more food. I want Kelsey in my room in the next ten."

"Right, boss."

Shaken, I stood and turned. What I wanted to do was to run through the open door Baxter had just left through, find a window, and get the hell out of there. I didn't want an owner to come. I didn't want a new, fresh hell to be brought down on me, but most of all, I didn't want to leave Kelsey.

How was I going to get us out of the mess?

I only saw one option.

Death.

CHAPTER TWELVE

THE FOLLOWING DAY

SAXON

*W*hen I woke, I had fucking drool coming from my mouth onto the pillow. Rolling to my back, I wiped it away and glared to the ceiling. They'd drugged me. Fucking drugged me. Suffice to say, I hadn't slept in a god-arse long time, even when they thought I had, I didn't, and their drugging me told me they goddamn knew it. "Fuckin' cunts."

"Least you're alive and stronger now. We can make a safe play to get our girl back knowin' you won't crash on your feet from exhaustion."

I knifed up to see Stoke sitting on the end of the bed. Groaning, I rubbed a hand over my face. "What you doin' in here?"

"Came to make sure you ain't gonna give us shit about it. My woman was worried about you. Fuck, we all were. You been like a zombie gettin' around on your feet. You needed sleep, Vicious, and now you have, get your arse up and to church. We're goin' over shit before the run."

Goddamn, it was good to know I had people at my back. Even if they pissed me the fuck off. "Can I take a piss first?" I asked.

Stoke snorted and made his way to my door. "Yeah, while you're in there have a shower. If you don't, I'll send in Mrs Cliff to help you."

"Bastard," I shouted to the closed door, with him on the other side chuckling. I'd asked Stoke the other day how he could still smile with his brothers, laugh even. He replied, "Because of my woman. She gives me courage, strength, and a reason to want to smile and laugh. She keeps me sane when I feel things crashing down."

It was then I understood.

Nary, my angel, was the same even when she didn't know it.

Every time things felt like they were crashing down, I'd ride until I found Nary. All I needed was a glance at her smiling face, her warm eyes, and fucking beautiful body, and it'd calm me. She'd calm me. Hell, even when we were sparring back and forth, I enjoyed each moment because I got to hear her voice, see her eyes flare with annoyance, and sometimes hurt. Then I'd hate myself for hurting her.

Fuck. I had a lot to make up for.

After a quick shower and dressing in my usual biker boots, jeans, tee, and my club vest, I made my way into the common area where Malinda shoved a plate of food at me. "You need to eat before anything gets started."

Shit. I'd never felt so taken care of in my life. Each time they did, it warmed my gut.

As the women chatted around me, I quickly ate, and once my plate was clean, I offered my thanks and headed to the meeting room. When I entered, it was bustling with movement and talk. Papers were spread on the long table. Talon, Dodge, and Gypsy were leaning over a map talking low. While Gamer, Griz, and Killer were surrounding a computer. Others were arguing about what gear to take and how we were going to get there. A thrill of something pulsed through me. I put it down to excitement to get my woman back, excitement to take some lives. Whatever the reason, adrenaline surged through me.

Hours later, we had a plan. Gypsy had a piece of Beast's equipment, which was undetected to any device, in his ear for Talon to know what was going on. Couldn't believe a guy who didn't know us, owe us anything, was willing to walk in there with no weapons at all. The guy had balls of steel. Though he did know we had his back, and he trusted us enough to keep the shit storm about to happen out of his face while he secured Nary. The brothers and I would be at a safe distance away in the bushland surrounding the place, and when we got the words, "Let's get this show on the road," we'd be crashing Baxter's party and taking some lives with us.

Shit was about to get real, and I was looking forward to it.

FIVE HOURS LATER

NARY

My dooming fate had arrived. The previous day, I tried and tried to get Kelsey to agree with my plan, but she wouldn't. She even told me she'd do everything in her power to make sure I didn't stuff anything up. I'd suggested we start something, a very bad something, which would bring us a lot of pain and eventually, hopefully death.

I wanted it.

To die.

I understood why Kelsey had wanted it before.

Everything seemed at a loss.

And even though death scared the shit out of me, I'd prefer to have my free will and end things when I decided, not when someone else did.

What also helped ease my fear of death was doubt had slipped into my mind, telling me my family wasn't coming.

Kelsey, the strong beautiful woman, still held out hope

and pleaded with me to be safe and get help when I could, when I was out. I agreed in the end as she was becoming hysterical.

I knew what went through her mind though while she begged me to leave, stay safe, and try to find help. She planned to die.

Try as I might, I couldn't begrudge her for that. It was exactly what I would have planned if our positions were reversed. Little did she know, though, I wouldn't let her go on her own. If I had to, I would beg and promise my owner the world if he could get Kelsey out.

She made me realise fighting the men wasn't going to be an option. I would be locked up away from her and she, like myself, wanted to stay close until the end. She had begged me, and it was the last thing I could give her, promise her.

The tears on my face tracked down my cheeks, probably ruining the make-up I'd applied earlier. I'd also put on a red silky slip. Though the make-up couldn't hide everything: the scar, the gauntness, or the shaking of my body.

My lips trembled as I said goodbye to Kelsey. Each step destroyed my heart, damaging it beyond repair as I walked from the room, leaving her in that darkened hell all alone.

As we approached a door, I wiped at my face, stood tall with my shoulders back, and took a calming breath.

Please, please, please let this man be good.

Malcolm, who smirked over his shoulder at me, turned to the door and opened it. My heart was in my throat, and with the pace my breath was coming in and out of my body, I was sure I'd pass out soon.

Quickly, my eyes flicked around the room. It was like a living room, big with couches, a TV, and a coffee table. Baxter sat on the couch near the window facing me. Opposite him sat another man. He was huge like Beast or Dallas and had his hair tied back in a bun. Five other men stood around the room, one was Stan, so I guessed they were all Baxter's men.

I clasped my hands in front of me and stepped in. My feet stilled, and I came to an abrupt halt. I didn't want to walk further in. My chest ached with my heavy breath.

It wasn't right.

Nothing was right.

I was about to be sold.

To never see my family again.

A sob caught in my throat. I held onto my stomach as chills broke out on my skin.

"Nary," Baxter called. "Come here."

The man who sat opposite Baxter stood and turned to me. My eyes widened at how good-looking he was. I bit my bottom lip. Even the hottest man could have the devil running through his veins.

The man grunted. His eyes narrowed. "This the bitch the Hawks are going crazy for?"

Tears brimmed and then fell. My heart broke once again knowing there would never be a chance to get Kelsey out. His words just confirmed it.

Doomed.

Clenching my jaw, I flicked my gaze to the side. One of Baxter's men stood there and laughed after Baxter did. My eyes trailed down to his gun tucked into his jeans at the side.

"Yeah, that'd be her," Baxter said.

"Don't give a fuck anyway, boss wants her. He gets her or her family is dead."

My head came up, eyes to him. *Shit.* Had he seen my gaze on Baxter's man's gun? My shoulders slumped forward. I couldn't do anything, and it killed me. I couldn't save Kelsey, myself, or my family.

I was stuck with no choices.

"Get your ass over here, bitch," the man demanded, then looked to Baxter. "You got the money. I'm taking her now."

"Not just yet." Baxter smiled and stood. "You gotta sign some paperwork. All transactions are marked and signed off."

"Fine," he bit the words through clenched teeth. His eyes came back to me. "You dumb, bitch? I said get your ass over here, now."

A new nightmare.

That was what he was.

Slowly, I made my way over and around the couch to be at his side. When he looked down at me, I raised my chin and glared. I thought for a second I saw his lips twitch, but when I glanced there, they dropped in a frown.

"How'd she get the bruised eye, healing lip, and scar?"

"Sorry, man, had to teach her a lesson, but the scar ain't from any of us. It was from my cousin, stupid bitch obviously didn't heed his warning so he shot her," Baxter explained. His hand came out, and Stan placed some papers in them.

"Right." My owner's man laughed. "Fuckin' stupid women never learnin'."

"Damn right." Baxter grinned and then looked back down at the papers in his hands. "This ain't the right fuckin' contract, dickhead. Go get it," he barked at Stan, who shuffled out of the room.

A hand gripped my jaw. I gasped as my owner's man turned my head to face his. "Pretty little thing, might have to ask boss if I can keep you." He leaned in and sniffed. "Fuck, you smell delicious." In further until his nose hit my neck. My heart beat near out of my chest at his next whispered words, "Name's Gypsy. Here with your family, Nary. Stoke, Saxon. Be good."

My family.

Goosebumps spread across my skin.

Stoke. Oh, God, my dad was out there.

Saxon. I caught the whimper by biting my lips between my teeth and closed my eyes tightly to stop the tears. A happy shiver raked over my body as Gypsy pulled back.

"Yeah, gonna ask for a taste of you." His eyes went to Baxter where he clipped, "Let's get this show on the road. I have her, and boss said nothing about signin' some shit."

"Don't start being a dick 'cause you have a hard-on for her. Just wait a few seconds more." His eyes snapped to one of his men. "Where in the fuck is Stan?"

"I'll go find him."

Baxter rolled his eyes. "Yeah, do that, idiot." He ran a hand over his head. "So, what's your boss got planned for her?"

"Dunno, but I do know what he told me. If you fuck this up, he's willing to come here and take your business from under you."

"Ain't gonna happen," Baxter yelled. His face turned red as his eyes went to another man. I went to look but was suddenly taken to the couch with Gypsy on top of me. I let out a cry of surprise and my stomach bottomed. "What the fuck?" Baxter got out before the door burst open. I tilted my head back to see four men dressed in black run in. Shots were fired and Baxter's men started falling to the floor, and Baxter himself backed up until he hit the wall.

"You good?" Gypsy asked, I looked up at him and was about to smile until I remembered Kelsey.

"You have to help me. Kelsey. She was in the room with me. Please, you have to get her out. Please," I begged, my fists gripping his tee.

He knifed up off me and nodded before he started for the door.

"Gypsy?" Talon asked. I'd know his voice anywhere. Sitting up, I turned in time to see him pull a balaclava mask from his head, as did Dodge and...

"Dad!" I cried.

"Do not fuckin' move," I heard Dodge snarl.

However, nothing else existed except for my dad. I was running before I realised and then stumbled, but he was there, taking me into his arms. Tears ran freely down my face. A cry caught in my throat, turning into a whimper.

"Baby girl, I'm here. We're here. Jesus fuckin' Christ. My girl. I got you. I got you."

"How in the hell—" Baxter started.

Talon growled. "You gotta realise by now, motherfucker, no one fucks with Hawks."

Bang.

My body jolted from the sound. I turned my head to the side, resting it against Stoke's chest. Saxon had Baxter against the wall. A destroyed TV lay at Baxter's feet. Had Saxon hit him with it?

"You touched her. You fuckin' touched her."

My hand covered my mouth.

Saxon.

He was there. He'd seen the photo.

Oh, no, no, no.

Saxon. Not my Saxon.

Looking fierce and protective as he pulled a knife free of his jeans and drew back his arm before plunging it into the wall beside Baxter's head. "With what I'm gonna do to you, you'll wish and pray for death, but I won't let that happen. It's time to suffer for what you've done to her. It's time to fuckin' suffer."

Dad laid a jacket over my shoulders. I shrugged into the arm and zipped it up as more men filed into the room. Saxon stood back and let them take Baxter. His eyes came to me, and they softened in a way I had never seen before from him. At least, not directed at me.

Though I wasn't ready to deal like I thought I was. I wasn't ready for anything.

My body stiffened.

"What, Nary?" Dad asked.

Looking up, I whispered, "Kelsey." Then I ran from the room.

CHAPTER THIRTEEN

AFTER NARY LEFT

KELSEY

*B*rendan, one of Baxter's men, had come into the room a little while after Nary had been taken out for her owner, and closed the door behind him. I was already feeling the loss of Nary. Still, when he entered, my stomach sank even more because I knew what he was there for. Even if Baxter didn't know, they still shared me around and threatened me with death if I ever told Baxter what they were doing.

Death.

I should have accepted it a long time ago.

Was I a coward that I hadn't?

It felt like it.

Then Nary showed, and with all the talk about her family, hope had filled me once again. So much hope. Nary made things shine. She made me smile and placed a need to survive in me, a need to live even when each day was filled with pain in more ways than one. Physically and mentally.

However, since I watched the only light I'd had in the last eight months walk from the room, I wished for death once again.

I jumped when Brendan's belt hit the ground. What I should do was just lay there and take it; at least it would be less painful. Something I'd learned over time. Instead, I found myself scooting up the mattress on my behind until my back hit the wall. I cried silently as I heard Brendan's zipper slide down. The room was lit only by the light on Brendan's phone. Though even with my eyes closed, I knew what was going on. Being locked away for eight months in the dark had strengthened my hearing. I wished it hadn't.

A hand curled around my ankle. I let out a cry when I was roughly pulled down the mattress.

"Fuck, you need a shower. You stink," he complained.

Suffer.

Covering my face with my arms, I cried as his hands shoved my legs apart. I cried as I heard him shove his jeans down, and then I cried as he lay over me.

"What the fuck?" he yelled and pulled back as something hard hit the door. He laughed. "Idiots." He was over me once again when suddenly the door gave way and crashed loudly to the ground.

I screamed and shoved at Brendan, who was struggling with getting off me and doing up his pants at the same time.

Blinking, my eyes finally focused on a large man, one I had never seen before.

"P-please no," I whimpered as he stalked towards us. I saw his jaw clench as he glanced down at me in his approach.

"Who in the hell are you?" Brendan barked as he finally stood beside the mattress.

Still the man didn't stop. He came right up to Brendan, gripped his head and then twisted.

Brendan's body hit the floor. His lifeless eyes staring up at nothing.

A scream built inside of me. This was it. I was about to die, and yet I still wanted to fight.

For what?

For nothing.

There wasn't anything or anyone to fight for.

I bit off my scream of terror and snapped my mouth closed. Instead, I took a deep breath and closed my eyes. I arched my neck, so he could grab it easier and nodded once. Acceptance filled me, calmed my heart and shaking body.

Death was better for me.

It would finally bring me peace. It would stop my body from aching, my heart from breaking and take away my mind from the nightmares I'd endured.

"Kelsey?"

My head jerked back, my eyes opening wide.

"My name's Gypsy, and I'm here with Nary's family. I'm

gonna take you to Nary." His hand reached out, but I cringed back. "Kelsey, I'm not gonna hurt you. I promise." His eyes looked less harsh than they did when he'd entered the room. "Fuck, baby, what did they do to you?" His gaze was on my thighs. On the scars.

I tried to shift my nightgown down when I heard screamed, "Kelsey?"

"N-Nary," I whispered. "N-Nary?" I called and struggled up. Gypsy was there. He'd helped me. "Nary?" I cried, my voice caught with fear.

Fear with what was to come.

Fear of the world out there.

A hand touched my waist, and I jumped. "Shhh, it's okay," Gypsy said. He was there again, a man I didn't know. A man who came in and... saved me. He saved me.

He was safe.

I was safe.

"Oh, Kelsey," Nary sighed.

My eyes moved from Gypsy to the door. Nary was visibly shaking as her gaze flicked from me, to Brendan, to Gypsy, then back to me. Only my eyes widened, and I cringed back. Gypsy's arm tightened. Even when I pushed back, I didn't move because of Gypsy.

So many men.

So many angry-looking men were standing behind Nary.

She stepped in, her hands up in front of her. "Kelsey, it's okay. I'm right here."

"No," I whispered and frantically flung my arms out to

shove Gypsy. His arm loosened, and I moved back again and again until I was standing on the mattress in the corner of the room.

"Everybody get the fuck out," Gypsy roared. I covered my ears with my hands and squatted.

Through hooded eyes, I saw no one had moved.

"Nary—" a man started.

"Dad, please, you're all scaring her." That big man was her dad?

"Nary—"

"It's fine. Let me just get her out to a car."

"Nary!" The room quieted, and Nary turned to her father. "Tell me this isn't the room he kept you in."

Her head dropped forward, her eyes to the ground. "Dad," she whispered.

"He locked you in here?" another man snarled. That one younger than the rest, but even scarier. His body was tense, his hands clenched at his sides and his mouth thinned. Before he yelled, "In here? Fuck me, fuckin' hell."

Another said, "There's no power, no toilet. Jesus, is that a piss bucket?"

My hands couldn't block out their voices. I wanted them blocked out. I wanted the room quiet and dark, but the light shone through the open door. I hunched in on myself; my head hit my knees, and I closed my eyes.

"Knife, shut the fuck up," Nary's dad clipped. He turned his eyes to his daughter. "Who is she?"

Nary sucked in a breath and said, "Her name is Kelsey… Dad, she's been here for eight months. Baxter—"

My eyes sprang open wide as I looked up and screamed, "No!" I reached a hand out to her, only to drop it along with my eyes when everyone turned to me. "P-please, Nary."

She strode towards me. Gypsy moved in front of us, blocking my view from the other men. Kneeling on the bed, Nary's hands came to my arms.

"I'm sorry. I won't say anything. I promise." Tears spilled onto her cheeks, and I watched them run down her neck. "We need to get out of here," she whispered.

"I-I don't think I can."

"Oh, Kelsey." She looked over her shoulder and asked, "Can you please leave?"

"No," I cried. "Not him." I pointed to Gypsy. A need inside of me to have him at my side was strong. He was safe. He'd *killed* a man to keep me safe.

"All good, darlin', I'm not leavin'," Gypsy told me from over his shoulder.

"I ain't goin' anywhere either," another man growled.

"Vicious, out," Nary's dad ordered. I heard this Vicious man suck back a breath ready to argue.

"You also, Dad," Nary said before anyone could say anything.

"Nary, I just got you back. I'm not leavin' your side."

Nary looked back to me. I nodded. He was her dad. He wouldn't... He should be safe also.

"Nary, don't think I'm goin'—"

"Saxon, please. I want to get Kelsey out of here."

Saxon. Nary's Saxon. She'd told me all about him, how much she loved him even after he was being mean to her. I could understand it though, after everything she'd said. He was always there, always protecting her, and it told me he was also protecting her from himself for some reason.

"All right, clear the room. Gypsy, you good to help Kelsey?" a man with dark messy hair asked.

"Yup," Gypsy replied curtly.

Saxon's pained eyes looked longingly at Nary one last time, and just as I was about to shout he could stay, I found myself biting my tongue, holding it back, and he stalked from the room. I just couldn't handle them all around me. Too many men. Too many angry men, surrounding me, suffocating me.

"I-I'm sorry," I whispered. "I'm sorry," I said again, my voice breaking.

"It's okay, honey," Nary reassured me. She stood and bent over. Her hand gripped my arm and slowly she helped me stand. My legs shook under me, but I took a step off the mattress, and then Gypsy was there. He ignored my flinch when his hand wound around my waist. He ignored my sniffles, my tears, and my tremoring body as he guided me slowly towards the door. Nary didn't leave my side and I was thankful. I couldn't have done it without her.

We came to stop at the door as Gypsy let go of me for a second. He pulled off his leather vest and then his thermal top. My heart beat frantically as he placed it over my head. Nary helped me pull my arms through. Warmth I hadn't felt for a very long time filled me.

Silently, with Nary's dad following, we made our way

out of the room. I cringed back when the light hurt my eyes, but Gypsy was there, his arm around my waist again.

"Kelsey, are you good?" he asked.

Blinking, I shielded my eyes for a moment until I was more adjusted and then nodded. We started walking down the hall opposite the bathroom. Once outside, the cool night air touched my skin. I stopped. Nary and Gypsy stopped with me. Ignoring the movement of so many men around me, I felt safe with Nary close, so I tipped my head back and looked to the stars.

Tears brimmed and then fell. I closed my eyes and drew in a deep shuddering breath, the cool, fresh air tickling my skin.

"Kelsey?" Nary said from beside me, her hand squeezing mine. I loosened my grip in hers a little. I hadn't realised I had been holding her so tightly.

Tipping my head down, I turned to her. My bottom lip wobbled. So much... I was feeling too much, and it was hard to take it all in. My mind spun while my heart danced wildly in my chest, and even with the warmth filling me deep within my stomach, my body shook.

With a small smile on my lips, I stuttered to Nary, "I-It's beautiful."

"What?" she asked on a whisper, tears in her eyes.

"Feeling free."

Closing her eyes, her lips thinned as she nodded. When she opened her gorgeous green eyes again, she ran a hand over my hair. "It is beautiful."

CHAPTER FOURTEEN

NARY

The ride in the van to the compound was silent. I sat beside my father, his arm around my shoulders where I rested my head against his chest. Though, I still had my hand clasping Kelsey's as she sat next to me. Behind us, in the other free seat, was Gypsy, a man I didn't know, but was grateful for him being there. What he did for Kelsey was unrepayable, but it was certain the two of us were the only ones who could keep her from having a panic attack.

As soon as we'd climbed in, Gypsy's hand was over our seat and he gently rested it on Kelsey's shoulder. At first she'd jumped, until she'd settled into it and leaned into my side. The only other in the car was Pick, who was driving. His eyes kept flicking to me in the rear-view mirror. I knew he wanted to say something, but he held back, and I appreciated it. Not only was I drained, but I was a ball of mixed emotions, and my stomach was playing dodgeball from it all. I was nervous to see everyone, even when I was glad my family surrounded me. However, I couldn't help but think of who exactly saw that photo Baxter took. Not only that, but I worried how they would treat me once I told them everything that had happened to me. I didn't want to be a fragile woman. I had been strong before everything. I wanted to go back to being that woman. Still, I was scared I wasn't going to be.

And Saxon.

He was there.

He was beautifully scary.

His reluctance to leave my side threw me. Shocked me even. *Another emotion to add to my large list.*

What would happen next? I didn't know. All I knew was I was grateful to be free. Like Kelsey had said. It was beautiful.

A GASP CHOKED MY THROAT. I straightened, coughing, raising my hand to my chest as my heart beat scary fast behind my ribs. For a second, I didn't know where I was, until Dad, next to me, gave my shoulder a gentle squeeze and said, "You're okay, honey."

Turning to look at him, I offered a small smile and a nod. I glanced beside me for Kelsey. She wasn't there. I spun to the back seat as I heard the side door to the van being pulled open. In the back seat, I found Kelsey curled up on Gypsy's lap.

"She wouldn't sleep or relax," Gypsy said quietly, his brows drawn down, his lips pinched tight in concern.

"Thank you," I whispered.

My name being cried out in a scream had me facing the front, and through the windshield, I saw my mum running out of the compound and straight for the vehicle. There were many other cars around us, but I knew what gave it away to where I was. All the men, my family, surrounded it.

My body ached, but it gave me what I wanted. I moved fast out of the van, climbing over Dad before he had the chance to get out since he was closest to the door.

"Nary," Mum cried, her hand covering her mouth. Tears ran down her cheeks as she stopped just in front of me. "Honey," she breathed.

"I'm okay," I murmured, and next I was crushed to her chest. I buried my head into her neck as I bawled.

My mum.

I was home. Safe.

"I was so worried, honey. So worried for my girl." She sniffed and tried to pull me back to look at me, but I clung to her. I wasn't ready to let her go and she knew it, so she held me tighter, closer.

"Sis," was said quietly beside me.

Lifting my head, my eyes landed on my brother. My brave brother who had tears in his eyes. I moved into his outstretched arms. More crying, more belly dipping and heart breaking as my brother broke with me. He cried and mumbled into my hair, "Jesus, fuck... Jesus, fuck. You're back. You're here. They got you back."

Nodding, over and over into his chest, I gripped him to me and said, "I'm okay. I'm good."

"Josh, let's get her inside, yeah?" Dad suggested from beside us. His hand came to my shoulder and pulled me tenderly back to tuck me under his arm. Over everyone, I saw Gypsy walking into the compound with Kelsey in his arms. She mustn't have woken, even through all the commotion.

Dad started for the doors and everyone followed. Mum came to his other side where he wound his free arm around her shoulders. Josh was at my other side, and he took the hand I wasn't using to wipe my face.

We only came to a stop when Saxon stepped in front of us. His eyes... I couldn't work out what it was. Though it seemed a fire had been lit in them, they also held concern and fear.

"Fuck," he bit out. His head tilted to its side and through a clenched jaw, he clipped, "Brother?" His hands fisted at his sides. He shifted from one foot to another, and yet his body threw off tension. "Please," he hissed low.

Looking up, I saw Dad lift his chin, before he said, "Why don't you take Nary in, Vicious?"

My eyes widened. This was what he was asking for? Why?

It dawned on me. Saxon had been scared *for* me, concerned *for* me. What I saw in his eyes was his true emotions for the first time.

The man before us stalked right up to me, Josh, and Dad. He moved in and I was swept up into his arms, carried bride-style into the compound. Tears formed once again—really they were always present, ready for my control to slip, allowing them to fall. Glancing up at Saxon, as he ground his teeth together, I slowly reached a hand up and touched his jaw. His eyes flicked down to me. "I'm okay," I whispered. His reply was a grunt. His eyes narrowed when he glanced back up to watch where he was walking down the hall.

He didn't believe me, and really, I didn't believe those words myself. I *was* more than okay being back with my family, but what had happened to me, to Kelsey, had damaged us and I knew a part of me would never be okay again.

So I moved my hand to his chest where I felt his heart beating frantically behind his ribs. He walked us into the common area, and a loud murmur of voices broke out as soon as I was spotted. Saxon planted me on my feet and then stepped in front of me. He moved his hand behind him to touch my waist.

"Stop," he ordered on a growl. Over his shoulder, I watched Josie, Low, Mrs Cliff, and other club members' women come to a halt on Saxon's words. "She needs rest, food, and water. You can see she's… okay. But leave the fawning until later. She's been through enough."

My head dropped forward, hitting his shoulder. I bit my bottom lip to stop the wail wanting out of my throat. He understood. How did he understand?

I'd already felt too much, and everything was climbing on top of me, weighing me down. I wanted to talk to them all, to show them I was fine, but I was tired and highly strung from all I'd already gone through.

"Vicious," I heard Dodge say. "Get her into a room. We'll welcome her back later." What he left off was "question her later."

"Trey," Low's quiet voice was heard in the silent room.

"Little bird, you'll get your girl soon. Yeah? Josie, yeah?"

"Yes, Dodge," Josie answered.

I lifted my head when Saxon moved and once again, I was swung up into his arms. I rested my head against his chest as he swiftly walked from the room and down the hall, which held the bedrooms. Near the end, he stopped and using his hand that held my legs up, he opened the door and then kicked it closed.

My heart stumbled.

I was in his room. I knew it was his from the smell.

He moved over to another door and stood me on my feet. "You want a shower?"

"Yes," I whispered, my eyes to the floor. "But... Kelsey?"

"Gypsy will keep an eye on her and come get you when she wakes, or we'll send her in here."

My hands restlessly played with the zipper of Dad's jacket.

"Angel." His voice was soft and it had my head lifting to meet his gaze. Never had he called me angel. The way he said it, the warm look in his eyes sent my belly dipping, and caused my head to muddle even more.

His hand reached up to touch my face. Why I cringed back, I didn't know. I didn't understand it. But I did, and I saw the pain slash through his eyes. He lowered his hand and took a step back.

"No," I pleaded and quickly took his hand in mine and tugged it up to lay his palm flat against my cheek. "I'm sorry. I don't know why I moved back, but I *do* know I can trust you, Saxon."

He watched as his thumb ran along my scar. His eyes came to me, and the warmth bled back into them before he said, "Have a shower. We'll talk soon."

"Thank you, Saxon," I whispered. "Not only for being one to get us… out, but for also knowing what I needed. Time."

"They'll want to know everything, like I do, but you take the time you need." With that, he leaned forward and touched his lips to my forehead.

My pulse beat hard. This was what we should have been like at the start. When he pulled away, I knew he'd seen the hurt in my eyes because he flinched.

"Angel, things will change."

"Saxon—"

"No, Nary. I fuckin' promise things will change. Time is all we need to sort some shit out."

My eyes widened. "What are you saying?" I whispered.

He shook his head. "Get a shower, angel. We'll talk soon."

"Saxon—"

"Shower," he ordered and opened the door to the bathroom.

With a roll of my eyes, I grumbled, "Fine." It was then he gifted me with a chuckle and a smile. My eyes widened, only to soften, and I slid my hand to his chest. "Saxon," I murmured.

His jaw clenched, and then I was in his arms. "Fuck, angel. Fuck. You're back. So goddamn glad you're safe and I'll make sure it stays that way."

Tears filled my eyes as I nodded against his chest. I couldn't talk. I couldn't do anything but cherish the moment.

Would this Saxon last?

I wasn't sure, but I could hope.

Maybe he'd woken up when I'd been taken.

Guilt stirred low in my belly. I closed my eyes tight and took a deep breath. Time was what we needed. I had to help Kelsey work her way back into the living.

I also had to speak with Jerimiah because even if things didn't go where I wanted them to with Saxon, if I was strong enough to make it certain Saxon knew how I wanted things between us, I had to let Jerimiah know everything.

My heart didn't belong to myself.

It never had.

It belonged to Saxon Black.

CHAPTER FIFTEEN

SAXON

*S*he had been in the shower for fifteen minutes when I heard her emotions take over. She tried to keep it quiet, but she couldn't and I knew, I just fucking knew she would be sitting on the shower floor, her arms wrapped around herself to try to contain her cries.

And she'd be doing it so it wouldn't worry me.

I wanted to charge in there, take her in my arms, and hold her close, let her break against me so I could help piece her back together. I didn't. She was naked and, fuck, after what she no-doubt went through, having a man, any man see her naked would not go down well. Stalking to my bedroom door, I pulled it open and stopped still.

"She needs me," Malinda said.

Malinda, Stoke, and Josh were standing out in the hall

waiting. With a nod, Malinda rushed by, her arms full of clothes and other shit, and went straight into the bathroom. A squeal of shock from Nary and then loud, painful wails of agony slipped through the room before Malinda closed the bathroom door.

My head dipped, my hand moving to the back of my neck where I rubbed as my stomach filled with an aching need to go to her. A need to ease her torment.

"Shit," I clipped. My gaze lifted when Stoke and Josh walked into my room.

"I know, brother," Stoke said, his gaze hard, his jaw clenched, same as Josh. They were feeling it along with me. They sat on the end of my bed. I closed the door and put my back to it before I slid down it until my arse hit the floor.

Another loud shriek of agony erupted from behind the door. Then Malinda saying something.

Fuck. Fuck me. I placed my head in my hands and closed my eyes. My woman's pain was killing me on the inside. My throat felt thick while my soul felt crushed. My stomach stirred up a storm.

"I'm going to kill him," I mumbled.

"Not alone you're not," Stoke gritted.

Raising my head, I looked to him and then Josh. Yeah, they were feeling it.

"I want in," Josh said.

"Josh—" Stoke started.

"No!" his son yelled.

"Keep your voice down," I ordered on a snarl.

Josh's glare swung to me. "He did shit to my sister. *My*

sister. I want to wrap my hand around that fucker's neck and look him in the eyes while he fights for his breath." He looked back to his dad. "You can't deny this from me."

"I can." Stoke sighed. "Fuck." He faced his body to his son, tagging the back of Josh's neck and said, "This is somethin' you have to live with for the rest of your life. Doin' this shit can fuck a person up. I get you want to do this for Nary, and I'm goddamn proud you do. I just don't like my kid reachin' into the dark so soon."

"Dad," Josh mumbled. "You taught Nary and me we stick up for each other and our family. No one fucks with us, but especially no one fucks with Hawks. I'm eighteen. I ain't fifteen any longer. If I'm reaching for the dark, I want to. Hell, I'd be glad to because… he touched her, he messed her up. Anyone can see it, and right now, I'm listenin' to how much anguish is inside her. What *I* couldn't live with is if I sat back and done nothin'."

Stoke studied his son's face. After a while, he nodded. "Okay, you come with us when it happens."

Josh reached up, his own hand going to the back of his dad's neck where he pulled and their foreheads hit. "Family first."

"Family first," Stoke repeated.

The bathroom door opened and Malinda walked out. Once she closed it behind her, she faced her husband and took a few steps towards him before her face crumbled. Stoke was in front of her in seconds. As Josh and I stood, Stoke wrapped his woman up in his arms.

"Not yet, love. Wait until she can't hear. Not yet," he

whispered into Malinda's hair. Her whole body shook with silent sobs.

"Declan." Her voice broke on a whisper, and she gripped her man tighter. "T-they touched her, hurt her, s-starved her. My baby, my girl, went through hell. It's too much. It hurts too much. I-I... oh, God."

My hands came up and gripped my hair. I closed my eyes as her words penetrated my mind.

Jesus Christ.

Fuck.

Shit.

Malinda let out a shuddering breath, tilted her head back, and said, "She wants to tell her side. She wants to get it over with."

Stoke turned to Josh and ordered, "Get Talon and Dodge. No one else."

Josh wiped his palm down his face and nodded, leaving the room quietly.

"Love," Stoke began, and when he had his woman's eyes, he went on, "Need you to go to the girls. But fuck, love, I wanna be there for you."

"Don't," she said, shaking her head. "Be there for our girl. Later you're going to have to help me." Her eyes came to me. "You take care of her also."

"Always," I clipped.

She smiled sadly. "I know, honey." With one last lingering hug and a quick lip touch from her man, she walked from the room.

Stoke sat back on the bed, his head in his hands. "Fuck

me." He raised his head and looked to me. "You sure you wanna hear this?"

Crossing my arms over my chest, I leant back into the wall and said, "Everything. So I know where I have to take care and be cautious."

The bathroom door opened and Nary with her long, wet hair walked out dressed in jeans and a long-sleeved top. Her feet were bare. I went to my side table and grabbed some socks. Turning around, Stoke was already in front of her whispering something to her, his hands cupping her cheeks. I let them have their moment, and when I saw them done, after he brought her into a hug, I went to them. Nary's eyes hit mine first and then Stoke's. I held out the socks and said, "Put them on."

She nodded and moved back, going to the bed to sit down. My bedroom door opened. Talon walked in first, followed by Dodge, and then Josh.

"Josh," Nary called. I watched as she caught her brother's eyes and then shook her head.

"Nary—"

"Please. Please, Josh, for my sake. I can't have my baby brother in here for this. It's bad enough with Stoke and..." Her eyes flicked to me for a second, and then they went back to her brother. "Please."

He sighed. "Okay." Josh walked from the room, closing the door behind him. Stoke moved to sit next to Nary on the end of the bed. Dodge went to the only lounge chair I had and sat. Talon pulled out the chair at my desk and lowered himself into it. I went and sat on the floor, leaning back against the wall closest to my woman.

Stoke, probably knowing his girl like I did, leaned forward, resting his elbows on his knees so she didn't have his eyes through what she was about to say. I shifted mine from her to the floor.

"I would like to only say this once please, and then... I need to forget. I need to live."

She waited, and it was Talon who replied with, "Of course."

She sucked back a big gulp of breath and started, "When they took me, I was tasered so I wouldn't know the destination. I woke to a dark room. I couldn't even see my hand in front of my face. It was there I met Kelsey. She'd been stuck in that room for eight months. She told me Baxter kept her for himself." Her voice quieted, and she whispered, "The things he did to her... She would come back to me beaten and with blood between her legs. She wanted to die and..." I moved to sitting at her legs where I took her hand. She sniffed, and I caught her nod before my eyes went back to the floor. "I wanted to die at the end. I was weak, where Kelsey was there for longer and what she'd—"

"Babe, don't," Dodge ordered. "What happened to you is as fucked as what your girl went through. Don't matter you were there less. Got it."

"Yes," she murmured. Her hand gripped mine tighter. "Kelsey said Baxter usually stuck to homeless girls so no one would miss them. She couldn't work out why I was taken." She sighed. "I found out why. It wasn't only because you knocked him back, Talon, or that Dodge bested him. He was Cameron's cousin."

"Fuck," Dodge clipped. "The dick who wanted Josie?"

"Yes."

"Jesus Christ," Stoke grumbled.

"He'll get what's coming to him," Talon said. Looking to him, I saw his eyes were on Nary. They were soft as he went on, "But, honey. We need to know what happened in there."

"Talon—"

"No. One way or another you gotta get that shit out, and we ain't your girls, I know this, but we want to hold that burden with you. No one else has to know, girl. Give it to us to hold. Give it to us to take on, Nary."

"I don't—"

Squeezing her hand, I glanced up to catch her eyes. "Angel," I said softly. "Give it to us."

"You will all lose it. I've seen it happen. I know what this will do to you all."

"Baby girl," Stoke started. She turned to him. "We will lose our shit, but it won't happen in front of you. We will lose it because of that fucker. It will make us crazy in anger, but none of it will change the way we care about you or treat you."

Shit, fuck, shit. I didn't want to hear, but I knew I had to.

She nodded and sucked in another breath. "They did *everything* except… he, Baxter, he wanted me to stay pure for my owner, that way they could get more money for me." The room filled with a thick fire of rage. It rolled off us all in waves. "Um, when they took my photo, I begged for him to not send it to you all. I-I tried to refuse it. That was when he hit me, and because I fought back…" She fell silent. "We didn't eat or shower for four days after that, not until I'd found out I was sold."

She sucked in a shuddering breath. I stood, picked her up, and sat her on my lap, cradling her head against my chest as her body shook. "Fuck, angel. You're safe now," I murmured against her hair. I felt her nod, only my eyes were looking from one brother to the next. They were all fighting what I was to keep our cool.

Baxter was going to pay tenfold for what he'd done.

How-fucking-ever, he wasn't going to get the easy way out with death. Shit no. I'd bring the idea to my brothers for Baxter to be turned over to the cops after we'd had our time with him. He needed to live his life out with days filled with pain and hell.

We had brothers on the inside. They would make certain of it. They'd keep an eye on him day and night to make sure he couldn't end his own life, and they'd make certain Baxter knew what fear was.

The fucker did not deserve easy.

The bedroom door banged open. Dallas entered, yelling, "Cryin', screamin' girl down the end. Nary, we need you."

Nary gasped and was off my lap, running to the door in seconds. I quickly followed her, and in the hall down the end, we heard the ear-splintering pierce of Kelsey yelling Nary's name.

As we came to the door, Nary paused only a second before she was up and standing on the bed with a scared

Kelsey. With her arms out in front of her, she whispered shit to Kelsey.

"I was only sitting in here when she woke while Gypsy showered. I didn't do shit," Dallas said from beside me.

Looking there, I saw Melissa standing in front of him. She slowly turned and glared up at him. "You big arse, you would have told her not to freak or cry, or some other stupid shit." She pulled back her leg and kicked him in the shin.

"See, it's okay." I heard Nary say. "The men here won't do anything even if we do something to them."

"Fuck, tiny woman. You—"

"Shut it, Viking man, and get out."

"Gladly," he snarled in her face, only his head tipped back to the ceiling, and he cried, "Why me?" Melissa sent him a wink and a kissy face.

The banter, the small smile on my woman's face helped cool the fire raging inside of me. No matter how much I wanted to race from that room and deal with Baxter, my woman was coming first. I wasn't leaving her side until it felt right. *Then* I'd deal with Baxter alongside of Stoke and Josh.

Family first.

CHAPTER SIXTEEN

NARY

$\mathcal{K}$elsey had calmed a little when she saw me. She calmed even more and sat down on the bed with me when the woman I didn't know kicked huge Dallas in the shin and he did nothing to her in return, well, except shout in her face. Once he stalked from the room, most of the other bikers left along with him. All the way, teasing Dallas. Not Saxon though. He stood just inside the door leaning against the wall. His eyes were on me, warm, and yet, I saw the storm brewing in them. The storm started when he'd heard what had happened to me, and I knew if Dallas hadn't interrupted us, the storm could have taken over Saxon.

Then again, I wasn't sure if Saxon would have let that happen. He seemed changed. His hot head and bad-tempered attitude seemed under control when I was around. Yet, in the past, I was the one who'd brought it out in him.

My mind spun in confusion.

What exactly was going on in that mind of his?

It was something to worry about later. Right then, I wanted to take care of Kelsey.

"You okay?" I asked.

Her gaze took in Saxon, Dad, the woman I didn't know, Josie, and Low. Dallas must have gone on a screaming rampage over a woman crying, calling for all the reinforcements he could get.

"Y-yes, I'm sorry. I was confused when I woke," she whispered.

"Honey," the new woman started, "Dallas would freak anyone out. Don't worry about it." She moved towards the bed, her hand out in front of her, and once I took it, she said, "I'm Melissa by the way. Julian, my gay BFF, got me here to help look for you. Only because of the screwed-up situation, I couldn't make any deals because I'm a woman. Which was why I got Mason, Gypsy's president from the Rebel Wayfarers MC in America, to help us out." After she shook Kelsey's hand, she moved back a step.

"Thank you, we appreciate everything," I told her. So that was how Gypsy came about. His accent had told me he wasn't from Australia. My family had gone above and beyond to find me. It was something I doubted I could repay, yet I hoped to one day.

"Pleasure is all mine or else I wouldn't be here to torture Dallas." She smiled.

"Are you and he...?"

"Hell no!" was shouted from the hall.

Melissa snorted and said, "He wishes. But I'm not going to be around for much longer."

Josie stepped up, her hand to Melissa's shoulder. "I hope you'll stay for a little while still. I would love to hear more stories of my brother-in-law."

"I'm sure I can think of some. Too bad his little one got sick and he had to leave. I would love to have embarrassed him more."

Low laughed and shifted closer to the bed. "Julian never gets embarrassed."

Melissa rose her brows. "You'd be surprised." Her eyes went to Josie. "Hey, where are your men? I thought they always stuck to you like glue?" She glanced back to Kelsey and added, "The men here are mighty fine, don't you think?"

Kelsey shrugged and ducked her head, a blush lighting her cheeks. I was sure there was one man she thought fine, only he wasn't a Hawks man. Which worried me. She trusted Gypsy because he'd saved her and killed a man who had hurt her. She clung to him like he was her security blanket, so what would happen when he left to go home?

It worried me, among other things.

Looking at Low and Josie, I watched them talk to Melissa as Kelsey listened. She learned and got shocked, her gasp told me so, about Josie's *two* men. My friends seemed normal, which made me think I was stupid to have thought they would've treated me different. Actually, I had been stupid. They'd gone through their own hell and came out on the other side, which gave me hope Kelsey and I would be okay.

Their eyes met mine. I smiled sadly and said, "I'm sorry for earlier."

"Don't you dare, girl. We totally get it." Low nodded.

"We really do." Josie smiled. She glanced over her shoulder to Saxon and Dad and asked, "Can we have some girl time, please?"

Dad snorted. "Knew it was only a matter of time. Gonna go see your mum, Nary. You good?"

"Yes, Dad. Thanks." He gave me a chin lift and walked out. My eyes moved to Saxon, who was still leaning against the wall with his arms crossed.

"Pretend I'm a girl."

My heart warmed. He didn't want to leave me.

Melissa and Low burst out laughing, while Josie, and even Kelsey, giggled softly. I smiled and shook my head at him, then said, "That's actually impossible to do."

The corner of his lips tipped up. It was gorgeous to see. I'd never seen it directed at me, only at the younger Hawks' kids or his biker brothers.

"Out!" Low ordered.

His eyes narrowed on her, the same look I'd seen a million times, and yet it never scared me; it never put me off him. We all had issues, and maybe sorting them out with a special someone could help. I had a hankering I'd be Saxon's special someone.

His words earlier gave me reassurance I could be.

"Fine," he snapped. "I'll be out in the hall." He turned, moved into the hall, spun to face the room, and then slid down the wall opposite the room to sit on his butt. He then raised a brow at Low. She grumbled something under her breath about alpha men, went to the door, and closed it.

"Something's changed in that guy," Low commented as she came back to the bed and then sat, facing us and crossing her legs. Josie and Melissa also climbed onto the bed, while Kelsey and I moved back to make room, leaning our backs against the headboard.

"I agree with Low and I'm sensing it's a good change," Josie whispered, not wanting the man in the hall to hear her.

"He says he wants to talk," I admitted.

"Talk is good." Kelsey smiled shyly.

Grinning back, I nodded and said, "It is."

"You should have seen him, Nary." I caught Josie's eyes. "When he first heard, he lost it, big time. Pick told me it took a lot of brothers to take him down to the ground." My heart beat crazy in my chest at her words. She went on, "They had to lock him up for a while until he calmed. Then when Stoke arrived, he asked where Saxon was. I'm not sure what Stoke said to him, but Saxon came out with vengeance burning brightly in his eyes."

"It's true," Low added. "Girl, he hadn't slept, or ate, unless he was forced to and when we thought he was sleeping, apparently he wasn't. In the end his brothers had to drug him." My eye widened. "He was damn pissed, but he knew he'd be no good in the fight to get you back."

"That guy is fierce," Melissa said. Low and Josie nodded.

Then Josie continued, "Billy also told me that when Saxon went in to where you were, he was a machine. Took man after man down in any way he could."

Saxon fought for me.

Things were going to change between us, and I could tell from the way my girls were talking, it was going to be in a big, beautiful way. A change we couldn't rush into because it was something I wanted to last forever.

"Honey," Josie whispered. "Are you okay?"

Biting my bottom lip, I nodded, only the tears in my eyes told another story. I gripped Kelsey's hand in mine, and I offered to them, "At least, we will be with time." My eyes met Kelsey's. Darkness lingered in hers, and it scared me. I knew she feared where her life would lead since being free. All I could comfort her with was the fact I'd be by her side while we struggled together.

"We all know hardship in this room," Low said, a sad smile on her lips, her eyes on Kelsey's. "We've all been through our own version of hell." Low looked to Josie who nodded. Low, in a quiet voice, unlike her usual one, then told Kelsey of their ordeals. Towards the end, Kelsey was crying in my arms, and Low finished with, "So we know, girl. We know what you've been through, and we also know there is light at the end, and the light we've found is in the men who honour us to call our own. Only, I realise it's not only that, it's our family. Even if we're not blood related, we're family. We hold strong, and, honey, while you go through this, we will help *you* hold strong as well. You have us, sister, and never forget it."

The room fell silent and Kelsey nodded into my shoulder, her eyes on Low.

"Well, fuck me. I think I need a Valium after all that," Melissa said, her own eyes shining with tears. "I love that you all have this now and that Julian is a welcome part in the family, even by those bad-boy bikers. You all deserve the best."

"So do you," Josie said. "We haven't known each other long, Melissa, but you should know you've been placed into our family web."

"I appreciate it, babe. However, I'm not going to be around much longer."

"Still, no matter where you go, you ever need Hawks at your back, we got you," Low told her.

Melissa's eyes hit the bed, and she mumbled, "Thanks."

We gabbed for a little while longer, but once they saw my eyelids drooping, they hugged me and let Kelsey and me rest. As soon as the bedroom door opened, my eyes landed on Saxon and his were already on me. He stood and when Low, Josie, and Melissa were out the door, he came in.

"You need sleep," he stated.

"Yes." I nodded. "But would it be okay if we go to your room with the joining bathroom where Kelsey could have a shower before we fall asleep?"

"Yeah, angel." He moved to the side of the bed just as the door behind him opened again, and Gypsy was standing there.

His eyes were on Kelsey, and since she was close beside me, I felt and heard her sigh of relief. "Sorry," he offered. "I had to have a shower, darlin', and then speak to Mason." Kelsey nodded, but said nothing. She was just glad he was back.

God, how was she going to be once he was gone?

The men walked behind Kelsey and me down the hall and into Saxon's room. As I guided Kelsey to the bathroom, I said over my shoulder, "Can one of you find my mum and get her to grab some clothes for Kelsey?"

Gypsy sent a chin lift and left, closing the door behind him. By the time I had the water running warm for Kelsey, there was a knock on the bathroom door. When I opened it, trackpants and a long-sleeved tee, like mine, was shoved through. "Thank you," I said before closing the door once again. Turning around, I placed the clothes on the basin and asked, "Will you be okay on your own?"

"Yes." She nodded. I moved to the door again until she called, "Nary." Looking to her, I saw a small, sorrowful smile. "You will never know what you did for me... back *there*. You saved me, and I want you to know, I-I'll make sure to cherish the days, months, years to follow because you have given me this chance to live. You have shown me compassion and hope. You have me feeling emotions I haven't felt in a long time, even in that place. T-thank you, for everything."

Through watery eyes, I grinned and said, "We're in this together, and you'll always hold a place in my life and heart, Kelsey."

"Same to you."

"Have a nice shower, honey."

Her smile changed to a sweet one. "I-I'm sure I will."

After closing the bathroom door behind me, I lifted my eyes to see only Saxon in the room sitting in his desk chair, and before I could ask where Gypsy was, Saxon said, "He's grabbin' a bite to eat."

"Are you, um, do you, that is—"

"Angel." My eyes flicked up from the floor. "Get in the bed. Your girl can have the other side."

"But, this is your room."

He looked to the bed and then back to me. "Havin' and knowin' you're in here, my room, eases something inside of me. I'd prefer you in here taking care of Kelsey."

Oh, my God.

Did he just say that?

"Okay," I whispered and then moved from the door to the bed.

"Your mum sent some sleep pants. They're on the bed."

Picking them up, I was glad for the soft material to sleep in. Glancing over my shoulder, I saw Saxon had spun his chair to face the desk. Quickly, I removed my jeans and pulled up the sleep pants. "I'm decent," I said and pulled back the blanket, climbing in. I rolled to my side so I could face him. "Thank you." Suddenly, I found it hard to keep my eyes open.

"Fuck."

Blinking open my eyes, I asked softly, "What?"

His warm, hooded eyes were on me in his bed. "Nothin'."

He grunted. "Get some sleep, angel. If I'm not here when you wake, your mum will be, promise."

I hummed as my eyes drifted closed again. "I like this Saxon, a lot," I mumbled, not that the words really registered in my mind or the fact I had said it aloud.

"This is the way I shoulda always been with you."

His words drifted through me before sleep took me under.

CHAPTER SEVENTEEN

SAXON

*S*eeing her in my bed did something to me. Blood
rushed to my head and dick. I was a guy, so it was
bound to happen, especially when I'd been picturing it for a
goddamn long time while I had my cock in hand. I closed
my eyes, took a deep breath, and leant back in the chair.
Right then wasn't the time to have a hard-on, not after what
my woman went through.

When the bathroom door opened, I sat straight and
looked to Kelsey, ready to fly if she freaked without Nary
awake or Gypsy in the room. First, she took in the sleeping
woman, and then her eyes came to me. "S-she was very
tired."

I tipped my chin up in response. "Gypsy will be back

soon. He's gone to get food for you." I was letting her know she wouldn't be in the room alone with me for long.

She nodded, then timidly moved to the sofa chair and sat. "S-she spoke of you in there." Kelsey moved her eyes to mine for a second before they shifted back to Nary. "She's an amazing woman. Strong, protective, happy, full of hope. She's beautiful."

"She is."

"You've been mean to her."

Fuck.

Nary had told her.

"But she still gives her heart to you."

My body stilled. Hell, I even held my breath.

"You need to treat her b-better."

"I will."

"I can already see the change you've made through what Nary's said." Kelsey looked at me, and then her eyes narrowed. Christ, I was proud of the woman myself. "She didn't say it, but you've always been her dream. Please don't crush it for her."

"All I can do is hope I won't."

Her eyes studied me, until she moved them back to Nary. "She deserves the best."

"Agreed," I clipped. I wasn't sure I was the best for her still, yet, I was going to try to be.

The handle jiggled just before the door opened and in it stood Gypsy holding a tray. As he entered, I stood and said, "Here, man, sit there. I'm gonna get Nary's mum to come in to be here when she wakes. I got some stuff to do."

Gypsy nodded. He knew what I had to do, so he replied with, "All good, brother." As I walked out the door, I heard Gypsy say, "Darlin', come eat somethin.'" And I wondered how Kelsey was going to go after the man in there left. Fucking grateful he'd come to help us out. Didn't care we owed Rebel Wayfarers something because Gypsy was a good guy, and so I knew he'd handle Kelsey with care. I just didn't know which way he'd go about doing it.

Hell, I found with every step I took, I wanted to turn myself around and go back to my room to watch Nary sleep. Still, I didn't. Payback burned in my veins, and first, I wanted to chat with my brothers.

As soon as Josh, the last brother I wanted in the meeting room, entered, I closed the door and sat at the table with Talon, Dodge, Killer, Dallas, Stoke, Handle, and Josh. Griz had headed back to Ballarat already to inform everyone there how things went down. We didn't want to risk going through it all over the phone or by text. Other brothers were floating around, catching up on sleep, or eating.

"Gonna go in there with Stoke and Josh," I informed them. Talon and Dodge gave me a chin lift. Handle nodded. Killer and Dallas neither did nor said anything. "Before we do, need you to know we're gonna make him bleed, make him wish we'd take his life, but we won't."

"What?" Stoke snarled.

"He doesn't deserve to die. He needs to be dealt pain,

torture, and fear every day for the rest of his fuckin' life. If he tries to kill himself, which he will, we put a stop to it. He fucked with Hawks. He took a person in our family. He doesn't get the easy road."

"How you plan on doin' this?" Dodge asked.

Looking to them all, I answered, "Let Lan and Parker take him in for the shit he's done. We have brothers in there to keep an eye on him, and I'm sure they'd be happy to deal with him every day."

The room fell silent, and then Killer spoke. "Vicious has a point. Death is too easy for him." Killer's eyes hit mine. "Fuckin' hard to make that decision. I know I'd be wanting to end the man who took my woman and did shit to her." I went to butt in, until his hand came up. "However, the choice you've made is smart, because I know if I'd killed him, I'd end up regretting it. You'll see pain in Nary's eyes, you'll see fear, and you'll want to kill that man over again and again. At least this way, you'll know each and every motherfuckin' day, he'll be suffering, and the knowing will help ease the hurt you'll feel when you see Nary struggling on her bad days."

"I agree," Dallas clipped.

"So do I." Dodge nodded.

"Agreed," Talon said.

Looking to Stoke, I saw his jaw was tight, his eyes narrowed and filled with fury. "Thank fuck you thought of it before I got in there. I think knowing that man will suffer every fuckin' day for taking our girl is better than anything."

"Agree also," Josh bit out, then added with a goddamn

smile, "Since Mum's with Nary, we getting some payback in now?"

Yep, he was a good brother. Actually, I needed to see how he was going to react in that room with Stoke and me before I gave him my full approval.

What we were about to do wouldn't be pretty.

STOKE'S hand came down on my shoulder before I opened the door to where the fuckhead Baxter was being held. Looking back, I saw Stoke's eyes were on his son's, and he asked, "Last time, you sure you wanna be involved with this?"

Josh straightened to his full height, and the guy was tall. He nodded. "Yeah, Dad. I'm in."

"Right." Stoke tipped his chin up. "If you wanna leave at any time, you do it, and no one will think any less of you."

"I'm good," Josh stated.

Stoke glanced to me and nodded. I opened the door and entered. Baxter sat on a cot in the corner of the room, with Beast and Knife standing guard near the door. As soon as we entered, they left with Knife saying, "Have fun."

I watched as Baxter stood. His eyes and posture held no fear. I would soon change that. If anything, the man looked bored.

"Your cousin was Cameron," Stoke said.

"I see my sweetheart has been talking." He smirked. "Yeah, he was, and he left me a note saying what he was about to do. I didn't get it in time to help, but if I had, let's say things would have been different. The whore he wanted would have been his, and I would have taken some lives of the Hawks MC, instead of *his* being taken."

Stoke snorted. "That's bullshit. You both would have failed, but I wish to fuck you had received that note earlier and tried, then you wouldn't have had your hands on my daughter."

"Didn't know whose daughter she was. I'd hoped she was connected to Dodge in a way. Still, no matter, it fuckin' worked out. I got to have a taste of her." Stoke's arm came out to stop my approach. I wanted to carve the guy's guts out. Baxter chuckled. "How's the business going? I heard a few closed down after some fires."

Stoke shrugged. "They're fine actually. Helped us get a start on some renovations, which was something we've wanted to do for a long time. So *you* helped us."

He didn't like hearing that. His jaw clenched, his body tensing, and his eyes narrowing on Stoke.

A knock sounded on the door behind us. Josh moved to answer it, and while the other person closed the door again, Josh turned back around to us. In his hands, I saw our tools. I smiled.

Pliers, a baseball bat, knives. It was time to get to work.

I bit back a laugh when I glimpsed fear in Baxter's widening eyes, before he could school his features into a bored look.

"Josh, get the chair over there," I ordered, pointing to the steel chair in the corner. Josh moved to drag it into the centre of the room. "You gonna sit?" I asked Baxter.

He snorted. "Why make it so easy for you."

A clatter of shit brought my attention to Josh dumping our tools on the floor, all except the baseball bat. "You know, Dad, I should really get back into baseball. I kinda miss it," he said plainly, while swinging the bat around and around in his hand.

"Any time is a good time for a practice, son." Stoke grinned.

"Cool." Josh smiled at his dad, and fuck, the kid was fast. He strode to Baxter, pulled back his arm, and swung hard, slamming the bat into Baxter's knee.

"Fuck!" Baxter screamed as he hit the floor, his hands cradling his knee. Josh pulled the bat high over his head, and the fucking thing made a swishing sound as he swung it down fast onto Baxter's shins. His cry of agony filled the room, and hell, it was music to my ears.

Though I wanted more.

Walking to them, I grabbed Josh's bat before he swung it again and shook my head. Leaning down, I lifted Baxter and dragged him to the chair. "I want to get his shit done so I can get back to your sister," I told Josh who didn't look happy I'd stopped him. His brows were drawn down, his chest pumping hard with each breath in and out. The adrenaline had kicked in. "Grab the pliers," I said. "Stoke, you hold the fucker down."

"Right, Vicious," Stoke replied and came forward. He

stood behind the chair. His arms curled around Baxter's chest, holding down his arms.

As soon as Josh slapped the pliers into my hand, I took hold of Baxter's wrist. "Josh, help your dad hold him. The fucker is gonna squeal like a monkey."

"Stop, fuck. Don't. Jesus," Baxter cursed as Josh leaned over and applied pressure to Baxter's arm.

Sliding my hand down to grab his index finger, I said, "What we're gonna do, you'll wish you were dead. Though nothing we do will satisfy me enough for what you did to my woman." I laid the tip of the pliers to the tip of his fingernail, and slowly lifted the pliers, his fingernail coming with it. Baxter's screams would have been heard out in the hall. Only when I did a third finger did his screams turn into whimpers and pleas.

"Josh, a knife," I demanded.

Josh lifted up, went to where he'd dropped the tools, and tagged a knife. As he strode back, he asked, "Can I do it?"

"What?" I asked.

"You were gonna take his fingers, right?"

"Let him," Stoke said.

It was time to see what Josh was made of when it came down to the dirty shit.

"Fine," I bit out. Even though I wanted to be the one to deliver all the pain to the prick, I had to remember I wasn't the only one hurt by losing Nary. I gripped Baxter's arm as he tried shouting, cursing, and moving, but we held tight as Josh carved off all his fingers.

Blood pooled on the cement ground. "Dallas," I called.

The door opened, his head peering around it. "Soon as we say, need someone to come in and stop his bleeding. Can't have him bleed out before we deliver him to the cops." Dallas nodded and shut the door.

"W-what the fuck you talkin' 'bout?" Baxter asked. His exhaustion was showing. His brow was drenched in sweat. He opened his eyes before reclosing them more slowly. His body lounged instead of the stiff form it had been at the start.

Knowing he wasn't going to move—he was unable to from the smashed-in shins and knee—Stoke stood tall and moved around the front. "You're going to jail for what you did. Every woman you took deserves a chance to be free from the hell you delivered upon her. The cops will get all your files. They will find the women, and then they'll be telling them you'll serve a life sentence. What they won't know, and if a chance arises, Hawks will fill them in, is that every day for the rest of your life will be filled with pain. We have brothers in there itching to make it happen." He leaned in and got in Baxter's face. "You should have known not to fuck with us like your cocksuckin' cousin. Now it's a lesson you'll learn every goddamn day."

"I-I'll tell the police what you've done to me."

Stoke chuckled. "You won't be able to once we've finished. Especially since we'll have taken all your fingers and tongue."

Baxter blanched. It was funny to see him try to stand and run. We all stood there waiting and smiling. Some would call it sick the way we enjoyed inflicting pain, but I didn't care. Not after what he'd done to Nary.

"Suggestion," Josh said.

"All ears," Stoke answered.

And while Baxter yelled his fear, Josh shared with us his fucking brilliant idea.

"It shouldn't have to be only Hawks who have to put up with him on the inside. I suggest we carve into his forehead child rapist."

"Fuckin' perfect." I grinned. Prisoners frowned upon motherfuckers who touched children.

Stoke slapped his hand on Josh's back and said, "You'll do good, brother."

There it was. Josh passed, and in my eyes, it was with flying colours.

It was time to finish what we'd started, so we could hand the prick over and I could get back to Nary.

Her life would be beautiful from then on.

I'd make sure of it.

Fuck.

Then I remembered what I had to tell her.

CHAPTER EIGHTEEN

ONE WEEK LATER

NARY

*T*he week flew by. Kelsey and I both spent it resting, eating, and talking. My friend also got to know Mum, Low, Josie, Mena, and Mrs Cliff. We both got to know Melissa. Saxon and Gypsy never hovered too far away, yet they seemed untouchable, unapproachable. They treated us like we were more of a security detail than people they wanted to be around. Though, that wasn't totally true. Both men shared tender looks our way, both spoke softly towards us, yet, I still felt a distance between us.

I understood it.

In a way.

It was because they thought us fragile, and we were still, somewhat. Kelsey and I slept in the same bed and still in Saxon's room. Both of us woke through the night as the terror of the nightmares we'd had consumed us. It was after the third night, both Gypsy and Saxon slept in the room on the floor with us. It actually helped ease some of our fears.

The nightmares had been new for me. I had thought I would have got them, like Kelsey, in the place we'd been held, but I hadn't. So when I was back under the roof of my family, who protected me fiercely, I presumed I wouldn't wake in fright.

I didn't understand it.

Especially since we knew Baxter and his men were no longer a threat. His men were dead, and Baxter was in jail. Which was what he deserved more than dying. Though at first, when Saxon had told me Baxter was still alive, I wanted to run to the room and deal with him myself. Then, after Saxon explained his decision, I understood. Actually, I was grateful for Baxter still living and going through his own personal hell for the rest of his days, rotting in jail. I knew his time in there wasn't going to be a walk in the park. Saxon, along with my dad, had promised me Baxter would pay each and every day.

And yet the fear, even small, was still there.

I knew if I were still feeling it, it would be touching Kelsey worse. She hid it well most of the time, but on the occasion, I'd see darkness in her eyes. She was trying, like I was, and really, it was all we could do after what we'd been through.

"A-are you okay, Nary?" At first, I thought Kelsey's stuttering was caused by her ordeal. I soon learned it was a natural stutter, and I was sure I wasn't the only one who thought it cute. She gripped my hand as we walked down the hall for lunch in the common room at the compound, with Saxon following. Gypsy was out somewhere doing... something. Most likely talking to Mason or his friends, who were taking care of his business while he was away.

"I am, honey. My mind just drifted."

"Are we going out the b-back after lunch?" Kelsey took every opportunity to be outdoors. I was thankful the weather was warm enough to do so. We spent a lot of the afternoons just sitting outside, either with the grass under us or at one of the many park benches the MC brothers had set up some time ago. We would talk, read, or lean back and enjoy the sun shining down on us.

It made us realise we were free and helped warm us from the inside out.

"Heck yes." I smiled. "I heard there's bad weather on our way so we have to enjoy it as much as we can."

"We will." She grinned. Only to cringe back when we stepped into the common room and it erupted in greetings. My hand let go of hers to wind around her waist so I could hold her close as my eyes took in the women and few men in the room.

A smile lit my face. I gave a reassuring squeeze to Kelsey's waist and told her, "These people are more family members from Ballarat." Hesitation filled her eyes, but she nodded. I added, "I promise you will love them."

"I trust your opinion," she declared and then finally relaxed.

"Go to the posse, angel, before they go crazy." Saxon's advice drifted from behind me. "Kelsey can stay by me until it's done."

"Until w-what's done?" Kelsey asked.

A laugh abruptly left me. "You'll see," I said and then made my way to my friends.

They surrounded me. With a combination of tears, hugs, and coos, they all thanked the high heaven I was okay.

Julian stepped back and said, "I was so ready to go commando, and not in the 'losing the undies' way, but the 'alpha male' way, and come with the hot biker boys to get you. But then our baby girl got sick."

Then Zara added, "I would have been here sorting them all out, but Talon threatened me to stay behind with the kids. I mean, I know the men can do wonders, but there's nothing like the muffkateers to help out. Thank God for Julian finding Melissa."

"My girl is amazing." Julian clapped and then threw himself at Melissa for a hug. "I'm kidnapping you. You're not leaving me ever again."

And as Deanna and Clary went to say something at the same time, Ivy interrupted, "We were all so worried about you. I lost count of the times we called each other crying or got together becoming blubbering messes, and even when Griz said everything was good, we just had to come see for ourselves. And you seem okay, but we know what things are like after terrible situations." Her voice lowered. "The problems it can cause a person on the inside. *We* know. So we wanted you to know you're not alone. Anytime you need any of us, we're there. You just call, text, email, even send us a message via a pigeon, and we'll get our behinds to Caroline Springs in seconds. Well, not seconds, since it takes an hour, but you know what I mean, don't you?" Tears sprung to her eyes. "It's so good to see you."

Nodding, tears filled my own eyes as my pulse raced. I said, "It's really good to see you all also. Thank you for coming, and for having your guys come help—"

"Don't give us that shit. We're family. Family fucking helps each other. So there was no question when the men woke us and told us they had to get to Caroline Springs. We just let them go, of course we would," Deanna said.

"I know. Thank you."

Deanna sniffed. "No thanks needed either."

Smiling, I nodded. "I'm grateful for having such an awesome family."

Deanna winked and said, "So you should be."

Clary came to my side and wrapped her arms around me. It had been only two months since she'd given birth to her and Blue's little boy, Austin. I hadn't had a chance to meet him yet, and I couldn't wait to see him. I was about to ask when she said, "Anyway, we thought a girls' day was in order. Drinks, while we talk girl stuff, paint nails, do face-masks, and—"

"Just no waxing," Low called as she entered with Josie and Mena. "Mena gets into trouble around waxing."

Julian let out a burst of laughter, while Mena blushed and cried, "Low!"

"That's a story we have to hear." Zara grinned. "But don't worry, nothing will leave the room, and the men are at Dodge's with all the kids." She looked to Saxon. "You may have to—"

"Not a chance," he clipped.

She smiled. "I thought you would say that."

Saxon grunted and crossed his arms over his chest.

"What Clary didn't mention," Deanna started, and then announced loudly, "was we brought porn."

"Hell Mouth?" Saxon groaned.

"Relax, Vicious. It's *Magic Mike*, a movie about hot stripper dudes."

I had to laugh. Looking over my shoulder, my eyes met Kelsey's. I reached a hand out. "Come meet everyone."

Hesitantly, she came forward, and in a quiet voice, she said, "Hi." Even though she was about the same age as Deanna and Zara, her timidness made her appear younger.

Which could explain why Deanna yelled, "I'm adopting her." Zara, Clary, and Ivy groaned. Deanna pointed at Kelsey and said, "You, you're my new sister. Not that we wouldn't be sisters anyway because once you become Hawks, you become family. But what we'll have will be stronger. You come to me if anyone fucks with you, and I'll deal with them."

Kelsey licked her dry lips. "Ah, o-okay."

"Good. I think— Holy shit, who in the fuck are you?"

Kelsey and I turned together to see Gypsy walk into the room. He came to an abrupt stop behind Saxon.

Saxon ran a hand over his face and warned Gypsy, "Just go with it, and they'll settle down eventually."

Julian gasped. "I have never been a lov'a of man-buns, but you have just convinced me I'm wrong." He skipped towards Gypsy, who gulped and narrowed his eyes. Julian's hand came out, and he said, "Hey there, sex-bomb. My name is Julian, and you will be my—"

"Julian," I called. He glanced at me and I shook my head. I wasn't sure how Gypsy felt about gay men, but I didn't want to cause any problems for either of them. Julian pouted and walked back over to Melissa's side. I turned back to my girls. "Everyone, this is Kelsey." They didn't get close, but they all said their greeting differently. Some even told her how glad they were she was out and safe.

She cleared her throat. "I couldn't have done it w-without Nary or…" We all saw her flick her gaze to Gypsy who was talking quietly with Saxon.

"And that's Gypsy," I added. All eyes turned back to said man and eyed him appreciatively.

"Should we get this party started?" Low asked.

THE AFTERNOON, even if we didn't get outside, was just what we'd needed. I hadn't seen Kelsey smile or giggle so much, and I was so grateful for my friends. We drank, though Kelsey and I didn't have much. We ate, talked, and caused the guys to cringe sometimes. Admittedly, Julian caused that reaction most of the time, especially when we were playing truth, and he asked us at what age we all got our periods.

What the day brought me was peace. As if a weight I hadn't known surrounded my body, had lifted. Watching my friends, listening to them, and spending time with them was something I didn't know I needed.

It was late when their men came to collect them, and I learned all the men from the Ballarat charter were once again heading home with their women. Except Mum, Dad, and Josh, they were still in town, staying at Dive's. Mum was enjoying it because she loved the time cuddling cute Koda and getting to know Mena. Melissa had also decided to head back with Julian for a while. She wanted to spend time with Aeila before she came back to Melbourne and flew back to Sydney.

Once the last person left, I turned to Kelsey. She smiled big. "I love your family."

Laughing, I shook my head and told her, "Our family now."

"Yes," she whispered. "Our family." Her teeth bit down on her bottom lip, and her eyes flicked over to Gypsy. Both he and Saxon had been quiet most of the day, though they never left, and if anyone tried to touch on the subject of what happened when we were in our hell, the men had soon shut them down.

Kelsey's eyes grew soft as she watched Gypsy. So, I could tell, even though Kelsey had agreed she was a part of my family, I wasn't sure she honestly felt it. She knew we accepted her, cared for her, but I was sure she would have been happy even if it were only Gypsy as her family. Not that she wanted to be related to him because she was crushing big on him. Then again, it could all come down to the fact she saw him as safe and trusting.

Shaking my head, I ducked to hide my knowing smile and started towards Kelsey. I took her hand in mine, and when our eyes met, I asked, "Did you want to watch another movie in Saxon's room?"

She nodded. "That sounds nice, and w-would it be okay if we had some ice cream?"

"Of course. I may be in a food coma from all the pizza and ribs, but I still have, and will always have, room for triple chocolate fudge ice cream." I slipped my arm through hers and tugged her towards the hall, knowing the men would follow.

"Darlin'?" Gypsy called. When we turned together, he added with eyes only for Kelsey, "Gotta make a call. Be back in a sec.'"

"Okay," Kelsey whispered.

My eyes moved to Saxon to see he had a frown on his lips and hard narrowed eyes to the floor. He wasn't happy about something, yet when he looked up, he sent me a chin lift and a small smile. He was protecting me, no doubt concerned if I saw he was worried, I'd worry also. The idiot man didn't understand I would always worry if he was, because my heart was his, his life was mine. Anything he went through, I would as well.

CHAPTER NINETEEN

SAXON

*M*y eyes were on the ground as I followed the women down the hall to my bedroom. My thoughts were somewhere else though. They were on what Gypsy had just told me. He'd decided it was time to head home in the next few days. It'd be a fucking sad day to see him go, but I understood. He had his own business to take care of. He was a good, honourable brother, and I was goddamn glad I got to meet him. Hell, I was even glad we owed a favour to his president because what they did for us deserved us repaying them in some way.

However, his other words had caused my stomach to twist in worry. Gypsy was going to see if his president was down with it first, and if Mason was, Gypsy was going to put the idea out to Kelsey, to see if she wanted to go back with him. He'd hoped a change of scenery would help her come out of her shell more. What worried me the most and had my stomach tightening even more, was thinking on how Nary would feel if Kelsey left. It could set Nary back, and there was a high chance Kelsey would leave because she fucking adored Gypsy, even if she was hesitant with him. The concern my woman had for her girl helped Nary. It kept her distracted from the hell she'd gone through. Since she'd been back, she hadn't cried or let her emotions out, except that first night. Even when she woke screaming some nights, she didn't tear up. She'd check Kelsey and settle her, and then she'd lie back down and eventually drift back to sleep.

Without Kelsey around, I could only hope I'd be enough to keep Nary in the light.

Our talk was coming soon. I'd been putting it off for the right moment, but hell, there was never a right moment with what I had to say. I needed my woman to understand I'd be there for her always. Even after I shared my shit, I'd still make sure I wouldn't be far. I'd always protect her.

Goddam, I hoped I was enough for my angel.

(This part is written by MariaLisa deMora)

MASON

The phone woke Mason, and he twisted on the mattress, swiftly silencing the ringer. Willa stirred beside him as he rolled out of bed, thumb already sliding on the screen. Once in the hallway, he spoke, "Yeah?" He hadn't even looked at the number, knowing a call coming in at that time of day had to be important.

Stalking through the house, he glanced into Garrett's room, seeing his son sleeping, arms flung wide, covers rumpled. Gypsy spoke into his ear, pulling Mason's attention away from his boy, the no-nonsense tone putting Mason on high alert. "Need your input, boss."

"You got it," Mason said, making his way to the kitchen. He flicked on the light over the sink, leaving the rest of the room in shadows.

"You know why I was here, know what was going on." Not a question, because Mason did. He was the one who had sent Gypsy to Australia in the first place, hand-picked as a solution for the problem. He waited, knowing Gypsy didn't need any prompting to keep going. "You know who I am, Mason. The kind of man I am." Gypsy sucked in a breath, his reticence at odds with the need in his voice. "Need to ask what you think."

"Think about what, fucker? Spit it out." Chill air bit across his bare shoulders, and Mason was ready to crawl back into bed beside his wife, not stand on the cold tile of his kitchen floor listening to one of his men floundering around an ask.

"The gal, the one we scooped up along with Nary." The tone of Gypsy's voice changed, became filled with gravel. "Kelsey. She... she's come to trust me, boss. She doesn't have anyone here. No one except Nary, and that girl has to get on with her life. Kelsey would be... not in the way, because Nary would never make it that way, but they're stuck. Saw it clear today, because I saw a little glimmer of what they could be, what they will be when they move on. Mason." He heaved a sigh. "I gotta come home, but I can't see myself leaving her behind. I want... no, I need to bring her with me."

Curious, Mason asked, "What the hell are you asking, Gypsy?"

"I bring her with me, she's mine. I'll make it so she don't have to leave. Not talking a visa, boss. Talking she'd be in my life. Which means she becomes mine. Some of that'll be her choice, of course. Woman like her, one who had so much stripped from her, anything more than on paper has to be her choice. But fuck, Mason, she's mine, and that means she's Rebel. I'll take her any way she gives herself to me. Gonna take resources to get her... home." Gypsy paused, and Mason waited. "I'm bringing her, just needed you to know."

"Those words are more telling and less asking, in case you wondered," Mason joked. "She matters to you, then bring her. We got enough old ladies to help her get settled."

"Can you... do you think Willa'd be able to pick up some things for my house?" Tentative now, Gypsy sounded like he wasn't as sure about this one.

"You askin' if my woman would be willing to go shopping? Brother, you cannot be serious." Mason snorted a laugh. "That's like asking if she needs to keep breathing. Email what you want her to get, she... we'll make sure you have everything, brother. This woman means something to you?"

"Yes." The answer came quickly, a firm affirmative.

"Then she already means something to me. Got your back, man." Mason grinned at the doorway, seeing Willa's shadow as she made her way towards him. "Fate, brother. Tricky bitch, yeah?"

"What?" Gypsy sounded like he was on the move, probably to go find Kelsey and talk her into a change of hemispheres.

"You had to go clear around the world to find your woman."

(This part is written by MariaLisa deMora)

GYPSY

He walked to the door of Saxon's room, looking in at the group resting on the bed. In the middle, Nary sat close to Saxon's side, eyes on the TV. Saxon had his hand on her wrist, absently circling it with his thumb, holding her in place, not that she had any intention of going anywhere, his eyes also on the TV. Kelsey, on the other side of Nary, had a pillow bunched underneath her head. Even though he hadn't made a sound, those pale blue eyes were fixed firmly on Gypsy. *Me.*

It was always like that. Didn't matter where they were, or what was going on around them, she found him. With her eyes, or sometimes, and fuck but he loved when she did this, she'd sidle into him and get close. If he initiated, she'd let him hold her hand, and even when he could feel the pulse of her fear pounding in her wrist, she'd hold on. Leaning into him if he slung an arm over her shoulders, the quiver in her muscles feeling like she was fighting flight, but Gypsy knew it wasn't escape from him. The depths of her fear made it so he tried to keep himself clamped down, fighting against going hard from the nearness of the woman.

She needed a change, and he knew it. Saxon knew it, too. He was the only one other than Mason that Gypsy had talked to about her. Standing there quietly, he gave Kelsey a chin lift, one shoulder wedged against the frame, and she offered him the sweetest smile. Beautiful, so fucking beautiful. *Fuck, I'd do anything to make it so she had a thousand reasons to smile every day.* Gypsy indicated the hallway with a tip of his head, and she glanced up at Nary, then back to him. With a murmured excuse, she rolled off the bed and walked out of the room.

He was waiting. She got close, staring up at him, and he suddenly wondered if she understood what it did to him when she did that. Trusting without saying a word, getting close so she could feel just a bit safer, because he was the one who made her feel safe. Ever since that first day, Gypsy had felt the weight of that trust like a blessing, balancing it against the lust he felt every time he touched her. "Wanna talk to you," he told her and watched as her eyes widened. Not in excitement. Fear. *Fuck.* "Come with me, Kelsey."

Lips pressed tightly together, she nodded. "O-okay."

"Nothing bad, darlin'. Promise." His words seemed to give her a little relief, and she nodded again. Not giving her a chance to avoid his touch, he reached down, stroking her arm from elbow to wrist, then clasped her hand. He waited, eyes on hers, hoping she saw what she needed in his. It was slow and shaky, but she did it, and Gypsy smiled proudly at her when her fingers curled around his. He'd killed for her, and yet she never feared his hands on her.

Leading her through the house and out back, he stood, looking up at the stars for a moment, marvelling again at the difference in the patterns. Without trying to sort his head out, he started talking, "My boss, president... Mason, he sent me on this gig, you know. He's a good man. He'd like it here, I think." Gypsy knew he was rambling, but he was so fucking nervous he couldn't control his mouth. He'd been a damn cop who had interrogated murderers and racke-teering mobsters and still couldn't find the words to talk to this woman. *Because she matters,* he thought. *Because I want her.*

"Sounds n-nice." She was trembling again, and that killed him. *Give anything to make it better.*

Time to move this forwards. Gypsy kept his voice gentle when he said, "I like it here." Smiled when she squeezed his hand, then frowned as a shiver wound down her body. "Darlin', you're cold. Shoulda said something." Tugging on her hand, Gypsy urged her towards him, and she came, one trusting step after the other until she was close. He shifted so her back was to his front, and slowly, so slowly she could have easily avoided him if she wanted to, he wrapped his arms around her shoulders, cradling her slight body to him. "Better?"

"Y-yes." Her head was tipped to one side, hiding her face against his arm. Gypsy stifled a groan when he saw the arch of her neck, delicate and beautiful, and made for his mouth to fit *there*, just where the muscles of her shoulder created an angle. *Perfect for me. Fuck.* He pulled up a memory of her rescue. Bruised and frightened, struggling out from under that bastard, and only moments later she had trusted him. *Me.* Strong, and braver than she knew.

He had to get this right, couldn't risk frightening her with what his body wanted from hers. Curves she hadn't had when they'd met pressed against him, and he nearly released a groan when she shifted, her ass against his cock. She'd been a slave for weeks... months. He couldn't expect her to come back all at once. *But I can help her get a little farther, every single day*, he thought.

"I like it here," he repeated himself, then finished, "but I gotta go home." As if she'd been shot through with electricity, she stiffened, freezing in place. "Not right this moment, but soon, Kelsey. Very soon." So still in his arms, and he wasn't sure if the heart he heard pounding was his, or hers. *This could go so wrong*, he thought. *Or it could go right.* "Home for me is America. Have you ever thought of visiting, darlin'?" Hair trailed across his skin as she shook her head; beautiful and dark, her hair was so sleek. "Not thought of it, or wouldn't consider it?"

A shrug, her shoulders lifting and brushing across his chest in a caress she didn't even know she offered. "Darlin'." Gypsy didn't know what he wanted from her, but it was more than that simple movement. He needed her to make a choice, a clear decision to go with him. *Please, baby.*

"Never th-thought I could." That at least was not an outright rejection, and might speak to a desire.

"Would you want to? Want to come with me?" Gypsy's throat clenched tightly, and he had to force a swallow to continue. "Want to come home with me?"

"You… you won't l-leave me?" Her voice broke, and that tipped the scales for him. She might fear many things, but she wanted to be with him more than anything else. *She picked me.*

"What'd I tell you the first time I saw you? Huh, baby?" He didn't wait for Kelsey to find the words because they were written on his heart, and he desperately wanted her to know he remembered. "I ain't goin' anywhere. Not without you."

CHAPTER TWENTY

NARY

J watched the bedroom door open, and Kelsey came through. I couldn't quite work out the expression on her face. It was a mixture of concern, relief, and excitement.

Though my attention was dragged from her when Saxon stood from the bed and said, "I'll let you both get ready for bed and talk."

Talk?

We had to talk?

About what?

The way Kelsey flicked her gaze around the room, not meeting my eyes, and the way she nibbled on her bottom lip told me the talk, I knew nothing about, was going to be big.

Had Gypsy upset her? I'd hurt him if he had.

Actually, I couldn't see him even trying. He'd been wonderful with Kelsey. So much so, I was sure he had feelings for her.

My body jolted when I heard the bedroom door snapping closed. Saxon had already stepped out.

"Nary," Kelsey whispered. She walked to the end of the bed and finally met my gaze. "Um, I-I have something I need to say."

"Are you okay, honey?" I asked, climbing to my knees.

She nodded and smiled. "I am." She sat on the end of the bed, then moved forward. When she sat in front of me, I planted my behind on the bed and took her hand in mine.

"What is it? Because I was sure you were fine before you left the room with Gypsy, and now you come back, and you're unsure about something you want to tell me. I'm worried."

"Please, don't w-worry. I'm only unsure because I'm worried what y-you will think of it."

"What?" I asked quietly, giving her hand a squeeze.

"Gypsy just s-spoke to me. He told me he has to go back home soon—"

"Oh, honey, I'm so sorry," I interrupted.

She shook her head, licked her dry lips, and said, "He wants to take me with him."

"What?" I yelled. My heart jumped. I could already see the answer in her eyes: She was going. Leaving. I rubbed a hand across my chest. It ached for a different reason. Not because she was leaving; I knew it would be the best choice for her. She had a connection with Gypsy and he with her, so I wouldn't stand in the way of it.

What was churning my stomach was fear. We'd been there for one another. We knew what it was really like. We were in it together. We helped each other. We were... weak together.

Tears filled my eyes, and blinking through them, I saw Kelsey was also crying silently. She nodded and sniffed. "I-if we keep ourselves wrapped up together, I-I'm afraid we both won't learn how t-to live again."

Kelsey, my sweet friend, had come to the same conclusion I had. It wasn't only the men who were our safety. We were each other's. Only, I never realised it was in a bad way. I realised then that if Kelsey stayed, I wouldn't get back to who I was. I wouldn't go back to uni, move back into my apartment, or get on with life. Helping Kelsey would be what I focused on. We both knew this.

"Are you sure?" I asked, my voice breaking at the end. I didn't want her to be sure, because I wasn't myself. Not for Kelsey, but for myself. If she went, I would have to face reality. I would have to move on and... God, was I ready for it? I didn't know and that scared me the most.

"Yes," she said and then pulled in a deep breath. "W-when Gypsy said he was going home, my whole body..." She shook her head. "My heart felt hollowed, and it hurt me, here." She lay a hand over her chest. "I know I'll miss you so much because you have been... you're amazing, Nary." She looked down to the bed, then back up, and smiled sadly. "But I know I can't go a day without seeing him."

Nodding, I offered, "I know what you mean." I was the same with Saxon. Every morning when I woke, I sought him out. Every step I took, I looked for him, and every time we were apart, I wanted him near. "As long as you're happy, that's all that matters. I'll miss you dearly, but we can call, Skype, and message each other every day."

My shoulders slumped. I wanted to take the words back and tell her not to go, tell her to never leave me, but I would be doing it for a selfish reason, and I meant what I said. Her happiness was all that mattered.

"I-It's going to be—"

"Scary, but exciting. Gypsy is a man of honour, of trust. I know you'll be in safe hands with him. He's also hot as well." I fanned myself and watched Kelsey shyly smile while her cheeks heated.

"I think so also."

"What, about him being hot?"

Her eyes widened, and then she giggled. "No, I-I meant he's very trustworthy."

"He is. And, honey, he's very lucky to have you going back with him, but you're also lucky because it's obvious he thinks the world of you."

"Yes." She grinned. "Luck i-is finally shining."

"It is," I said softly.

THREE DAYS LATER

Kelsey and I were sitting out the back on one of the picnic tables talking and enjoying each other's company before she flew out with Gypsy the next day. I couldn't believe she was going still, and my stomach did a pity dance at the thought of being away from her, but it would be for the best, for both of us. I just had to keep reminding myself.

I moved my eyes from Kelsey when I heard the back door to the compound open. When I flicked my gaze there, I froze. Jerimiah had just stepped out. I shifted my gaze to Saxon, where he was working on his bike not far from us with Gypsy. I saw his head rise and then the fierce glare directed at Jerimiah. He dropped whatever tool he had in his hand and started for my ex. With my heart in my throat, I stood and quickly made my way around the table.

"Nary?" Kelsey asked.

"Honey, stay there a second, I just need to—"

"Get the fuck outta my sight," Saxon roared, stopping right in front of Jerimiah.

"I just need to talk—"

"I don't give a flying fuck what you need. She no longer concerns you. You lost your right to even be near her." Saxon shoved Jerimiah back.

"Saxon," I called and quickened my pace over to them. Saxon didn't listen to me. He got in Jerimiah's face and whispered something I couldn't hear. Then shoved him back a step. "Stop!" I ordered, coming to their sides. I laid a hand on Saxon's arm. He looked down at it and then up to me. I begged, "Please, I need to talk to him."

His eyes softened. "Angel—"

"Please," I whispered. Urging him to understand and hoping he knew, even though Saxon and I hadn't sorted what we were to each other, I wasn't going back to Jerimiah.

"Fuck," Saxon cursed on a growl. He turned and stalked off towards his bike. Looking there, I noticed Gypsy was long gone. I glanced over my shoulder to see him sitting with Kelsey, and Kelsey's worried gaze was on me. I gave her a reassuring smile and then brought my attention back to Jerimiah.

My soul ached. He looked terrible, tired, and withdrawn. Dread flipped my belly. I should have asked someone to have him come to me a long time ago.

No. I should have had the lady balls to seek him out myself, but I was scared because I didn't want to hurt him, yet, I already had.

"Do you want to sit down over there?" I asked, pointing to another bench seat.

"Sure," he replied and offered me a small smile. He followed me silently over, and I didn't have to look to know Saxon watched us the whole way. I could sense his stare burning our way. I made sure to sit across from Jerimiah, even though I wanted to sit next to him, to hug him, and tell him how sorry I was.

Instead, once we were both seated, I reached across the table and took his hand with my shaky one. Something was thrown to the ground in a clatter behind me. I couldn't let

Saxon bother me though. Jerimiah and I had a history. It was time we sorted it out.

"I'm sorry," I whispered. My eyes down on our hands, watching his thumb rub back and forth on the top of my hand. Something that once would have sent butterflies to my stomach, I found no longer did.

He scoffed. "What are you sorry for? I'm the one who's sorry. If I hadn't have listened back then, you wouldn't have... Fuck, Nary. You were taken. I should have protected you. Shit, it killed me to know my girl was in the hands of that motherfucker, and there wasn't anything I could do."

Tears filled my eyes. I shook my head back and forth. "No," I cried. "Please, don't take anything that happened on board. You aren't at fault. It was my stupid move that got me taken. It wasn't your fault, Jerimiah. Please understand that. I'm so sorry to leave you thinking it was. I should have come to see you after... when I was back. It's not your fault." I finished on a whimper and dropped my eyes to the table. Our hands gripped each other tighter.

"I was so scared for you," he admitted quietly.

"I'm okay," I said automatically. He tugged my hand. I moved my eyes up to his pain-filled ones and gave him a sad smile, then added, "At least, with time I will be."

"I know you will. You've always been a strong woman." He sighed, glancing over to Saxon and then back to me. "I'm in Hawks now."

"Jerimiah—"

"Don't, baby. I know." He flicked his eyes to Saxon once again and then back to me. He cursed under his breath and rubbed the back of his neck with his free hand before he said, "I just wanted to say since I'm in Hawks, you'll be seeing me around more and with uni still." He shrugged. "If I can, I want to be in your life, Nary."

"Jerimiah," I whispered.

"He has always been your happy ever after. Shit, anyone can see it, and I know you two ain't there yet, but I know a guy like him, a stubborn prick." He laughed. I smiled. "He'll make sure you get the world, and you deserve it, baby."

"So do you," I said. His head jerked back, his brow lifting in question. "You deserve the world, Jerimiah. You're gorgeous, strong, sweet, smart, and if a woman doesn't bring the world for you, then my sisterhood need their heads checked."

He threw his head back and laughed. After he settled, he clasped both his hands around mine and said, "If I didn't think I'd get my head ripped off, I'd hug you, baby." I giggled. He smiled warmly at me. "I know you have your girls, your family, and him, but if you ever need to talk, I'm always there for you."

"I know, honey, and it goes both ways. Even if Saxon hates it, I'm there for you, Jerimiah."

"Appreciate it." He let go of my hands and leaned back. "Now, before my head explodes from the bad juju vibes he's sending my way, I think I better get outta here."

It was my turn to laugh aloud. I stood as he did, and even though Saxon was watching, I strode around the table and hugged Jerimiah tightly. "Don't be a stranger because of him."

He snorted. "Never. I enjoy messin' with him too much."

I smacked his arm after he shifted back. He smiled, leant in, and kissed my forehead. I felt heat at my back, and when Jerimiah stepped back, he sent me big eyes.

"See you around," I said, stating right there, in front of the alpha man at my back, that Jerimiah and I would be friends.

Jerimiah winked and replied, "Lookin' forward to it." He started off, and then he called over his shoulder, "Later, fuckface."

"Get lost, dickhead," Saxon yelled.

Once he'd left, I turned to face Saxon. His eyes were already burning with annoyance down into mine.

Smiling, I said, "Everything's fine."

He studied my face and grunted.

"Saxon, Jerimiah and I are friends. You need to understand that." When he still just stared down at me and I saw him clench his jaw, my own frustration took hold. I narrowed my eyes and waited for him to say something, anything. What also was edging my patience over the ledge was when he promised he was going to talk to me nearly two weeks ago and he hadn't yet. I wanted to know where I stood with him. Was he going to treat me like a friend or more? Finally, I threw up my hands and said, "I don't know why I even bothered to tell you that anyway. It's not like it has anything to do with you."

"Angel," he warned.

Leaning up into his face, I snapped, "What?"

His lips twitched. "We'll talk soon."

Rolling my eyes, I blew out a breath and returned my gaze to him. He was smiling. "You said that a while ago, Saxon."

"We have time to wait. You just need to know I ain't backing away from you. I won't treat you like shit ever again. Things have changed. You've seen it. Just wait a little more, angel. After your girl is gone. For now, enjoy your afternoon and the goin'-away party tonight for them."

"Tomorrow then?"

He chuckled, shaking his head. "Maybe."

"Saxon," I bit out.

"Angel," he growled. Crossing his arms over his chest, his eyes narrowed. "Should we talk about you and him still being friends?"

Snorting, I said, "No, because it's happening."

"We'll see."

"No, we won't."

His eyes suddenly softened. He dropped his arms, only to bring his hand up. With the backs of his fingers, he ran them gently down my cheek. My heart stumbled.

"It's good to see my angel still has fight in her."

My eyes widened. He was sparring with me to bring her out, to bring me back. I dropped my forehead into his chest. His hands slid to the sides of my neck. "Saxon," I whispered.

"Been waiting for her to show, and now she has, you ain't taking her away. No matter what or where you are, you should fuckin' know you can always be her. Even when you're scared. When you feel the fear tightening your throat, you *can* be her. Still, I get it. I know she'll retreat at times, and when those times come, I'd be happy to bring her back so you can shine and be who you are without feelin' those darker emotions again."

"Saxon," I choked.

He squeezed my neck. "You'll be fine without Kelsey, angel. I'll make sure of it."

Sniffing, I pulled back, and through watery eyes, I met his gaze. "You will?"

"Fuck yeah. Be right with you. Along your side."

I would have burst into happy tears with the weight of devotion I felt for Saxon, if it wasn't for his teasing smile before he said, "Now, go be with your girl. I'm gonna go hunt that dickhead who thinks he can be friends with you."

I narrowed my eyes on him, and snapped, "Saxon."

He chuckled. "Good, she's still there after me layin' some heavy on her. Now, go be with your girl, angel."

Even though I rolled my eyes, and shoved at him, I did it gently and with a smile on my face before I went back to Kelsey.

CHAPTER TWENTY-ONE

SAXON

*I*t was the next day when I stood out front with Gypsy while our women were off to the side whispering to each other, hugging, and saying their goodbyes. The previous night had gone well. The party was wild like it always was when it came to Hawks celebrating, but the girls stuck close to one another and still, even with the sour note of Kelsey leaving, they enjoyed their time.

Glancing at Gypsy, I saw his eyes were on the women. "You think you're doin' the right thing, takin' her with you?" I asked.

His jaw clenched and he nodded, meeting my stare. "Fuck yes, I see it no other way. If I left without her, I'd be worried the whole damn time. She's it for me."

"Good to hear, brother." I held out my hand to him. He

unfolded his arms from his chest and thrust his hand out, but I didn't grip it. I took hold of his wrist. He grabbed mine before I brought him in close for a swift hard pat. Pulling back, I told him, "Can't ever thank you enough. Fuck, you goin' in there without a weapon and just us at your back to get my woman… Christ, I seriously can't thank you enough. Ever need me, I'm there, and I'm not just talkin' 'bout what the club owes yours. *You* ever need me, just fuckin' ask, man, you got me?"

"Honoured, brother, to have the chance to help you all out and to find my peace." His eyes moved to Kelsey and back again. "Honoured."

"We'd better pry those two apart so you don't miss your flight."

He chuckled. "Could be a task, but I bet you're right." He let out a shrill whistle, and the women looked over at us. "Darlin' we have to get movin'."

Kelsey grinned at her man and nodded. Then they went back to hugging and talking.

Laughing, I said, "Right, I'll grab mine and you take yours."

"That's a better plan."

We started their way. They saw us coming, so Nary turned, stepped up to Gypsy and hugged him tightly. "You promise to take care of her?"

"With my life."

My woman pulled back and grinned up at him. "That was a good answer."

Reaching out, I grabbed the back of Nary's jeans and

tugged her back into me, so her back collided with my chest. "Woman, they hav'ta get goin'." Glancing at Kelsey, I gave her a chin lift and said, "Keep in touch, yeah?"

"Yes, Saxon." She nodded. "Um, t-thank you for letting us stay in your room."

"Don't mention it," I replied.

Gypsy grabbed her bag off the ground, not that she had much; what she did have was extra clothes Nary had. Kelsey didn't want to go shopping for new stuff. "We'll talk soon," Gypsy said.

"Yeah, brother." I nodded once.

They started for the waiting taxi. Gypsy didn't want us at the airport. He wanted to settle his woman in with just the two of them, wanted to see how she was going to cope without Nary being around. Hell, I was sure Kelsey would be fine. Pure devotion was all I saw when she looked at her man. It might take a while for them to be what they needed to, but they'd get there.

"Bye," Nary called.

Kelsey turned and waved. Nary blew her kisses and gripped my arm as I slid it around her waist. Both women— I didn't even have to look at Nary's face to know—had eyes shining with tears.

Nary kept waving until the taxi turned out of sight. Leaning forward, I rested my chin on her shoulder and said, "It'll be good for her."

She sighed. "I know."

"You were her crutch and she yours."

She nodded. "I know."

"You'll worry and so will she, but you'll both shine eventually." She said nothing, only gave me another nod. Fuck, the next few days were going to be hard on her. I wasn't sure she was ready for our chat. I didn't want to lay my crap on her when she was raw from losing Kelsey. "Angel, let's get outta here for a while."

She stiffened. "Where?" she whispered.

"Wanna take you somewhere for lunch."

"I'd like that," she whispered.

Christ, I fucking loved the woman in my arms.

EVEN THOUGH I wanted Nary wrapped around my back on my Harley, I decided to take my truck instead. The drive was quiet, my woman's mind occupied with thoughts of Kelsey and her leaving.

Pulling into a car park of a restaurant, I climbed out and made my way around to her side. She already had the door open, so I reached in, my hands to her waist, and helped her down. Then I took her hand and led her in through the front door.

Once seated at a table for two, I grabbed the menu she'd picked up out of her hands, and when she looked up, I asked, "You doin' okay?"

"Yes." She smiled. "I'm just taking it all in. I never imagined I'd ever be sitting across from you at a table on a date." Her eyes widened. I smirked as she tried to fix what she'd said, "Not that this is a date. I mean, it's just lunch, and friends go to lunch all the time. I ate lunch with Kelsey every day. Maybe I should call Low, and Josie, and see—"

"Angel," I interrupted.

"Saxon?"

"I've been in love with you since the first time I saw you."

Fuck. Had I just blurted that shit out?

"What?" she breathed.

Christ. I had just blurted that shit out.

I shifted in the chair, suddenly uncomfortable under Nary's shocked gaze.

"You were thirteen and had just started high school. I saw you in assembly on the first day, and I was fuckin' taken by your beauty."

"What?" she screeched. I flinched and then watched a blush rise to her cheeks while she looked around saying, "Sorry," to the other customers.

When her eyes came back to me, I went on, "Knew you were it for me from that day, but I pushed you away."

She leaned in and hissed, "You were an arse."

I winced. Nodding, I said, "I know, and every fuckin' day I will regret how I treated you. I fucked up big time, and every time I cut you, it tore at me also. Shit, angel. When you started crushin' on me and wanted an in with me after I helped with the fuckhead Malcolm, thought I was a lucky bastard because you wanted *my* time. Then I got home and my dad spewed some bullshit, and I didn't want that to ever touch you." She sucked in a deep breath. I continued, "You're goddamn stunning, strong, and fiery when you want to be, loyal, and... hell, the list can go on forever and

I'd never get to the bottom of how good you are." I glanced away, out the window and then back. "But I'm tainted, and what I need to say to you tonight, what... Shit, the thing I have to tell you tonight... it could change everything." I snorted. "And being the selfish person I am, I wanted you to know it's always been you for me first. Since the day you sat next to one of your friends, threw your head back and let out a laugh so loud people looked, but you didn't care. You kept on gabbin' with your friend like nothing mattered."

Tears filled her eyes. "Why are you telling me this here, right now? And what the heck, Saxon? You've been in love with me since I was thirteen? What am I supposed to do with that information? Oh my God." She slumped back in her chair and covered her face with her hands.

Motherfuckin' hell.

Why in the hell did I say that shit? It was the wrong place and time.

My woman was crying because of it and I was being a bigger dick for just sitting there.

When I scooted my chair back, Nary pulled her hands from her face, wiped it, and glared at me before she spat, "Don't you dare move. We are sitting here talking about random crap while I try to process what you just told me. We are eating, and goddang it, we are going to enjoy our bloody first date."

What I wanted to do was pull her over the table and take her mouth with mine. However, I didn't think she'd be up for it without beating me black and blue first. What I also wanted to do was throw my head back and laugh my arse off. Though, that could also lead to me getting beat up.

Instead, I smiled and said, "Sounds good, Viper." Her eyes flared. I'd called her Viper when she'd tackled me to the ground trying to save me from her dipshit stalker who had a gun pointed at me.

"Wipe that smile off your face and find a waiter. I'm hungry."

That time I did laugh. "Right. My angel is hungry. I better feed her."

"And, Saxon,"

"Yeah, gorgeous?"

"I saw you that day also. You were down the row from me dressed all in black. You had a scowl on your face, and I couldn't help but think how much sexier you would look if you smiled." I stiffened, my pulse racing. Then she went on and blew me the fuck away. "I fell for you that day, and no boy compared. I watched you from afar, and I thought you hated me, but I didn't care. I admired you. I still do because you're fierce, handsome, strong, and worth knowing. The day you pulled Malcolm off me was when I knew no one else would do for me. And even when you pushed me away, I never stopped caring about you. You've always been it for me, Saxon Black." She smiled. "So I know whatever you have to say tonight, I'll listen and then after it, I'll still be there. Nothing you say, no matter how terrible you think it is, will take me away from you. Not now, not when you've finally shown me who you really are, not when my heart is 100 percent owned by you, and I'm glad it is."

"Fuck, angel," I bit out.

"We'll need to take it slow... I'm not ready—"

"Angel—"

"But I know one day I will—"

Christ. Why in the hell was she talking about what I think she was talking about in a goddam restaurant and causing my dick to go rock-hard? I interrupted before I shot my load in my jeans. "Gorgeous, how about we talk about that after I tell you my shit."

"As long as you know I'll still be around after your talk."

I rolled my eyes. "We'll see."

"No, Saxon Black. I know."

My lips twitched. "We'll see."

"Don't make me angry again on our first date. I really don't want to call Mrs Cliff to harm you."

"Shit, don't call that woman."

She giggled behind her menu. "I heard she told you she could teach you things in the sack."

I shuddered. Nary laughed again.

We sat back, enjoyed the food and the time with each other. I also let what I needed to say slip to the back of my mind. My woman was liking our first date, so I was there doing it with her and not stuck in my mind.

CHAPTER TWENTY-TWO

NARY

*M*y mind had been muddled since the man who had stolen my heart, when I was sixteen, told me he'd been in love with me even before I'd fallen completely for him. Yes, I had a crush on him at thirteen. I'd always thought he was good-looking, but he had been too scary to approach, so I'd admired from afar.

Why he'd kept me at arm's length obviously had something to do with his father, and it had been big enough for Saxon to have been scared enough to push me away every time. I needed to know his past so we could move on. Since he'd shown me who he actually was, there wouldn't be a chance I'd let him go. I wasn't losing what we were already gaining.

No matter how dark he thought it was.

No matter what, he was mine in each and every way, and when he finally talked with me about it, I would prove to him I was staying at his side forever.

Along with a muddled mind, my belly was acting as if a choir was singing, and every note they hit sent a pleasant quiver inside of me.

I couldn't stop smiling. Throughout lunch, my mouth was constantly tipped up. My skin seemed to heat as my mind played his words over and over. *I've been in love with you since the first time I saw you.*

He was in love with me.

With me.

I wanted to squeal with glee, but I also wanted to hit him upside the head, kick him in the shin and balls for being a prick to me for five years.

He stopped his truck in the compound car park and I sensed him turn towards me.

"You ever gonna stop smiling?"

Heat hit my cheeks, and I shook my head, peeking at him through hooded eyes. "Probably not."

He sighed. "Fuck," he clipped and I turned to him, my eyes searching his handsome face. Worry was clear as day in his eyes, his dipping brows, and his thinned lips.

"What?" I asked, still smiling, because even with him worried, his words of love were turning over and over in my mind.

He licked his lips and then placed a sad smile upon them. Silently, I watched his hand come up and cup my cheek. His thumb stroked my skin, and then he shifted his hand so he could glide his thumb across my bottom lip. My heart went wild in my chest. It seemed to chant, "Kiss me, kiss me, kiss me."

Unfortunately, my mind picked that moment to muck everything up when concern swooped in and crashed the choir in my stomach. Instead, it dropped when I thought if I was moving too fast after everything that had happened to me. Would he think I was…? God, I didn't even know myself. Was I wrong to want his touch after everything? Was I wrong to feel so attracted to him and want his kiss after everything? Was *I* moving too fast? Was it wrong to want to kiss him, to hug him? Would he see it as me using him to try to forget? I wasn't, I knew I wasn't, but I worried he would see it differently and not understand how happy, how excited he made me when he smiled at me, when he spoke softly to me, or touched me with care.

"Where's the smile gone?" he asked. I jolted out of my thoughts and met his gaze as he went on, "'Cause I was thinking I fuckin' love seein' it on your face, knowin' I was the cause of it, but I'm goddamn worried it will be lost to me forever when I tell you what I have to." He clenched his jaw. "You deserve to smile every day, angel, and I'm fuckin' praying it'll still be me causing them after tonight."

Maybe I needed to step back a little and let him lead. If anything he did to me triggered something inside of me from my time in hell, it would pain him, and I didn't want that happening. The last thing I wanted was a rift between us. I knew Saxon well enough to know if I freaked out, it would wreck him.

So, I shrugged. "I guess you'll just have to wait and see."

"Now she's holding something back from me. Been watching you a long time, angel. I know when somethin's on your mind, and it just ran through some thoughts real quick. Only, the thoughts weren't good because you didn't come out smiling at the end."

Rolling my eyes, I looked away. Only his fingers slipped to my chin and tipped my head so I had to meet his gaze. "Hit me with them, angel."

"What do you mean?"

"Tell me the thoughts that made you frown so I can help you through them."

I narrowed my eyes. "Maybe after you tell me your thoughts, and no, Saxon, I'm not talking about your thoughts *now*. I'm talkin' about what you think you have to tell me that will drive me off."

He smirked. "Well played, gorgeous, but wait until tonight."

"Why?" I snapped.

"Because your dad texted me while you were in the dunny, and he wants his girl at Dive's for dinner. Dive and Mena have gone back to Halls Gap to grab some stuff. They're stayin' overnight, which means your mum has the run of the kitchen, and she wants to cook for her girl."

Slumping back in the seat, I crossed my arms over my chest. "Fine, take me there so I can spend time with them."

"I'm stayin' for dinner also."

Snorting, I said, "Of course you are."

"We'll talk tonight, angel. Spread everything out on the

table, and if you think you can take it, we're moving on, and when we do, it'll be together. Meanin' everyone will know you're my woman." He snorted himself. "Not that you haven't been since the first time I saw you. It'll be better now I'm not being a cockhead."

Another snort. "The party's still out on that, because right now you're being one."

He jerked his head back. "How?"

"Wanting to hear my thoughts and worries when you won't share."

"I'm sharing. It'll just be tonight."

Sitting up straighter, I glared again. "And you expect me to just spill my guts when you order it, but I have to sit back like a good girl waiting for when *you're* ready?"

He raised a brow. "If I say yes, you gonna crack it more?"

"Yes!" I snapped.

He shrugged. "Don't matter. I like it when you're riled. It's you, and I love you being you. Makes me want to shut you up with a kiss." He threw open his door and got out, leaving me with my jaw dropped open and wide eyes.

Rolling down my window, I yelled, "Where are you going? I thought we're going to see my parents?"

"I'm gettin' you a goddamn jacket because it'll be colder when we leave there."

Flopping back into the seat, I clipped, "Well, really."

Then my smile came back. He cared. He loved me. We fought and I enjoyed it. We were both stubborn, and our words may get rough, may come loud, but I knew it would never again get out of hand where I would end up hurt.

When he returned and threw my denim jacket between us, I was still smiling. He took my smile in, groaned, and muttered, "Fuck me."

I giggled, watching him while he started his truck as his lips twitched.

WHEN WE ARRIVED at Dive's, Mum came out the front door wearing an apron, waving wildly. Stoke soon followed. He rolled his eyes at Mum, then leaned against the door frame with his arms crossed over his chest.

Saxon was already out of the truck and around at my door opening it before I had the chance to do it. He took my hand as I slid out and then continued holding my hand as we walked together to the front door. I took in my mum's gaze. Her eyes were on our hands, and they grew misty and soft.

She blinked as we got close and smiled, taking the few steps to us where she wrapped me up in her arms.

"My girl."

"Mum," I whispered into her hair. Like mine, there was a lot.

"How you going, honey?" she asked.

"Better. It was hard to see Kelsey go, but I'll be okay."

Pulling back, her hands rested on my shoulders and she studied my face. A small smile formed on her lips, and she nodded. "You will be. Now, come help your mum in the kitchen while the guys chat." She turned and threw her arm over my shoulder, leading us to the door. "Hey, Saxon."

"Malinda." He sent her a chin lift.

We paused at the door where Dad was. "Don't I get any lovin' off my daughter?" he asked, raising a brow.

Grinning, I said, "Of course," then wound my arms around his waist.

"Saxon, come on through and grab a drink," I heard Mum order and sensed them move off, but I just kept holding onto Dad. I wasn't sure if it was for his benefit or mine. "Josh!" Mum scolded from inside. "Get your feet off the coffee table. This is not our house."

"Jesus, Mum, we're at Dive's house, not the Queen's."

Both Dad and I chuckled. When he moved back, his hands came to my cheeks. I placed mine on his wrists. "Can already see," he muttered, while looking at me.

"What?" I whispered.

"You, my girl, coming outta the darkness to be herself again."

"Dad," I whimpered, tears pooling, my bottom lip trembling.

"Fucked up, what happened, but my girl is strong. Nothin' will beat her down, not when she has us at her back and that kid in there who would do anything to keep her safe and happy." He smiled. "Can already see his magic workin' now he's not being a dick." I snorted a laugh. Dad's expression sobered. "You may need to be strong again when he tells you his past—"

My brows pulled together in confusion. "How—"

Dad shook his head, slid his hands to my shoulders, and I dropped mine to his waist. Dad interrupted with, "He didn't tell me. I found out, and I know, you being my girl, you can handle it, and I know when you do... when you show him once and for all he's worth your love like you've *always* been worth his, it'll be fuckin' beauty for the rest of your lives. He'll make it so, and so will we. But my girl is also stubborn like her ma, so I know she'll do anythin' to make it happen."

"I will." I nodded.

"Be happy, my girl," he said and leaned in to kiss my forehead.

"I'm getting there."

"Good." He grunted. "And if Vicious does anything to fuck it all up, which is highly goddam doubtful, I'll take the guy down myself."

Laughing, I hugged him again. "I know you will."

"Now, we'd better get in there or your mum will worry I've got you crying out here."

"It was close."

"Don't tell her that. She'll have my balls," he said and opened the front door again. I wasn't sure who'd closed it before, but I was grateful for the peace to have that moment with Dad.

CHAPTER TWENTY-THREE

NARY

*D*inner was going well, though I noticed Saxon had been quiet since I'd left him with Dad and Josh in the living room. I couldn't help but wonder what had happened to cause the frown on his lips and the pinched brow. I didn't have to wonder long. It was after we'd finished eating and were sitting around the table talking when Saxon sucked in a breath and announced, "I realised somethin'."

"That you had a brain?" Josh asked, sniggering. I kicked him under the table, which made him yelp, and Saxon flicked him the finger while Mum glared at her son.

Saxon smirked. "Known that all along, idiot."

Josh rolled his eyes. "Whatever."

My man flicked his eyes to the table for a moment as he

LILA ROSE

took a deep breath. He then looked back up. With his sad eyes on mine, he said, "Realised I should probably tell you all together what I did when I was fourteen." My body stilled, my heart beating like a jackhammer. He licked his dry lips and went on, "It's mostly why I pushed Nary away and caused her five years of pain, but she wasn't the only one I hurt. Through her, I would have caused you all pain because you all care about her so much."

"Saxon, you don't—" Mum started.

His eyes went to her, and she shut her mouth. Saxon nodded. "I do. Need this out in the open because you all mean everything to Nary, and she means all to me. So I need your... I need to know, if what I did, if you all can... if you'll let me be with Nary after it. Because it's what I want. She's what I want, always has been, right from the start."

"First day of high school," I whispered. I heard Mum suck back a shuddering breath.

My man smiled. "Yeah, angel."

"You talk, brother, we'll listen," Dad said. He already knew something, and I think having Dad know it helped Saxon continue.

"Right." Saxon nodded. "Since I was four years old, my mum used to beat me." Mum reached over and took my hand in hers. I squeezed tightly and bit my bottom lip. I would not break down on him. I tried my best to keep my composure as he continued. "Small things I did pissed her off, so she'd beat me for it. She'd scream at me day and night for draggin' her down." He clenched his jaw, only to unhinge it and sigh. "It went on like that for ten years. My

214

dad knew what she was doing. He just didn't care, and when I was young, just a fuckin' toddler, I went cryin' to him, and he told me to man up. Each time he came home to me bloody and bruised, he'd tell me to, 'man up'." Saxon lifted a hand and rubbed the back of his neck, his eyes on the table. "One day, when I was fourteen, I'd had enough. I guess you could say I manned up." He glanced up. "We were in the kitchen when she started on me. I'd accidently spilt some milk and she, fuck, she picked up the microwave and threw it at my back. It knocked me forward against the sink, and when I was leaning over, she picked up the milk bottle and kept hitting me in the back of the head with it." Saxon shifted in his seat, leaning forward, his elbows to the table. "There was a knife in the sink." His voice was low and cold. "I picked it up and spun around, forcing it in her gut. She gasped. Shocked I'd done it. I was shocked as well, so I pulled it out. I didn't know I'd hit something vital. She fell to the ground and bled out while I watched."

"Fuckin' hell," Josh whispered.

"What'd your dad do?" Dad asked.

Saxon snorted. "He came home and called the cops, said it was self-defence and that was the end of it."

There was more to it. I knew. I could sense there was, but what he'd said in front of my family was enough for the night.

Finally, he looked to me. I shook my head and asked, "This is why you stayed away?"

"I got my mother's blood on my hands, Nary," he clipped.

"No," I whispered. "What you *had* on your hands was your torturer's blood. She wasn't your mother."

"She's right," Mum said, just as quiet. Tears filled her eyes, and she leant in to touch Saxon's arm. "No mother should hurt their child. She didn't deserve you. What she did was inhumane. She obviously wasn't right, and for you to deal with that on your own... her death wasn't your fault. Your father got one thing right. It was self-defence."

He sat back, Mum's hand fell to the table. He shook his head. "She gave birth to me and I killed her." His voice was rough.

"Bullshit," Dad snarled, his eyes hard. "You didn't mean to kill her. You were fuckin' fourteen. A kid. It was an accident. That's all it was. You didn't do it in cold blood. It was an accident, but one deserved."

Mum sniffed. "The past is the past. You've shown us what you would do for our daughter, how you care for her, and keep her safe. I'm honoured to know she's in your hands."

"Besides," Josh started. We all looked to him. "She's had a girl hard-on for you for years, 'bout time you two got your act together. My sister is no fool. When she hooked her heart to yours many years ago, she knew what she was doin'."

It was at that moment I couldn't have been prouder of my family.

Standing, I walked around the table and stood beside Saxon. He shifted to have my eyes. I held out my hand, and he took it. "You're stuck with me now."

He applied pressure to my hand and asked, "Can we get outta here?"

"Yes." I nodded.

Everyone walked us to the door. Dad stood off to the side with Saxon for a moment. He grabbed the back of Saxon's neck and tugged him forward until their foreheads touched. He muttered something we couldn't hear. Saxon nodded but said nothing. Dad added something. Saxon's jaw clenched and he nodded again.

Dad pulled back and said, "Get our girl back."

IT WAS quiet in the car. I left Saxon to have his thoughts, but I took his hand on the drive to the compound. He never let go until we came to a stop in the car park. Then I asked quietly, "What did my dad say to you?"

"He was privileged to have me as a brother, but to also have me as his daughter's man."

"And?"

He groaned. "Let's get inside."

"Saxon," I pleaded.

"He told me to lay it all out, and I will, just not in the truck. Come inside with me."

"Okay."

On the way to the room, we were greeted by a few brothers who were lazing around. Not sure if they sensed the tense atmosphere surrounding us, but they didn't hound us for more of our time. We kept walking down the hall and into Saxon's room.

While he paced, I sat on his bed and waited.

He came to a stop and faced me, his hands on his hips. "What I didn't say in front of your 'rents was when my father came home and saw Mum layin' on the floor dead, he calmly boiled the kettle and threw it over me, telling me to tell the cops it was self-defence. I had the bruises to prove it, but he wanted more to show them. I did, and then my dad held it over me for the rest of the time I was there. I had to do what he said. He got me to steal shit all the time, and then he continued to beat me like my mum had. At least it wasn't as bad." He shrugged. "Nary," he started, and I watched him gulp. "The boiling water, it landed here"—he pointed to his chest—"and here," then his stomach.

Anger rose up inside of me, my temperature suddenly high. "He is not your father. He's a monster like your mother. You have us, you have me."

"Angel," he said quietly. "What I'm saying is I'm scarred."

Narrowing my eyes, I snapped, "So what? So am I." I gestured wildly to my face with my hand.

"Babe," he groaned. "This is a different type of scarring. It's fuckin' ugly."

Sighing, I told him, "I used to think mine was as well. The pain I'd been in was terrible. At the time, I didn't want to live. I thought nothing would be worse than what I was going through. I was wrong. What happened to me and Kelsey was worse, and they leave scars as well, only no one can see them."

I stood from the bed. "I've learnt scars, no matter on the inside or out, are pretty." He scoffed. I stepped closer to him and whispered, "Saxon, they're beautiful because they show what a person has been through. They're beautiful because they show how a person has come out of their nightmares with scars, but still they're living and proving that no matter what anyone will do to them, they can live on and be happy."

He closed his eyes towards the end. His jaw clenched tightly and he breathed hard through his nose, flaring his nostrils. Stepping closer again, I laid my hands on his chest. He flinched. I ignored it and slid my hands down to the bottom of his tee. There I gripped and slowly pulled his tee up. He let me, but still he didn't look at me. When I had it free from his body and his arms came back down, I moved my gaze from his face to his chest. I couldn't help it. I sucked in a breath and tears sprang to my eyes. His skin was puckered and patterned in burn marks.

"Not what you expected?" he asked quietly, but hard. Looking up, his eyes were open and on me. He flinched again when he saw my tears, and then he went to move to pick up his tee.

I grabbed his arms and cried, "No." He stopped and stood tall, his eyes now hard. I shook my head. "It hurts me to look at them." He snorted and went to move again. I pressed my hand on his chest and then leant in to touch my lips there. It was his turn to suck in a breath. Glancing up, I said, "It hurts me to look at them because I know you would have been in a lot of pain, and I would never want that for you. They're you, Saxon. They aren't ugly. They're you, and it shows me how strong you really are."

"Fuck," he snarled low and then ran a hand over his face. "How'd I get so lucky to have you?"

Smiling, I said, "We're both lucky. We've been through so much, yet we still find each other at the end. We're fated, meant for each other. And the hard times we've been through, and will probably go through again when you annoy me, are sent to test us, but I know we'll come out better for it at the end."

"Angel." His voice sounded pained. "Fuck, Nary. Goddamn, I do love you."

"And I you, Saxon Black." Again, I kissed his chest and then asked, "Will you sleep in the bed beside me?"

His eyes flared. "I can't. I won't… It's too soon to—"

I glided my hand to cup the back of his neck. "I know we're not there yet. All I want is to feel you with me."

He nodded. "I can do that."

"Thank you."

I went to the bed where my nightie was under the pillow and then looked to see Saxon had his back to me, only he was bending to pick up his tee.

"Don't put that on, please," I begged.

He nodded and sighed. "Okay."

Quickly changing, I told him when I was decent and then moved past him to the bathroom. After closing the door, I readied myself for bed and then stared at myself in the mirror.

The day had been huge. Having Kelsey leave, to Saxon

taking me to lunch and telling me he'd loved me, to arguing there and then in the car. Then with my parents, and finally in the bedroom. I was drained, exhausted. As I was sure Saxon was as well.

Still, after everything, I found myself smiling. I was about to sleep in a bed with the man of my dreams. My hand slapped over my mouth, and I giggled behind it. How he thought I would think him ugly after seeing the scars was beyond me. If anything, his hotness skyrocketed, and one day, when it wasn't so fresh, I would tell him.

Biting my bottom lip, I went to the door and opened it, only to stop still. Saxon sat in the bed leaning against the headboard with the blanket pulled up to his waist, and his gorgeous chest was bare.

"You good?" he asked roughly.

Shaking my head to clear it, I smiled and squeaked, "Yes."

"Nary?" he bit out, not believing me.

"Sorry." I waved my hand in the air and slowly approached the bed. "It's just, I've always dreamed of opening a door to see you waiting for me in a bed." Smiling so wide it hurt, I finished, "Actually, having it, seeing it for real, is better than any dream."

Wow, was that a blush hitting Saxon's cheeks?

It was, and witnessing it sent my belly fluttery.

"You're crazy." He smiled.

Nodding, I shifted back the covers and climbed in. Saxon slid down to lie on his back, and before he could move again, I moved in and rested my head on his chest, curling my arm over his stomach. I quickly tipped my head to his chest and pressed my lips there with a gentle kiss.

"Crazy for you," I whispered. My words got me a squeeze from his arm around my shoulders.

Blissfully, we drifted off to sleep together.

CHAPTER TWENTY-FOUR

TWO WEEKS LATER

SAXON

*L*ove. It was a fucking funny thing, only because I never thought I'd feel it so strongly for anyone besides Nary. But shit, the way Stoke, Malinda, and Josh had been that night at Dive's house had been... Christ, amazing. I held so much guilt and hate inside me for what I'd done. Didn't realise my own dad had fuelled those emotions, making me hate myself even more. It was why I'd driven Nary away. Never thought I was good enough for her. Not only had she proven me wrong, but her family did also.

Since that day, Nary and I had spent just about every

waking and sleeping hour together. I was surprised she was content to stay at the compound in my room with me. But I also suspected she was holding herself back by not returning to her apartment she shared with Parker, and also with not going back to uni. Both of those subjects I needed to touch on with her, but after Parker saw me the other day, it was time to broach at least the first subject.

It was early. We were lying in bed, and I'd been awake for a while holding my woman in my arms as the sun started to shine through the cracks in the curtains. Nary stirred beside me and stretched, her arse pushed back against my erection.

Hell.

That was what is was. Hell. Waking up for the last two weeks with a hard-on. Still, I wasn't keen on getting into her panties until I knew she was ready. Shit, we hadn't even kissed, and there had been a fuck lot of times I wanted to, especially when she'd give me her attitude about random shit.

"Morning." She sighed. How she knew I was awake, I didn't have a clue. She sensed a lot of things about me. Like even before I walked into a room, her eyes would already be on the door as if she'd known I was coming.

"Mornin', angel," I muttered against her neck as she stretched again. I bit off the groan as she pressed back against me again. Before I did something stupid, I rolled to my back. Instantly, she rolled over and laid her head on my chest. Her hand lazily ran up and down my scarred chest and stomach. She honestly didn't give a fuck I was defective.

Made me love her more for it. I cleared my throat. "Gotta talk to you 'bout something."

Parker had told me that he was moving out of the apartment, and since he owned the building, he'd already shifted into the one on the top floor. He wanted Nary to come back, make that place her home for as long as she wanted. He'd also suggested I should move in with her. It was a big step, but shit, I was ready for it.

She tensed after my words. I glided my hand up and down her back. "It's all good, Nary."

"Okay," she said quietly.

"Parker stopped by the other day." Her body tensed again. "Wanted you to know he's moving out and you're gettin' another house buddy."

Suddenly, she sat up, her back to me and ranted, "He moved out? Why would he think to do that? I was thinking I would go back there eventually, and I would feel safer knowing he was there. Since he's not taking undercover work at the moment, he was going to be around more. But now he's moving out, and I'll be with some stranger. I don't think I can move back there… I think I should stay here, in this room with you, but only if you're okay with it. I mean I know we're together, and you've never told me to get out of your space, but if you want, I could move into another room here at the compound, where I know I'd be safe."

I knifed up, placing one hand on the bed at her hip, and I leaned in, resting my chin on her shoulder. "Angel, you can't stay here forever. You need to get back to where all your shit is."

"You want me gone and moved in with someone I don't know?"

"That's not what I—"

"No! That's okay," she mumbled and threw back the covers, climbing out of bed. "I get it. I shouldn't have stayed so long without talking to you about it."

"Angel, get your arse back 'ere."

"No, I uh, I'd better get some things together. I mean you're right. I have to get back to normal." She looked around the room. "And I really don't have much here." She shrugged.

I got out of bed. Thank fuck my dick had calmed, and I wasn't stalking to her with a tent in my boxers. "If you'd just let me finish—"

Her hand came to my chest to stop me. "I'm sorry. I've stayed too long—"

"Nary," I clipped.

"I'll have a quick shower—"

"For fuck's sake," I yelled, before my hands landed on her shoulders and I brought her close, crashing my lips to hers. At first, she froze, until I touched the tip of my tongue to the seam of her lips. Then she melted, but I didn't want her lost, so I pulled back and barked, "You gonna listen now?"

Her eyes were hazy and her eyelids low. Her breath came out in puffs, and then she nodded.

"Finally. What I was gonna say, your new roommate, it'll be *me*. Parker was givin' us the apartment together."

She blinked slowly, and then, Jesus, her eyes narrowed. "Are you *telling* me we're moving in together?"

"Yes," I hissed.

"*Telling* me?" she huffed.

"Angel, I was a dick to the woman I loved for five fuckin' years. I ain't waiting and losing more time with you."

Her eyes widened. "Oh."

Smirking, I said, "Yeah, oh."

"Well, okay then. I think I'm down with that, but…"

"What?" I growled.

"Do you think we can try that kiss again because it wasn't the best, and I need to know if this will work between—"

Fuck that. It would goddamn work. I pulled her in again, wrapping my arms around her waist where I picked her up and mashed our lips together. She sighed, and I took that chance to sneak my tongue into her mouth. As I slid her down my body, my dick hard once again, I stood her before me. Our lips and tongue got to know one another again, and if the moan from my woman was anything to go by, she was enjoying the moment.

"Get out of my way, Viking man!" was screamed just outside our bedroom door.

Nary whimpered when my lips left hers. I threaded my fingers into her hair and brought her head against my chest. She'd be able to hear my heart racing in my chest.

"Not until you fuckin' talk to me," Dallas yelled back at Melissa. I had wondered when she was going to show back up. When I'd spoken to Stoke last, who was back in Ballarat with the rest of Nary's family, he'd told me Melissa had decided to stay for a little while for a vacation.

Melissa scoffed. "Now you want to talk? I thought you hated to talk."

"Well, I decided while you were gone that you're my woman."

"*What?*" she screeched. Nary started giggling and then looked up to me with a smile in her eyes and on her lips.

"So you're not the only one who *tells* their woman instead of asks," she commented.

I nipped at her lips and said, "No, angel, and it's somethin' you gotta get used to, because it's a part of all Hawks men."

She shrugged. "I'll work out how to get what I want one day." She glanced to the side and then back. "Though, you in my arms, I guess I'm already getting what I want."

"Fuck, you're gorgeous," I bit out roughly.

Melissa started laughing in the hall. "You can't be serious."

"Yes," Dallas snarled.

"Well, I don't want you."

"Bull-fuckin'-shit. What was with all the flirtin'?"

"I liked teasing you. It made my day fun."

Dallas groaned, and I knew he'd be running a hand over his face.

"I'm here to say goodbye to Nary, Low, Mena, and Josie. Then I'm going."

"You ain't," Dallas clipped in a warning tone.

"I am," Melissa snapped.

"You leave, I'll come after you, and you won't like it."

Melissa snorted, and then came a knock on our door. I looked down at myself. "I'm gonna get a shower."

"Don't shower on my account," Melissa yelled through the door. "I like looking."

"Christ." I laughed. "She really is the female version of Julian."

"Tiny lady," Dallas warned.

"You still here, Viking man?"

"Right, I'll lay it out for you. I claimed you, you're mine and I'm yours. While that happens, you don't fuckin' flirt with another brother or any man at all. If you do, you pay for it, and if they try anything, I will fuckin' stab them in the goddamn eye. If you run, I'll find you, and there will be hell to pay. You hear me, tiny woman?"

"That's the most I've heard Dallas say," Nary whispered, her eyes wide.

Chuckling, I kissed my woman hard on the lips before stepping back to grab some clothes. On the way to the bathroom, I asked, "That kiss, was it good enough to agree to me movin' in? Not that you have a choice, but I thought I'd ask anyway so you don't get your panties in a twist."

She stomped her foot. "Saxon."

Laughing again, I opened the bathroom door and shut it behind me. On the other side, I heard Nary open the bedroom door, and then Melissa say, "Men, they're all the same possessive butt-munchers."

"Ah, hi, Dallas," Nary said.

"Nary," Dallas bit out, and then there was a loud smack.

"Hey," Melissa yelled.

"That ain't gonna be the last time you'll feel my palm if you don't listen and heel, tiny woman." The door was slammed closed. No doubt Dallas had gripped the handle and pulled it shut before he stalked off down the hall.

Crap, I realised my mistake. I should of showered in another room so I didn't hear the goddamn girl talk. Quickly, I threw on my tee and yanked the door open to the room and then froze when I heard from Melissa, "Well, shit, that man made me wetter than a dish rag."

"Fuck." I groaned. Stalking to my woman, I kissed her swiftly before I kept on walking to the bedroom door. "Don't wanna hear that sorta shit. I'm headin' to another room to shower."

Nary's hand covered her mouth to at least try to stifle her laugh. When she nodded, I was out of there.

"Wait!" Melissa yelled. "I could use some sex advice."

"Fuck no," I yelled, slamming the door behind me.

NARY

"So," I drew out. "It's really good to see you again." I smiled, and then we both burst out laughing. Stepping close, I tugged Melissa into a hug, and then I asked, "Did you want to grab some breakfast?"

She moved back and shook her head. "I would any other time, but I really am here to say a quick goodbye. I have to get home and back to work." Melissa worked at a software design company.

"What about Dallas?"

She snorted and rolled her eyes. "He's full of it. He'll forget about me in a day or so."

I bit my bottom lip and shook my head. "I honestly don't think he will. Dallas is rough, stubborn, and gets what he wants. Like all the men in Hawks. He has his eyes set on you, and I can tell you now, when you get home, check over your shoulder because he won't be far away to drag you back here."

Her eyes softened, only to narrow. "I doubt it, and if he does, he'll have a fight on his hands."

Giggling, I said, "I think he'll enjoy that."

She smiled. "So will I. Now, come give me another hug. I've already said a goodbye to the others."

"They're here early," I commented while hugging her.

"Yeah, they told me you're moving back into your apartment with Saxon, which is bloody exciting, so they're here to help."

"Really?"

Her brows rose. "Yes, why?"

"It was only this morning when Saxon *told* me he was going to be my new roommate."

She threw her head back and laughed. "The Hawks men sure do know how to get what they want, no matter what."

"Exactly." I grinned.

Again, she rolled her eyes. "Anyway, I'll miss you."

"You won't for long, if Dallas has anything to do with it."

"We'll see."

"Yes, we will." I nodded. She started for the door. "Melissa," I called. She turned to face me, her hand on the handle. "I'll miss you too, and thank you again."

"Anything for a sister." She smiled, winked, and walked out the door with a "See you on the flip side."

"See you soon," I whispered, because she was right. Hawks men did know how to get their way.

CHAPTER TWENTY-FIVE

ONE WEEK LATER

NARY

*S*axon was my dreamcatcher. The nightmares were gone. I'd been sleeping like a baby, and every morning I woke with a smile because I had my man at my back. The night after we'd moved in, we spent it with friends talking and drinking. Then he tried to go into the spare room to sleep. I'd yelled. He'd cursed and stomped into our bedroom. At least he'd been stripping off his clothes and climbing into *our* bed when I'd finally walked in.

He'd thought I would want to adjust being back in the apartment on my own. Stupid man didn't get that the only thing helping me adjust faster was him at my side.

Never in my wildest dreams did I think Saxon and I could be as we were. We were living together, we were happy, and even through our arguments, I knew I was safe. While he would never be a man who brought flowers home, who took me to fancy places to eat, he still showed his devotion every single day. He was a simple man who enjoyed our time together watching movies, talking, and even spending time with our friends or family. He was perfect. Better than I'd imagined, and I had pictured a lot about what we could be.

Only, I was ready to move into the next stage. I still wasn't sure if that made me the bad person in our relationship because I wanted to be with the man I loved after being violated. And I didn't know how to approach the subject about it.

"Nary?" Kelsey asked on the other end of the phone, gaining my attention.

"Sorry, honey. I was elsewhere."

"Saxon?" I could hear the smile in her voice.

Laughing, I said, "Yes. But I don't want to talk about him. I want to know everything that has happened since the last time we spoke." I moved from the bedroom and down the hall, with my mobile to my ear, to see Saxon sitting in the living room with his feet up on the coffee table. He was watching some bike repair show on the TV. It was Saturday, and Kelsey and I liked to call each other every Saturday since she'd been gone. We also Skyped in the middle of the week, just so we could see each other.

She was loving America. Gypsy made her move effortless. He was also a devoted man. I could hear how happy she was with every word. She was sounding confident as each week passed, but still, there were moments... We all had moments our dark times touched us. Even if it was a passing thought, or a loud noise in a quiet room, or even a memory set off by something we were doing or eating.

Dark moments would always arise.

At least with the people around us, we were able to beat them back when they came.

"T-things are good. I've been venturing out more. Gypsy takes me places when he has the time off and teaches me things about the area. I-I've finally met Mason and his woman, Willa." She giggled. "At first, I was so scared, Nary. H-he's very intimidating. But after seeing how he was with Willa for a while, I knew he was l-like the Hawks men. A man who cares deeply. I-I knew he wouldn't do anything to harm me." A voice in the background said something. "I-I know, Gypsy."

"What did he say?" I asked.

"He said he would have kept me safe anyway."

"Of course he would. But tell him to stop listening in on our conversation."

"Nary." She laughed. "Pardon?" she asked who I assumed was Gypsy. "Nothing." She sighed. "Nary said to s-stop listening in to our conversation."

I heard a bark of laughter. All of a sudden, his voice was close enough I could hear him. "Darlin', I bet your man is listenin' as well."

"Saxon wouldn't do that, Gypsy," I told him, which got me another round of laughter.

"Angel, Gypsy's right."

"Saxon," I snapped.

Both men chuckled.

"Nary?" Kelsey said, getting back on the line with humour in her voice.

"I'm here, honey."

"I nearly forgot to tell you. Gypsy s-said I could try working for him. See how I go."

I warmed at how hard Kelsey was trying. She was happy. More than happy. Even though Kelsey and Gypsy hadn't moved past any stages from a gentle touch or lip touch to the forehead or neck, she was madly in love with him, and from what I could tell, him her as well.

"Wow, honey," I whispered, "that is fantastic. But take every day as it comes, and please don't be disappointed if things don't go well at first." I didn't want her to get her hopes destroyed if she ended up having a panic attack or anything.

"I know, I won't," she quietly answered.

Moving into the kitchen, I looked out the window. "Honey," I said gently, "I haven't said this in a while, but I want you to know I'm proud of you."

"Nary." Her voice quivered.

"You amaze me, Kelsey. Moving forward right into living and reaching for things you want. It's beautiful, honey."

It also made me realise I was still holding back. I hadn't returned to uni because I... I wasn't interested in the journalism course I was doing. I wanted my life to mean something more, and it was time I set out to achieve it.

"I miss you," Kelsey said suddenly.

"And I miss you, but talking with you each week helps."

"Yes," she agreed.

"Kelsey?"

"Yes, Nary?"

"Are you smiling?"

She sighed contently and said, "Yes, always now."

"I'm glad."

"So am I."

"I'm going to let you go now."

"Until our Skype date."

"Yes. Bye, Kelsey."

"Bye, Nary. Adore you."

"And you." I grinned at our usual sign-off before I hung up and placed my phone on the bench. I didn't move. I remained staring out the window. After everything Kelsey had been through, I was ecstatic that she was finally getting her happily ever after with a man like Gypsy. A man who was caring and wanted to show her that living was worth it. A man who wanted to show Kelsey that everything in the world wasn't bad, and if she wanted peace in her life, he went out of his way to make sure she got it.

She was shining.

"Angel?" Saxon's warm front pushed against my back. His arms came around my chest, where he tugged me back so I rested my head against his shoulder. "You good?"

"Yes." I smiled. "She's happy. Safe and happy, just what I wished for her."

"He's a good guy, angel."

"He is. I hope one day we could take a trip over there to visit his home town."

"Hell yeah, Nary. Sounds like a plan."

"Good." I grinned.

Saxon leant down and kissed my neck. He was kissing me a lot lately. Every time we passed in a room or if he was heading out with a brother and left me at the compound with Low in the reception area. Every chance he got, he kissed me, and I loved it. His lips were made for mine. Every time they touched, a spark of passion would jolt through me.

"Heard she was gonna try out working for Gypsy."

"She sounds so excited about it."

"Hope it goes well then."

"So do I. Though, even if it doesn't, I know Gypsy will take care of her."

"He will, like I would you, which brings us, in a round-about way, to you and uni."

Sighing, I shifted to the side and admitted, "I know I've been putting it off." He raised a brow as he leant back into the bench. I rolled my eyes and moved to the table, then sat. "Yes, even when you've tried to talk about it in the past week." I bit my bottom lip, my eyes to the table. "I'm thinking I don't want to continue with journalism. It doesn't feel right for me any longer. It used to excite me, but... not anymore. And starting over could take time. I had money saved from my job at the movie theatre, but it's dwindling down, so I need to get back to work. Hopefully they'll take me on again. Then I don't know if I can afford to change my mind on my career choice so late in the game. Especially since I would have finished my course in the next year."

Lifting my gaze, because I heard his footsteps approach, I jerked back when I found him already in front of me. He picked me up out of my chair, and sat, placing me on his lap, so I was sitting sideways on his. I curled an arm around his neck to hold on while he moved his arms around my waist, bringing me in close to him.

"You're Nary May, you're Hawks, and you're my woman. You can do whatever the fuck you want, and we'd still be there at your back."

My belly twirled in pleasure. "But—"

"No buts, angel. What you wanna do?"

I averted my gaze to the side. What I wanted to do was so different from journalism, but I felt it would bring me peace to help others.

Saxon jiggled his legs under me. "Gorgeous?" Once he caught my eyes, he asked again, "What you wanna do?"

"I was thinking of doing something similar to Josie, only she wants to help young children. I would like to help women in domestic violence. Still I also want to help young adults, but then again…"

He jiggled his knee again. "Fuckin' awesome you wanna help women and such out, but what will it entail?"

Shrugging, I said, "A diploma in counselling, a certificate

IV in youth work, and a certificate in life coaching, and that should cover all my bases."

"How long?"

"Another year and a half, maybe two. Depends how I can do it all while working."

He gave me a squeeze and ordered, "Do it."

Snorting, I said, "It's that easy, hey?"

"Angel, what you wanna do, help women and children out when they need it most is a giving job. It's gonna be fuckin' hard though when you see cases you can't find an answer to or they won't listen to you."

"I know," I whispered.

"As long as you're prepared for it and it's what you want, then yeah, Nary, it's that easy." He kissed my neck, then nibbled his way up to my ear. It was there I froze from his next words. "My woman's been through hell. She wants something different in life, she gets it. Nothing you wanna reach for is untouchable. I'll make sure of it."

"Saxon," I said breathily. My hand slid up his chest where I took hold of his tee.

He shifted back to capture my misty eyes. "I believe you can do this, and when times are hard, I'll have your back, angel. I'll always have your back. Fuckin' love you." All I could do was nod. My bottom lip trembled and I watched his gaze roam my face. His eyes softened with tenderness as he slid his hand to my face and cupped my cheek. "Now, you gonna kiss your man before you start bawling?"

Narrowing my eyes, I snapped, "Saxon."

He threw his head back and laughed. I waited until he'd

calmed down and met my gaze again, only just as I was about to say something, he got there first with, "My angel goes from soft and sweet, to viper, in seconds."

"Saxon," I bit out.

He gripped the side of my neck, his eyes dancing with humour. "Wouldn't want it any other way. I love your sweet side, but I fuckin' love your bite. Now kiss your man before you show me your viper fangs again."

"Sax—"

"Kiss me, woman, and I'll even cook dinner."

"Fine." I glared and then smiled right before my mouth met his.

CHAPTER TWENTY-SIX

NARY

*S*omething dragged me out of my sleep. I slowly blinked open my eyes to see the room still held darkness. Light spilled in from the hallway, I assumed from the bathroom. I must have left it on when I'd been to the loo. I wondered for a second if it was the light that woke me, only to suddenly freeze when a hand *in* my panties pressed against my mound. Saxon's gentle snore behind me told me he was still asleep. He was unconscious and copping a feel. A wave of lust tingled through me when his hand pressed in tighter.

Still, I lay there and waited.

Waited for the panic to set in.

Waited for the dread to seep in.

Only, it didn't happen. It didn't happen as I knew it was

the man I loved behind me. The man who with only a glance or touch drove my hormones crazy with need, a need to want more.

So nothing could take me away and place me back there in that hellish moment because Saxon Black, the man I loved and who loved me back just as fiercely, was there with me.

With his arm over me, he pressed himself in close to my bottom. It was then I felt his hardness. I stifled my giggle, knowing he would be shocked when he woke. Until then, I was more than ready to play.

I *needed* to play. My clit pulsed with pleasure.

Excitement caused a flutter in my chest and my breaths to come in pants.

Slowly, I pressed my pussy forward onto his hand. Saxon mumbled something behind me and then, oh God, then his fingers dipped in harder against my mound and one finger slipped through my lips, straight into my heat. I clamped down on my bottom lip to stop my moan. Sleeping Saxon thrust his cock into my backside again. He groaned.

Pressing my hand to his arm, the one attached to his hand in my panties, I tentatively glided my fingers down to see if he would wake and realise what he was doing. No matter how he acted, I didn't want him to stop. I had waited too long to have Saxon Black touch me, and I was desperate to caress him right back.

When he didn't wake as my hand reached his wrist, I shoved my hand under my panties to rest flat on the top of his hand.

LILA ROSE

But then Saxon stirred behind me. He thrust in again and then jerked back. "Shit," he hissed. He shifted back, and it was then he realised where his hand exactly was. I heard his gulp of air and then, "Holy fuck," he whispered the curse, probably thinking I was still sleeping.

Gently, he started to move his hand up, his finger slipping from me, until I quickly moved my own and gripped his wrist, pleading, "Saxon."

"Fuck, Nary. Shit, sorry." He tried to pry his hand out again, but I pressed mine on his wrist.

"Please," I begged.

"Angel." He sighed. "I don't—"

I thrust up and pushed his hand down on me and moaned. "Saxon."

"Jesus," he cursed. "We shouldn't—"

"I want to."

His body was tense, and then he exhaled. It fanned across my neck, making me shudder.

He leant in, his lips just below my ear. "We don't have to."

"I want you to touch me."

His lips smiled against my skin. "I am."

"More," I demanded.

His body relaxed into mine, and then, God yes, his hand dipped down again, and he slid one finger in, up and down. "Fuck, you're wet for me."

"Y-yes." I smiled. "It happens when your man is feeling you up in his sleep."

His hand stilled.

244

No!

"You were awake?"

"Oh, yeah."

"Christ, you're primed." His voice clipped roughly as he sank his finger deep inside me, then pulled it back out and up to circle my clit.

"Yes." I breathed the word.

"That feel good?"

Was he worried about me?

God. All I wanted was for him to keep doing what he was doing to me.

I ground myself against his hand and then back against his hardness. He sucked in air and let out a curse.

"Yeah, my woman likes her man finger fuckin' her."

"Yes." I moaned. I kept moving on his fingers and back against him. Still, a need to touch him was urgent. Reaching back, I slid my arm under his and down, straight into his boxers.

"Goddamn," he groaned as soon as I circled my hand around his dick and tugged up and down once. I lost his hand. I made a mew of complaint until he ordered roughly, "Take your panties off." He shifted and moved behind me, while I pushed my undies down my legs. I threw the blanket off us and kicked my panties to the floor.

I lay back and Saxon moved in close again. I sighed when his hand touched my thigh and he forced it down to the bed. The other he hooked it over his legs.

His fingers tickled as they danced up over my mound and then higher, pushing my nightie along with it, until they came to a stop, and my nightie was scrunched up under my armpits.

"Fuckin' beautiful," Saxon murmured through clenched teeth. He cupped a breast, moulded it with his hand and then pinched my nipple, drawing a gasp from me. "Stunnin'. Give me your mouth, angel."

I tilted my head to the side and up as Saxon leant over. He claimed my mouth in a sensual kiss while he glided his fingers down my body and cupped my pussy.

"Mine," he roughly growled against my lips.

I agreed with a moan when he dipped a finger inside of me, then added another. My hand searched him out again, and I wound my fingers around his erection. He pumped his hips forward, his dick sliding in and out of my hand.

"Fuck," he cursed and ran his lips down my neck where he bit.

"Yes!" I cried and ground down on his fingers, fucking myself with them.

Finally, I was getting a taste of what we could be like in bed, and it was beautiful.

His hand disappeared from between my legs. Instead, he gripped my waist and pulled me up on him so I straddled his thighs. His hands gripped my nighty, where he then tugged it up and threw it to the floor.

"Wanna see your face when you come. Want you to see me, know whose hands are on you, and know with each touch from me you become mine more and more."

"Please," I begged. I then arched my back and cried out as he thrust his fingers deep within me. As I rode his fingers and his thumb circled my clit, I lowered my upper body and kissed, nipped, and tongued his chest.

"Christ, fuckin' perfect. Meant for me."

"Always."

"Shit, yes."

I could sense it building inside of me, in my lower belly. It swirled, dipped, and caused me to pant.

"Head up, Nary. Sit back and show me yourself."

Leaning up with my hands rested on the bed beside his head, I sank down on his fingers. A shudder ran over me, a small smile of pleasure lifting my lips, and then I pulled back up again. As I kept moving down and up, my eyes remained open and on my man under me. To see Saxon below me sent a thrill throughout me. Still, I needed to touch him, to grip him. I reached down for him, my hand circling him, pumping his cock.

"Faster," he ordered through clenched teeth. "Fuck, yes." His groan spurred me on.

"Saxon," I cried, throwing my head back. I couldn't stop. I wouldn't. I rode his fingers in me while I jerked his cock up and down.

"Eyes," he demanded.

Tilting my head, our eyes connected, I bit my bottom lip and moaned in the back of my throat as my orgasm overtook me. My walls clenched around his fingers while his thumb circled over and over my clit. I came long and hard, waves of delicious heat rolling through me.

Saxon cursed. His jaw clenched and his neck muscles tightened as the first shot of cum erupted out of him, landing on his stomach. I kept pumping as he slid his fingers from me. After the last drop of cum came out, I slumped myself down on top of him, not caring his jizz would be all over me.

His hands cupped my arse, then he said, "Wasted a long time. But that moment just made up for it."

I giggled and nodded against his chest. "You can cop a feel in bed anytime you like."

"If that's the outcome, I'll be copping a fuckin' feel every chance I can get."

LATER IN THE DAY, we were back in the apartment and I was on the phone to Josie, when I asked her, "Do you think I'm making the right decision?" I had just told her my choice of giving up journalism to study counselling.

"I think you should do what you feel is right. Is this what you want?"

I leant over the kitchen counter, moving the crossword I had started earlier aside as I contemplated my choice once again. More than half of me was dead set on the change. I wanted to help others. The only small part of me that hesitated was my concern that what if it wasn't something I enjoyed, making the whole subject change a waste of time.

"I'm 80 percent sure it is."

"Follow your heart, honey, and it will lead you the right way."

"I've searched all about it, and I know I do want to help

people. Most counsellors aren't people with a past like ours, and I think actually being equipped with the knowledge of how bad days can get would be more helpful than someone who is blind to it. Even helping Kelsey, gave me a sense of... goodness. Studying it all has led me to want to reach out to women in a violent domestic situation. Teens in the same situation. Ever since... Josie, I have a need to help people through their own hell because I know, like you do, what it can do to a person. If, in some way, I can help ease their burden, their fears, then I want to." I groaned. "I sound like a fool."

"No, you really don't. It sounds like you know what you want."

Smiling, I nodded and then because she couldn't see me, I said, "Yes, it does sound like it. Come Monday, I'm going into uni to change my courses." My whole body eased from a tension I held over the decision I needed to make, since I had finally made a choice. The right choice. My smile widened.

"I'm glad. Now tell me, how are things going living with Saxon?"

Heat touched my cheeks when the image of that morning popped into my head. "Good," I sighed.

Josie giggled. "That sigh sounds like a sweet one."

Just speaking of my man sent warmth throughout me. "It is," I admitted.

"Honey, I have another call coming in. I'll ring you back shortly."

"Okay, I'll stay close to the phone, ready for your call."

LILA ROSE

I had only hung up the phone and started back on the crossword when I sensed him.

"How'd it go with Josie?"

Glancing over my shoulder, I smiled. "Great. It helped make up my mind. I'm going to do it."

He winked. "Glad, angel. Really happy for you."

"Thank you. The support you give me... I couldn't do without it." A blush heated my cheeks and I looked back down to the crossword. "Um, do you know the point value for the letter H in scrabble?"

"Wouldn't have a fuckin' clue, but do you know how sexy you look leant over the counter?" he asked, his voice coming closer, and then I felt his hands at my waist. I went to stand, but one of his hands slid to my back and held me down, so I was still bent over the bench.

The phone rang. Saxon ordered, "Tell her you'll call her back."

Nodding, I answered, "Josie, I'll have—"

"Honey, I forgot to tell you. I heard from Mum the other day and she wants us to visit her. It will also give us the chance to meet Austin. I was thinking maybe next week..."

Josie's voice went to the background, because I concentrated on what Saxon was doing. He had flipped the bottom of my dress up over my arse and he was palming my cheeks. I bit my bottom lip to stifle my moan.

"Does that sound like a plan?" Josie asked.

Next my underwear was pulled down my legs, and he went back to rubbing his hands over my arse. My pussy grew wetter and wetter with each passing touch, and finally he dipped a finger inside of me.

"Nary?"

"S-sorry, I was distracted. Ah, yes, it sounds like a plan."

"Great, so Mum said she would organise lunch, and I know she would hate us bringing anything, but I'd still like to. Did you want to come over the day before we go and…"

Her voice faded once again when Saxon added another finger and thrust it hard inside of my slickness.

"So wet," he rumbled.

"Yes," I breathed.

"So what time suits you?" Josie asked.

Oh, God. I'd forgotten I was on the phone.

"Um, what for again?"

Josie giggled. "It's only a guess here, but is Saxon in the room with you?"

"Yes," I squeaked when Saxon bit my arse cheek.

"Honey," she started with humour in her voice, "call me back when you're free."

A tongue slid against my folds.

"O-okay," I stuttered. "Bye," I added quickly before I ended the call and dropped my phone to the bench. "Saxon," I cried as he spread my lips and tongued my clit.

"Seeing your arse bent over, I couldn't resist," he told me before kissing me down below again. I pushed back onto his mouth and was rewarded with a groan from him. "Soaked in juices for me."

"Yes." I nodded and then rested my head on the bench while my man ate me out. Then I heard the zipper to his jeans being lowered. I turned my head to the side so I could see him pull his cock free. He palmed himself.

"So fuckin' good," he said. "Goddamn, you make me so hard." He went back to kissing my pussy, driving his tongue in and out while his finger moved over my clit. The tightness was back. I was going to explode. I ground myself down on his face and finger. "Come for me," he ordered. "Wanna feel it on my tongue."

"H-hell," I cried, just before my orgasm burst and Saxon's tongue pushed back inside of me. "Yes!" I mewed.

As I came down, my legs felt like jelly. Saxon took one last lick, sending a shudder through me and then bit my arse cheek. Standing, I turned to face him to see he was still palming his cock. Quickly, I got to my knees.

It's Saxon.

I can and will do anything for my man.

He wouldn't force me, hurt me.

His hand dropped away from his dick when I took it within my mouth.

"Christ," he clipped out on a groan. "Shit, angel, you don't have—"

Shifting back, I said, "I want to." Then I sucked him in again. I cupped his balls and gently ran my hand over them.

"Yeah, fuck. Yes."

His balls shrank up; he was close. One of his hands slid down my back, and I shuddered in pleasure when he slipped two fingers inside of me and began pumping. He removed them, and I glanced up to his face to see him suck on his fingers while his eyes were heated and hooded looking down on me taking him.

"You ready?" he asked through clenched teeth.

Damn, he was one sexy man.

He cupped my neck. My eyes fixed on his, wanting to watch him lose control. At the first squirt of his cum, I drank back and kept on drinking when more came. He cursed, threw his head back, and pumped his cock into my mouth until the last drop touched my tongue.

His gaze returned to mine while I licked the tip of his dick before leaning back on my knees. Saxon reached out and pulled me to him. I went willingly and moaned when his lips crashed into mine in one hot and heavy kiss.

CHAPTER TWENTY-SEVEN

ONE WEEK LATER

SAXON

Standing from my knees, I looked down at my work and smiled. I'd just spent two hours airbrushing the final touches to a customer's Harley. He'd wanted a skull bursting out of some flames on the tank, which was what he got. Only, when he started his ride and it'd heat up from the exhaust pipe, he'd see the hidden skulls there also. I was fuckin' proud of it and was looking forward to showing the client.

Glancing over to the wall where the clock was, I saw it was close to closing time. Which meant my woman should be back soon with Josie and Low after a day of shopping.

She'd wanted me to go, but I did not shop for small crap for the apartment. Anything with a motor, fine, I was in. The rest, I was leaving up to Nary.

I was over at the sink washing my hands when I felt small hands at my waist.

"That had better be my angel and not a brother," I said with a smile on my lips.

My woman giggled behind me. I quickly dried my hands and turned, tagging her at the back of the neck where I pulled her forward so our fronts clashed. Leaning down, I touched my lips to hers. However, since it was Nary, the kiss went from mild to hot in seconds. Our tongues tangled, our lips slid over each other, and then after the dickhead brothers started catcalling, I bit her bottom lip before offering her a quick peck and then pulled back.

My forehead rested against hers, and I moved my other hand from her waist to behind her back where I gave the finger to the brothers still giving us shit.

"Missed me?" She smiled.

"Missed your mouth." I smirked.

She slapped my arm, nipped at my lips, then shifted back. "It's lucky you're pretty or I wouldn't put up with you."

"Lies. All fuckin' lies." I chuckled. "You'd have me even if I wasn't goddamn good-lookin'. I'd make sure of it."

She rolled her eyes. "That I believe."

Moving off, I curled my arm around her shoulders and started for the office. "How'd shoppin' go?"

"Good." She grinned. "The girls and I are about to take it

back to our place in Low's car, and then we thought about heading out for a drink tonight. Would you be down with that?"

"Sounds like a plan. I'll make sure Dodge, Pick, and Billy are up for it before I leave. Though I thought I was headin' back with you now." I stopped just outside the office.

"You can—"

"Vicious. Callin' a meetin', now," Dallas clipped roughly.

"Right." I gave him a chin lift, and he took off down the hall. Glancing back to my woman, I said, "Change of plans. I'll round up the guys, and you girls get ready at our place. We'll all meet you there before we head off for drinks."

"Sounds great. Oh, and ask Dive as well. I'll be calling Mena." With one last kiss, she turned to open the door as my hand slapped her arse. Fuckin' hell, I wanted my hands on her, and my fingers in her. When she looked over her shoulder with a smouldering look, I was ready to drop to my knees and taste her pussy. She winked. "Later."

"That had better be a promise," I called, walking off.

"It is," Nary yelled to me, and then I heard the office door close.

Entering the room, most brothers were there surrounding the table. I sat next to Handle and waited.

Dodge banged the gavel down on the table. "Dallas called this meeting, but there's also shit we need to go over for the club. Dallas first."

All eyes went to him. "I'm headin' to Sydney for a few days."

"What for?" Knife asked. Though his twitching lips

already told me he knew, like just about all of us, why Dallas would suddenly want to head off on a plane.

"You punks know why. Once I get my woman—"

"If!" Gamer yelled.

Dallas levelled him with a glare. "*Once* I get her. I'll be headin' back with her."

"Damn, brother, she's a feisty one. You sure you can handle her?" Billy smirked.

"If not, I'll give her a go," Knife announced. As Dallas slowly stood, Knife quickly threw up his hands shouting, "Joke, brother, joke."

"Right," Dodge called. "Wish you luck, brother. If you ever need anything, just fuckin' call, yeah?"

Dallas grunted. "Will do."

"Which means, some of you will hav'ta pick up his job while he's gone." Some groaned. "Fuck off pussies." Dodge glared. "Also, Fang called earlier. He's been takin' care of shit at the strip clubs that got hit by the fires and said they'll be finished with the renovations in about two weeks. Teasers has been expanded, which means we'll be bringing in more clients. We're gonna need to hire more girls to dance, and Julian is comin' down to teach them some new moves." He eyed us all. "What I'm also gettin' at is the place will need more security. Handle, you work it out with two other brothers. I want three on rotation. Even with the bouncers from the firm Talon uses, I want extra protection."

"The women must have golden twats or somethin'," Gamer said.

"This place will be the most upscale strip joint in all of

Victoria. Every prick will want to go there to see the best girls there are."

"Hell, can I live there?" Knife asked. For some reason, I glanced to a silent Beast sitting next to Knife, and I saw the scowl on his face directed at Knife. What it was about I didn't have a fucking clue. Though, something inside of me told me I didn't really want to know either.

Dodge, ignoring Knife, went on, "Beast, since Dallas will probably be away still when the club is ready, I need you to install your equipment all over it."

Beast gave him a chin lift. I'd often wondered why the brother wouldn't talk, but it seemed no one knew. We all accepted him the way he was, and he'd somehow get his point across with a look or a text. Even if those were only few, it seemed he just didn't like to communicate.

Shit, we all had our demons. It was up to him to share them so we could help.

"Anyone got anything else they need to add?" Dodge asked. The room was silent. "We're done then." He slammed the gavel down onto the table once again.

The room started to clear out. I got up and went to where Dodge, Pick, Billy, and Dive were.

"Nary was here. The women want to head out for a few drinks tonight. You all in?"

"Sure. Drunk Josie is a hell'va fun." Billy smirked. Pick rolled his eyes, but he did so smiling.

"I'll ask Mena when I get home, see if Jason or Blue's ma would mind Koda. Let you know later," Dive said with a chin lift before he left the room.

"I'm down. I'll throw the kids over to Dive's and get Jason to mind them. His girl and him love lookin' after the kids."

"Right. Gonna head back to see what shit my woman bought to make the apartment all girly."

Dodge snorted. "You didn't advise her not to go over-board before she left?"

Shrugging, I said, "Nope. I don't really give a fuck what she changes, as long as she's happy with it."

"Fuck. How'd we all get so whipped?" Pick asked. "Actually, don't answer it. I already know."

"Yeah." Billy grinned. "Love of a good woman."

THE MUSIC WAS PUMPING. The place was crowded, and usually that shit would drive me crazy. That night it didn't because I was watching my woman enjoying herself with her girls.

I stood at the bar with my brothers as we watched the women out on the dance floor moving their bodies to the music. Actually, I didn't have a clue what all the women were doing. I only had eyes for mine. She had her arms up in the air while her hips and arse swayed back and forth to whatever fucked-up song was playing.

They'd been at it for the last hour. My dick was goddamn hard.

"How long we been here?" Dive asked. His woman had

thrown herself into the girl group well. She looked at ease with them, and they seemed to love having her around.

"Too bloody long," Dodge groaned. I glanced to see Low dip and shake her arse with her head turned and eyes on her man.

My brothers and I had only a drink or two because we all drove, so we weren't really feeling it. Still, we'd stay as long as the women did because we wanted them to have a good time.

"Fuck off, Fang," was screamed off the side of us. We all looked there to see dickhead Jerimiah gripping a woman's arm and spinning her to face him. Before he got to say anything, she opened her mouth and yelled, "You left the club. You have no right to say what I can and can't do. Now leave me the fuck alone." She pulled her arm free and darted off through the crowd.

Jerimiah ran a hand through his hair and then glanced our way. His eyes narrowed on me, and he let out a curse before sticking his middle finger up my way.

Chuckling, I shook my head and even though I wanted to bite something back, I could see the concern in his eyes for whoever that woman was.

"You good?" Dodge called.

"Fine," he clipped, heading our way. Billy placed a beer bottle in his hand, which he swigged back.

"Woman trouble?" Dive asked.

"In a way." He shook his head. "I gotta get outta here."

"Hey," I called as he started to walk off. "You need anythin', you're Hawks. We got you."

His head jerked back, his eyes widening, and then he smirked and sent a salute.

"Aw." Billy smiled. "Our little Vicious is growing up."

Snorting, I rolled my eyes. "Fuck off, idiot."

"I've had enough," Pick stated. "We're gettin' our woman home." He looked to Billy who smiled big, and they both headed to the dance floor to claim Josie.

"I'm so down with that idea," Dive said.

"Fuck, yes," Dodge agreed.

Shit, I was ready to take my woman home hours ago. Thank fuck I wasn't the first to crash their party. Though, as the men led them away, the girls actually seemed eager to go.

Nary came bounding my way and threw herself against me, wrapping her arms around my neck. She beamed up at me and said, "Had the best night. Thank you, Mr Black. My girls rule da house." I chuckled. "Hey, I forgot to say to you, before I left the garage today, Low and Josie showed me some of your airbrushing work. It's freaking amazing."

Smiling, I kissed her and said, "Thanks, gorgeous. I think I do okay."

"No, no, no. Not okay. You rock that shit. You really do. Let's go home."

When she'd said home, meaning a place for just her and me, my fuckin' gut fluttered.

"Home sounds good." I nodded, unwrapped her from me, and took her hand, leading her out to the car. The whole way my woman hummed.

LILA ROSE

Once driving towards home, Nary asked, "Do you want kids?"

"Why you askin'?"

"I love kids. I love them all. The whole tribe of Hawks kids, and I'd love to have my own one day. Since you and me are together for-freaking-ever, I just thought you should know. I want to pop out your children."

Jesus Christ.

How lucky could I get?

"Yeah, angel. I want kids."

She turned to me and breathed, "Yay." She shifted in her seat so her whole body faced me, while she leaned the side of her head against the seat as she looked over at me. "I guess, well, we should, you know...." I took my eyes off the road for a second to watch her raise her brows up and down.

Chuckling, I asked, "What?"

"You know," she whined. Drunk Nary was fuckin' funny. "We should start practising making babies."

Fuck.

"Nary—"

"No, really. I'm ready. More than ready." She yawned. "Did I mention I had a great night?"

Thank fuck she changed the subject. My dick was urging me to pull over to the side of the road to take her.

When we parked at the apartment, I turned off the car and looked to her again. Smiling, because she was sound asleep, I reached out and swept her hair behind her ear.

262

When I trailed my finger down her cheek, jaw, and neck, she mewed in her sleep.

I was glad she'd drifted off. If she'd kept up the talk of sex, I wouldn't have been able to resist her, and I didn't want our first time to be when she was drunk.

It had to be special.

CHAPTER TWENTY-EIGHT

NARY

Saxon was in the shower a few days later when I heard his phone ring. We were about to head over to Josie, Pick, and Billy's place so I could help her cook before we visited her mum for lunch in Ballarat the following day. As I walked to the kitchen, my mind drifted to the previous night in bed. Saxon had been in a playful mood. I'd lost count of the different positions we'd tried for a sixty-niner. Some were laughable, and those times made us chuckle at our efforts. Others were... delicious. We couldn't seem to keep our hands off each other. Even though I had begged for him to be inside me, he wouldn't. He asked for a little more time, and since we were still experimenting with each other, I was happy to wait.

"Hello, Saxon's phone, Nary speaking," I said with a

smile on my lips. I hadn't even looked at the caller ID. I'd just wanted to answer it before it stopped ringing. So when no one spoke on the other end, I pulled the phone away to look at the screen. The number was private. Placing it back against my ear, I said again, "Hello?"

"Want to talk to my son."

My heart started to race. It was Saxon's dad.

"No," I said, my voice low. I then cocked my head to the side, listening for the shower. It was still running.

"Let me talk to Saxon, bitch."

"You will never speak to him again. Do you hear me? Never will you be a part of his life. You are dead to him."

"The little prick can't cut me out of his life. I know shit about that bastard that could land him in jail. It's obvious you care for him, so do you want him spending the rest of his life in jail? I'm out the front right now. He's living in some fancy fuckin' apartment, thinks he can just forget about his old man. He can't. Tell my idiot son to get his arse down here. I want a word."

He was there, at our apartment.

But I wouldn't let him see Saxon. I would not have Saxon be fed some bullshit from the man who was supposed to be his father.

Not if I could protect him.

"He'll be down in a second," I snapped into the phone and then hung up. I quickly called another number and prayed I could get rid of his father before Saxon even knew he'd stepped foot near us. When the person answered, I said, "Parker, please tell me you're upstairs."

"Am. You good, babe?"

My shoulders sagged in relief. "No. I need you to meet me downstairs to oversee something, please."

"Be there in a sec."

"Thanks." I sighed in relief and hung up. I nibbled on my bottom lip, wondering if I was doing the right thing. Should I just let Saxon deal with it? No. Saxon had protected me in so many ways; it was time I stood up for him. For my man.

Swiftly, I grabbed my keys off the counter and marched to the front door. Opening it, I nearly ran into Parker. He flicked his hair out of his eyes and asked, "What's goin' on? Thought I saw Vicious was home when I got in from my run."

"He is," I said, shutting my front door and heading for the stairs with Parker beside me. "Saxon's phone just rang. His so-called father is downstairs wanting to speak with him. Saxon's in the shower. He doesn't know he's here, and I don't want him to either. He's not... his father isn't a nice man."

"Say no more, babe. I got your back."

"Thank you." I smiled and even when my heart was just about beating out of my chest, and my belly was a ball of nerves, churning over and over, I opened the entrance and stepped out into the morning sun.

There was an old man with a beer gut, and grey hair back and sides, bald on top, leaning against an old Ford sedan. He straightened when he saw us. A look of confusion came over his face, pinching his brows together.

"What the fuck is this?" he demanded, crossing his arms over his chest.

"My name is Nary. I'm Saxon's girlfriend, and this is Parker, Saxon's friend. Saxon's in the shower right now, so he doesn't even know you're here, and I would prefer he didn't find out at all."

The man chuckled. "You can get the fuck back up there, you stupid cunt, and tell my—"

"Speak to her like that again and you won't know what hit you," Parker snarled. "I suggest you listen to her and then get the fuck outta here."

Taking a breath, I asked, "Why have you come here?"

"None of your business," he barked.

"Then go and never come back," I retorted.

"I'll wait until I see my son," he roared and took a step towards me. Parker went to stand in front of me, until I lay a hand to his waist and shook my head. The man in front of me didn't scare me. If anything, I pitied him. He was an old, mean man. It was all he would ever be. Saxon and I didn't need a person like that in our life.

My hands went to my hips. "Nothing you can say or do will make me go up and get Saxon. You're nothing to him."

"You don't know all of him. What he's really like."

I laughed without humour. "You think I don't know? I know it all," I snapped. The fool blanched. "How you let his mother beat him, and when he killed her, you then took over the job and made him do things he didn't want to do. It stopped when the Hawks MC took Saxon away from you, and I'm glad they did. I know you're a pathetic, little old man who will never have the chance again to treat Saxon the way you did. Saxon is *my* life now, and I won't let anyone harm him in any way."

He snorted. "You'll let a kid who killed his own mum touch you? A kid who's nothing but trouble, who's tainted like the dirt he is?"

Shaking my head, I said, "No. I'll let a man who did everything he could to find me when I was kidnapped and abused. I'll let a man who knows all of my trauma and takes it on like it's his own personal mountain to climb and conquer. I'll let a man who loves me with everything he has, touch me, care for me, and is there for me no matter what we face. Saxon Black is my man. The only good thing you gave him was his kickarse name. Now, you're just a stranger we don't want to know."

SAXON

I'd just gotten dressed after a shower when I went looking for Nary. Panic set low in my gut when I didn't find her anywhere in the apartment. I stood in the kitchen gripping my hair, when I noticed my phone on the table flashing. Picking it up, I saw there was a message from Pick asking us to grab some eggs on the way over. Anger warmed my body when the message didn't fucking help to find where my woman was. But then I noticed in my caller log that a call to Parker had been made about ten minutes earlier.

Without shoes, I ran from the apartment and up to Parker's door, banging like hell on it. When no one answered, I bolted down the stairs to go check if Parker's car was there, only to come to an abrupt halt when I spotted my woman outside with Parker... and my motherfucking father.

Stomping to the door, I pushed it open, and then, fuck me, Nary's soul-touching, heart-pumping, dick-hardening words hit me first.

Stepping out, I clipped, "She's right."

My woman jumped and spun to me, her eyes wide. Parker moved back a few paces with a smirk on his face.

I came to a stop beside my woman and curled my arm around her shoulders, tucking her in close. "I don't give a fuck why you think it's right to come near me. I don't owe you anything. I don't want you in our life, and since the day Stoke took me outta your place, I no longer know you. You don't exist to me or anyone in my life."

The old man's jaw clenched. He narrowed his eyes at me and said, "I can fuck up your little happy life—"

I threw my head back and laughed. "You hear that, Parker?"

"I did, brother. Not good, old man, to threaten him in front of a detective."

Dad went pale. "You're a detective?"

"Sure am."

Dad just about blew a vessel when he pointed at me and yelled, "Then you need to arrest him for the murder of his mum."

Parker snorted. "That case has already been to court and

269

was ruled as self-defence. Judge would hate it being brought up again for no reason at all."

"He stole. When he was younger, he took things off our neighbours. He—"

"Fool," Parker barked. "You standing here dirtying their footpath with this bullshit is a fool's act. Tell them the real reason you came here."

Dad shook his head. His body sagged, the fight leaving him. All I wanted was for him to get the fuck lost so I could take my woman inside to show my appreciation for her words.

"I need money."

"Oh, my God," Nary breathed beside me. "You think you can come here and ask your ex-son for money after the way you've treated him?" Her voice was high and agitated. Goddamn, my woman rocked. I kind of wanted to laugh at the ex-son business.

"Shut it, you fuckin' whore. You don't know what I had to put up—"

Suddenly before him with my hand around his neck, I forced him back to hit his car.

"Saxon," Nary cried.

"Parker," I bit out harshly. I glanced quickly to see Parker was holding Nary back, and then I turned my attention to the old, fat man in front of me. I loosened my hold on his neck, just a little, so he could breathe, and then I snarled in his face. "You don't know me anymore. You don't know what I'm capable of. So you need to learn now that I never want to see your face again. I'm not only me. I'm Hawks. I have a fuckin' army at my back, and if I can't get to you to end your life, one of my brothers will gladly step up. I don't like the way you spoke to my woman. She's been through enough. What you need to understand, the man who touched her, took her from me, lost his fingers and tongue. He can't walk properly because of the way me and my brothers worked him over. He can't go to the cops because he can't communicate. He's not the first one I've fucked with, and he won't be my last. If I see you again, you'll be just another fuckhead who couldn't keep his mouth shut." Searching his face, I saw it. Fear. And then I smiled. "You get me." Stepping back, I said, "Get the fuck outta here and never show your face again. You hear me, old man?"

"Y-yes," he stuttered before he ran around to the driver side, got in his car, and took off.

Turning, I looked to my woman, who was eyeing me back with soft, sad eyes. I didn't want her eyes sad for me. I didn't give a flying fuck he'd come and tried his shit with us. I was older, stronger, and I was better because I had my woman at my side.

"Parker?"

"Yeah, brother?" His lips twitched. Hell, maybe he could see the hard-on I had for my woman. She'd had my back, wanted to protect me. I didn't care how he knew I was in a mood to have my woman, but he did know, and he thought it was funny.

"Ring Pick or Billy, tell 'em we won't be over to help cook."

"Saxon?" Nary said, her brows raised high in confusion.

"Will do. Have a good day, you two." Parker grinned.

"We will," I said with a wicked smile. Nary took it in. Her head jerked back a little, still not knowing what was going on in my head. It was then I stalked forward.

Her hands came up in front of her. "Saxon, don't be upset with me. I was just trying to save you from seeing that idiot man."

My strides ate the path quickly, and then my woman let out a squeal when I picked her up and threw her over my shoulder. Parker's laughter was left behind as I made my way into the building and up the stairs, takin' two at a time.

I had our door opened, closed, and locked in a matter of moments before I was stalking down the hall and into our bedroom. All while my woman was over my shoulder trying to calm me down, saying she didn't mean for her to deal with my father. She was just looking out for me, and she thought it better if I didn't have to face him.

I flung her to the bed. Her back hit it and she scrambled to her elbows and kept on going, "...really, you shouldn't have to put up with him. I was trying to do you a favour—"

"Angel," I growled out low.

She blinked, and said, "Yes?"

"What you did for me, trying to protect me, what you said, meant a shitload. You know how much I love you?"

"Yes." She smiled, her eyes warming.

"Good. 'Cause now I'm gonna show you how much. Been holding off, wanted it to be perfect, have flowers, candles, and all that shit, because you deserve the best. But can't hold off any longer. Wanna be inside you, angel.

Wanna feel you wrapped around me. You ready to take your man?"

"God, yes," she sighed, and I just knew her pussy would be drenched for me.

"Get naked, angel," I ordered and pulled my tee off. It was comical how quickly she stripped. I had my button on my jeans opened by the time my woman was on the bed naked and ready.

Slowly, I lowered my jeans and boxers and kicked them off. I stood at the end of the bed, my cock still hard as fuck, while I admired my angel on the bed waiting for me. A frown marred my lips when I said, "Fuckin' hate that it's gonna hurt you the first time."

"It will be worth it. *You* are worth it."

Climbing onto the bed, my woman spread her legs, and I could see she was soaking for me. Dipping in, I kissed her stomach, and she shivered. Looking up, I said, "You say the perfect things to ease me." Kissing my way up to claim her mouth, she moaned. Pulling back, I admitted, "Realised, this being our first time together, it will be one to remember forever."

Her breath came fast. "It will be."

I took my cock in hand and swiped it against her slickness. "Always hoped to lose our virginity together and finally it's becoming real."

Her eyes widened. "You mean my virginity?"

Shaking my head. "No, angel. *Our*. Never had anyone before. I knew it wouldn't mean somethin' unless it was you."

"But all those—"

"A ploy. Never done shit with them." I kissed her neck, bit her earlobe, and added, "They weren't you." I chuckled. "Fuck, Nary, I can feel your heart race against mine."

Shifting back, I saw my woman's eyes were wet. "Gorgeous?"

She sniffed. "You really have loved me forever."

"Yeah, angel, and I'll keep lovin' you for the rest of my life."

"I love you, too, Saxon Black," she said and then lifted her hips so my cock slipped past her entrance.

"Christ, woman. Need to know, saw pills, you takin' them?"

"Yes." She grinned.

"Thank fuck, wanna feel you with nothin' between us."

"Then do it."

"Nary, it's gonna hurt—"

"Do it," she insisted. "I trust you to take care of me, and by that, I mean also making sure I orgasm."

Grinning, I said, "You're on." I thrust in fast. She cried out when I felt the tear inside her, but I kept going until my cock was all the way in. There, I stopped so she could catch her breath. Her eyes were closed tight, her lips thinned. Goddamn, I hated to see the pain on her face. "You okay?"

"Hmm." She then opened her eyes and smiled up at me. Pulling myself out a little, I watched her eyes widen, so I stopped. "It's okay," she reassured me. "It hurt a little, but it felt nice also."

"You sure?" My voice was gravelly because, fuck, it was

taking all my control to not just fuck her senseless. My cock was near exploding inside of her. My woman was so fucking tight and wet. He was enjoying it. Shit, *I* was enjoying it, but I wanted my woman to also.

"Yes. Please, keep going."

Shifting out again, all the way until the tip just touched her, I looked down and saw blood on my cock. My woman was mine and no one else's. I wanted to beat my chest and roar in elation. Instead, I sank back into her tightness. She whimpered, her eyes closing, and a cute smile touched her lips. Leaning in, I kissed her. She moaned as our tongues played, while I slid my cock back out and in.

Going to one elbow, I kissed her one last time and then slid my gaze down our bodies to watch where we were connected.

When my woman cupped my neck, I met her eyes. "You feel so good," she whispered.

"Christ, so do you." I got to my hands, over her and ordered, "Look at us. Look, angel." She went to her elbows and moved her gaze between her legs, watching my cock slide in and out of her. A sudden surge of wetness made her slicker. "You like watching us."

"God, yes."

"Fuck, woman. You're gonna make me come."

Leaning on one hand, I slowed my pace, thrusting gently in her, and rubbed at her clit. She threw her head back and cried my name.

"Jesus," I snarled as her walls clamped around my cock. "Nary, angel. Hell." I groaned as she kept coming, panting and moaning. I couldn't stop. My hips pumped harder and harder into her. "I'm... fuck, I'm coming!" I yelled and shot my cum into my woman.

I kept pushing inside, loving the feel of her, and grunting until I was empty. I slid out gently and landed beside her. She curled into me, tucking her head under my chin.

"Worth the wait. You're worth everything," I said, my voice low and rough.

"So are you," she whispered and tipped her head to kiss my chest. "Are we really not going to Josie's?"

Chuckling, I told her, "Fuck yes. When we catch our breath, I'm runnin' you a bath, takin' care of you, and then, if you're up to it, we're makin' love again."

"Hmm," she said sleepily. "I love the sound of that."

EPILOGUE

NARY

*E*verything was perfect. I couldn't stop smiling, and my stomach wouldn't stop dancing and dipping in pleasure. Saxon and I had spent the previous day making love in just about every room in the apartment. Just the memory of it warmed my body. I was a little sore, but it was worth it. When I'd told him that, after he asked how I was feeling, he'd frowned. He hated me being in pain, but it was a discomfort I cherished. Which was what I'd told him, and then I'd added how much I loved that I could still feel him between my legs. It would mean that he would always be on my mind. He liked that fact, if the smug smile was anything to go by.

I had so much to look forward to. Waking up and going to sleep with the man of my dreams beside me. Starting my new courses soon and having my job back at the movie theatre, so I wouldn't have to worry so much about money. Even the arguing with the man I loved, I looked forward to. Strange to most, but not me.

When we pulled into the compound at the Ballarat charter, I glanced at my man and asked, "I thought we were going to Nancy's for lunch?" I flicked my gaze to the clock on the dash. "We're already running late."

"We'll get there, angel. Just gotta see your dad about somethin'. You comin' in to say hi?"

Rolling my eyes, I said, "Of course, or he'll get mad if he finds out I'm in the car and didn't come in. Besides, it is my surprise party." I smirked.

Saxon narrowed his eyes. "It's a few days early. How in the fuck did you know?"

I giggled. "When I spoke to my brother last, I knew he was keeping something from me. When I threatened to tell Mum about the porn he has stashed in the garage, he caved."

Saxon ran a hand over his face and groaned. "At least we know he's a weak link when it comes to his sister. You're just gonna have to pretend to be surprised. Your mum's gone a little crazy."

"I will." I smiled.

"Good." He chuckled.

I met him at the front of the car, and we walked in together, hand in hand. Once through the front door, Saxon pushed me against the wall and claimed my mouth.

When he pulled back, I complained with a small growl.

"Never get tired of kissing you," he said with a smile.

"I hope you'll never get tired of doing other things to me also."

He shifted his head to the side and clipped, "Woman, never talk about that when your dad is close. He'll have my balls."

"It's okay. I'll tell him I like them too much."

"Nary," Saxon warned, but he was doing it smiling. "Come on." He took my hand again and led me down the hall.

"Surprise!" was yelled. I pretended to stumble back, as Saxon's arm quickly came around my waist to hold me.

"Oh, my gosh." I gasped, and then I took it all in, the food, the people. Everyone was there from the Caroline Springs and Ballarat charters. My mum was being held by Stoke. She had tears in her eyes.

Saxon's chin touched my shoulder. "You really need to invest in some acting classes."

I snorted and whispered, "Shut up." Still, I felt choked up; tears even filled my eyes. What they wanted to do for me, the surprise, the thought, even when I knew, it meant a lot. I turned into my man and buried my face into his neck. "Everyone is so amazing," I cried. I heard laughter at my back.

"Hey," Saxon said softly. Looking up to meet his eyes, he gestured down. Glancing there, I saw he held an envelope. "Happy birthday, angel."

With shaky hands, I took it and opened it. A gasp left my lips, and I lifted my shocked eyes to his. He'd given me two first-class tickets to LA. "But we can't afford this."

He chuckled. "Angel, I make a shitload with my custom designs. We can, plus we're meeting Kelsey there. She's coming for the weekend to see you."

"Oh… Saxon."

SAXON

Cupping my woman's face, I kissed her again. I was right before. I would never tire of tasting her lips.

"Go to your mum, angel, before she bursts with excitement, and don't forget, play dumb about the whole party."

She giggled. "I will. You may not think I'm a good actress, but I can fool my mother." She gave me one last peck before turning and starting for her parents.

Then I heard her mum yell, "You knew. How?"

Stoke snorted. "Let me guess, your brother."

Malinda screamed for her son and then went after him with Nary following. It gave me a chance to pull Stoke aside. Hell, not that I really wanted to. Nerves were eating at my insides. Still, I forced myself forward and came to a stop beside Stoke, Killer, Dodge, Talon, and Griz.

"Vicious, how's things?" Talon asked.

"Good," I mumbled and flicked my gaze to Stoke. He rocked back on his feet and smirked over at me.

"You wanna talk to me, brother?" he asked.

Rubbing the back of my neck, I said, "Ah, yeah." Then Dodge's phone rang. We all fell silent. No one would ring on the day of Nary's party unless something had gone down at one of the businesses.

"Yo?" Dodge answered. "Yeah. Fuck. Serious?" A pause and then, "I'll send some brothers your way. Pick 'em up at the airport." When he ended the call, he looked to us and informed, "That was Dallas. He wants backup in his situation. Apparently, Melissa is married already, but something ain't right with it all."

"I'd go, but I don't want to leave Nary yet," I said.

"Nope, I get it. Gonna send Beast and Knife."

"She never mentioned she was married," Talon stated. "Shit, Julian would have said somethin'. Whatever's goin' on doesn't sound good."

"If he needs more than Beast and Knife, I'll send some more brothers. Until they find out more, we'll just have to wait," Dodge said. "For now, I'm gonna go talk to them, you lot enjoy the party. And, Vicious, go and ask Stoke for his girl's hand already." He smirked and then walked off.

Air caught in my throat, and I started coughing. Stoke slapped his hand to my back while they all laughed. The other brothers made themselves scarce. I rubbed at my chest and met Stoke's glare. Then the fucker smiled and again slapped my back.

"Knew the day was comin'. Was gonna give you more shit before I agreed to hand my girl over to you, but shit, this has been a long time comin'. You've proven yourself to her, to me, and to Nary's mum. I trust you, Saxon, and I'd be fuckin' honoured to have you as my son-in-law."

"Christ," I clipped.

Stoke chuckled. "Go and get your woman and make her even happier."

Clenching my jaw, I relaxed it and said, "Thank you... fuck, for so much. If it wasn't—"

"No." He shook his head. "I may have helped. But it was all you who got to be the good man you are today."

Emotions got the better of me. I pulled Stoke in for my own slap to his back. After I shifted back, I nodded, turned, and found my woman straight away. She was in the middle of the floor with her girls surrounding her. I started towards her with my guts on fire from all the anxiety I was feeling. Still, nothing would hold me back.

NARY

"One last thing, angel," Saxon said from behind me. I turned, but he wasn't there. My hand was taken and my gaze travelled down. My breath caught in my throat as tears filled my eyes when I saw my man on his knee in front of me. "You mean the world to me, Nary May. I fucked up a lot with us." People laughed. "I still want the chance to prove to you every day for the rest of our lives how much I love you. Will you do me the honour of becomin' my wife?"

Words.

I had lost them. All I could do was nod, over and over. Everyone cheered. Saxon took hold of my shaking hand and slid a ring on my finger, then stood. He swung me up in his arms where he then proceeded to kiss me.

I had been wrong. Everything wasn't perfect; it was more than that.

It wasn't until later that day, I leaned into Saxon and asked, "Where's Dallas?"

He smirked and answered, "Forgot to tell you, he's in Sydney trying to claim his woman."

I threw my head back and burst out laughing.

Look out, Melissa. The Hawks men knew what they wanted, and they made sure to get it.

"You happy, angel?" Saxon suddenly asked.

Turning, I wound my arms around his neck and looked up into his eyes. "Very happy."

He smiled. "Why's that?"

"Because I have your ring on my finger. I have your love, your body, and I get to spend the rest of my days with you." I gave him a quick kiss, only to pull back and ask, "Are you happy?"

"Fuck yes. I was never meant to spend my days living without my angel in them, and now I don't have to. I got you, Nary May, soon to be Black."

With tears swimming in my eyes, I whispered, "I got you right back, Saxon Black."

CANDID INTERVIEW

WITH MASON AND HIS REBELS

By MariaLisa deMora

Rebel Wayfarer's Character Interview conducted Sept. 14, 2015, by Erin with FMR Book Grind and Turn The Paige Book Blog.

Today is the day that I, Erin, get to interview the hot, sexy, tatted men of the Rebel Wayfarers MC. I am so excited, and I hope that I don't babble too much. These men make me drool something fierce and I hope I can keep my wits about me to get through this. So here we go!

Erin: WOW!!! *I walk in the door and see the most panty-combusting group of men I have ever laid my eyes on. I am already having to wipe the corner of my mouth.* Hey guys! I am so happy to be here!
Gunny: Hey, Erin. Nice to meet you. How's it hangin'?

Tug, reaching out to smack the back of Gunny's head: You don't ask ladies how's it hangin', dillweed.

Gunny, turning to glare at Tug: Fuck you, old man. Since when do you get to tell me what to do?

Mason, standing and reaching out a hand, gesturing towards the couch nearby: Ignore them, pretty lady. Come on in, rest a spell.

Erin: I want to start off with a few easy questions. I would like to give anyone who is not familiar with you some background info. * thinking to myself that if someone doesn't know who these guys are they are living under a rock*. So in the interest of getting to know you, could you all please tell us what your "job" within the MC is?

Mason: National president, kinda like everybody's favorite uncle some days, and their worst nightmare the others.

Bear: Um. I...the bikes are what I do. Build bikes, customize them, work with the fab shops. My pretties, the guys call 'em. My sanity is more like it.

Slate: Fucking liar, Bear. You settle people's shit when needed, but yeah, you roll that iron for the club. Truth spoken there, I guess. I'm just a local guy, standing in the top spot in the Fort, makin' sure our shit stays tight there.

Jase: Hi Erin, I don't think we've met before. I manage several businesses in Fort Wayne for Mason Industries. Not quite the finance guy, but I am responsible for the profitability of things here in northern Indiana.

Gunny: Job? Club job? I work for the city. What the fuck you talkin' about?

Tug: Jesus, Gunny. Can you go for two minutes without fucking up? So sorry, pretty lady, he's like the unwashed cousin most days. I'm retired, you might say. Retired to the Fort, where clearly these barbarians need lessoning on how to behave.

Gunny: Fuck you, Tugboat.

Bear: Guys, can we just...

Mason: Shut it. Alla y'all.

Erin: Now I know that Mason is basically the centerpiece of this club *and what a glorious centerpiece he is (cue the drool)*. What was your first impression of him?

Bear: Yeah. Well, you see him. He just fills up space. I guess if we were doing a word association I'd say 'powerful.'

Slate: Scary as fuck! Standing behind the bar in Chi-town, the man bowed up at me when I used Watcher's name, flat out accused me of spinning tales. He was scary as fuck. Then, the man set me up, put me against some powerful people there, all so he could take my back. Fucktard. Love the man like a brother, but he's a fucktard some days.

Jase: I'd have to agree with Slate. My first impression of Mason was fear. Not on his part, nope, I don't think he can spell fear. Not that he's stupid or anything, cuz he isn't. Well, not all the time. Did you see the truck he bought for his boy, Chase? That's stupidity, for sure. Anyway, my first impression was fear on my side of things. The team'd gone into Jackson's after a game and I thought for sure Daniel, he was the captain of the hockey team in Chicago, I thought he had lost his mind when he took us to that bar. It belongs to the Rebel Wayfarers, for God's sake. Then, I dunno, things just settled out okay. Mason turned out to be one of the best men I could ever hope to know.

Mason: Y'all need to shut up this shit. Seriously.

Gunny: I was afraid of him, too, but not for the pansyassed reasons these bastages have spouted. I was afraid of him because he saw things, things people didn't want seen. Secrets that hurt when pulled to the surface. I was afraid when he would look at me, scared he could see the fear ball I tried to hide for so long. No, shut up, Tug. It's my turn, bastard. So fear, but also…like you wanted him to be proud of you, so you did better than you thought you could. Does that even fucking make sense?

Tug: Yeah, for once you're making a fuckton of sense, Gunny. Mason pulls the best out of everyone he latches onto. Now. Now that he's found his place, found his role, his calling. My first impression though? Tough mother-fucker. He'd been beat within an inch of his life, betrayed by someone he trusted, yet he came out of it with his fucking head high, not held there with pride, but with a sure belief that he could do any-fucking-thing he needed to. Tough motherfucker.

Erin: Now Mason, what were your first impressions of your brothers?

Mason: These men in this room with me today are my inner circle. The most trusted men. Trust them with my life, have done so, would do so again without question. Tugboat has known me longest, and I'm proud to call him, and the rest of these rat bastards, brothers. Tug saw a kid out of his depth and offered me wisdom, telling me that blood didn't always mean right. Slate, well, I've never met a man with a greater want to be part of something larger than himself. He makes people around him better by expecting better. That's a talent you can't train, needs to be gut-deep, and makes him a valuable asset no matter where he sets his ass.

With Bear it was…pain. That was my first impression, and you know it, brother. Don't look at me like that. You know it's true. You showed me your angels that first day, and the loss rang through that garage like the lash of a whip. He's moved out ahead of it, finally, that wave that kept catching up with him for years. Moved past the pain, accepting it finally so he could make room for something else in his life. Glad to see it, proud of you, brother. Jase – this dude is my court jester, always got a fucking joke to throw into the mix. Helps diffuse things, but don't let that fool you. Man is fucking tough. Hockey tough, he likes to say. I call it Rebel tough.

If Slate had the market on wanting, then Gunny held it for needing. Man found what he needed in the Rebels, fucking glad we were there for him, know he's there for us now. Any ask we have, he's stepping up to the plate, ready to knock it home for us. Love these men, my Rebels.

Erin: Mason, you have a knack for reading people and knowing where they will fit. It is almost like you are clairvoyant. What was the defining moment that you just knew these men would become your family?

Mason: Erin, didn't I just go over this? Pay attention, gal, I don't suffer fools. Each man holds a different place in the club, and that place evolves with need.

Tug: (not distinct)

Mason: I hear you, old man, don't gotta whisper. I know that was rude. Ya know, Tug says he's retired now, but that wasn't always the case. He was my sounding board for years, still is. Holds an important place in my life, my brother.

Finding that person to bounce things off of is critical, because when people hand you power like this, like the title of national president, it would be far too easy to get all cocked up and high on yourself. Like I just did with you, and I'm sorry, gal. That was uncalled for. I need people that I can trust to tell me when I'm fucking up, not to just suck my cock and tell me what a good job I'm doing all the time, because I fuck up. A lot. I just have good men in place to help me deal with the shit that comes from that fuckupism. Sometimes you see the need, and then look for the person to fit the role. That was Bear. I knew what I wanted, a garage that could turn out bikes people wanted, would beggar themselves to own. A business to support my brothers, and our club in a way that took some of the money worries away. Then I found Bear, and he was custom made for the role. Still is, loves his pretties. The man makes some of the damn finest custom bikes in any of a dozen states around here.

Jase was different. Captain didn't come to us so much as we pursued him. Wooed and won him, and I knew where I needed him, but had to get the shit in place for what I wanted him doing. I knew we needed him, the man, and found his niche so we could keep him.

Jase: Awww, you love me!

Mason, laughing: Shut the fuck up.

Erin: Guys, same question. What was that defining moment that you knew that Mason and the Rebel Wayfarers were your home?

Bear: Well. Crises make for dramatic stories, right? I was in Des Moines, and had gotten sideways with a few guys I was investigating for the club.

Slate: Sideways? That's a weak fucking description, brother.

Bear: My story, Slate. Leave it. So I'd gotten sideways and then in the middle of everything, Mason and Slate and a dozen other brothers sweep in to the rescue just like the cavalry.

Slate: Saddle up, motherfuckers.

Tug: Shut it, let Bear tell it his way.

Bear: So I'm layin' there in my blood listening to Mason's voice coming from across the warehouse, and I realize, I would die for this man. For Mason. For the club. I would die and count it good. Worth the cost. Rebels forever...

All, voices low, intense: *...forever Rebels*

Bear: Yeah, so that's when I realized it was more than I'd thought. That it was deeper than family. That there's a trust and truth behind the connection we have. My brothers. I knew it went both ways, that if needed, they would step in front of a bullet for me, too. I'm a fucking Rebel, man. It's not a label, not a posture of pride, it's who I am. Rebel to the core.

Slate: I can't do any better than that, man. Tears, brother. Got me wet in me eyes.

Bear: Fuck you.

Slate: Not my type, man. But, back to the question, I knew on day two, I think. But, I'm a stubborn fucker, so I held out. Mostly because for so long I'd wanted something like the brotherhood I found, so looking at it, watching the men…it all seemed too good to be true. Then the day I patched in, I nearly got fucked in the ass by someone who didn't get it, didn't understand the truth behind the letters on my vest: L&R, Loyalty and Respect. We settled shit that day, and I knew I'd found it, that it wasn't a fluke. This was the real deal, and I was lucky enough to be inside it.

Jase: I think the incident that solidified things for me was when the club members rescued Sharon, my sister. I wasn't anything other than a hangaround at the time. A friend of the club, but far from prospect or member. But, without knowing she was my family, they saved her because she was Rebel. She worked for the club, so she belonged to them, and they felt a responsibility to her that went bone deep. So they rescued her. Because it was the right thing to do. Not always the easy thing, but the right thing. I knew from that moment on that I'd never have to worry about losing the family I'd built, because they don't let go…won't let go.

Gunny: Everybody's fucking longwinded tonight. I lost my Marine brothers, found my Rebel brothers. Found my place. There, good enough?

Slate: Fucking poetry, Gunny. I'm wet in the eyes again.
Gunny: Fuck you.
Tug: Pretty lady, are you sure you want to deal with these buffoons? I'm a little older, graybeard status rides easy on my shoulders. Means I've seen shit, and dealt shit, and now just don't give a shit. But the Rebel Wayfarers is one of the best-run clubs I've ever been privileged to see, much less be part of. How could you not count them family?

Erin: I would like to get a little more personal and have a little fun with it. Are you game?
Slate, motioning to his crotch: How personal we talkin'?
Mason: Jesus, man. Tie a knot in it. You got Ruby, and she'll nut you if you don't watch your shit.
Slate: Truth. Nuff' said.

Erin: How many tattoos do you have and which one means the most to you?
Mason: Full sleeves on both arms, rib pieces both sides, club tat on my back. Some tribal stuff. Couple of smaller ones scattered here and there. I have a memorial tat on my calf, names of the family I've lost. The piece that matters the most is the phoenix. It reminds me every single day that life comes full circle. You rise in triumph and glory, and then things wind up in ashes. It's how you fight to rise again that can define who you are. Don't let things shove you around, make you into whatever circumstances would dictate. Like Jung said, 'I am not what happened to me…I am what I choose to become.' That means you get to choose what your

responses are, what your new life will be. Become what you want, direct your own destiny.

Bear: Um. I don't actually…

Slate: Pussy don't have no tats.

Bear: I just never wanted …

Mason: Sensitive point, Erin. Sorry. He ain't even got a club tat. Mother*fucker.*

Bear: I just don't like…

Mason: Not even a club tat. I even hooked him up with my favorite gal, Dagger, and he fucking stood her up. Made the motherfucker pay for the session anyway. Like I said, sensitive subject there. Move it along. Who's next?

Slate: Oh, me, me. Do me next! I have a *fuckton* of tats! Got an angel with bowed head, naked upheld sword and his chromed 9mm pointed down, with the phrase "My Brother's Keeper" on my left shoulder, then "the journey is the reward" on my left-hand ribs. Wanna see? No, okay. Check it, on my right forearm I've got "we live with the scars we choose." That's the one that matters most, we'll circle back around, yeah? Custom dragon on my chest, it's a big fucker, took a bunch of chair time, his wings stretch from shoulder to shoulder and his tail drops down to tickle my dick. Then I've got "the past is practice" in a tribal band on my left bicep, and the ever-ominous, "three can keep a secret if two are dead" on my right-hand ribs.

Told you I had a bunch!

Left wrist and forearm, "never let your fear decide your fate" and then alongside that an accompanying black line drawing of a compass that kinda looks like a dream catcher, feather tied to the southward-pointing vane. This one on my right shoulder is a blackbird. Sweet cheeks, I see you're overwhelmed at the sheer number. But there's a story for each of them, yano? You got the time, or if you're buyin' the beer, I'll story you for each of them one day. But another day, yeah?

On my back, reserved for the club, is my club tat, complete with rockers. Full color, that motherfucker hurt like a bitch. Finally, I've got "bleed with me and you will forever be my brother" low on my back, down below my club tat.

The one that matters most is easy, like I said. The tat I got for Estavez' daughter, Mela, to celebrate her ease in finding herself after a hard fucking start in life. Like Mason said, you can let what happens to you define you, or you can slough that shit off and take the lesson that matters most, live with the scars that are important. Choose to allow things to change you, live with those choices, make yourself a better person. "We live with the scars we choose." Profound shit, man. Pro-fuckin'-found.

Jase: I've got a bunch, too. Most of them unimportant. This one, the one on my right shoulder? Each date means something. The top one is the day I met DeeDee, my ole lady. Second is the day I patched into the club. Third is the day I retired from hockey. That fourth date is when she married my ass, made me the happiest man in the world. The final one is the day we lost a close friend. I got long arms, though, I can make room for lots more significant days. Just don't want any more like that last one. I'd rather have good days than bad, but it's important to remember both.

Gunny: Pass.

Slate: The fuck you mean, 'pass.' You don't get a pass, motherfucker.

Gunny: Pass.

Slate: Gunny, you can't—

Mason, with a scowl: Drop it.

Tug, pulling his shirt over his head, showing the tattoo on his back of a soldier carrying a fallen comrade in a fireman's hold, with block-lettered words below, 'Some gave all': My back piece. It's for my son.

Mason, reaching out to grip Tug's shoulder, silently.

Erin: What is your favorite part of a woman? *holy hell where did that come from?*

Mason, barked laughter: Titties. Love to watch them pretty titties bounce. Soft pillows to lay my head, handfuls to play with, mouthfuls to suck on. Titties all day long, baby. Don't give a fuck if they can pass the pencil test, or hold up a bottle of beer, or any of the other useless tests you women put yourselves through to see if your titties are pretty. Love any titties. Big, small, soft, firm, titties on a woman make me hard, every single fucking time.

Bear: Lips. I love Eddie's lips. She can communicate entire conversations without speaking, just with the way she holds her mouth.

Slate: Hair does it for me. Love to get both hands wound up in my Ruby's hair, using that grip to tug her. Pulling her head back and forth, working—

Jase: I like the whole package, but if I had to narrow it down to a single part—

Slate: Did you just interrupt me?

Jase: No, it was my turn.

Slate: It was not. I wasn't done talking about the blowjob.

Jase: We weren't talking about favorite sex act, Slate.

Gunny: Legs. No, I like a woman's arms.

Jase: Make up your mind.

Slate: Blowjobs, love 'em.

Gunny: Ass. Definitely ass. Love ass. Full on, fukerton. Look it up, man. Ass, definitely. Mmhmm. Love that ass on Sharon.

Jase: SISTER.

Gunny: Woman. *Mine.*

Tug: Hips and legs, I'm an ass man, too, but not the way Gunny means. I love the roundness and softness, the way a woman gives when I push. Soft and sweet, love to wrap my hands around her hips, pulling her back—

Bear: Shut up. That's my mother you're talking about.

Mason: MILF, man. Own that shit.

Bear: Shut the fuck up.

Erin: What is your favorite thing to do in your down time? *I can think of a few things I could do with these men!*

Mason: Spend time with my brothers and family. I don't know what 'down time' is, because I'm always 'on' but that's okay, because I love my family. Can't think of anything I'd rather do.

Bear: I'm back playing guitar and doing little shows at

Marie's. You should come by sometime, me and Slate's brother play almost every weekend. Benny, he's the lead singer for Occupy Yourself, you might have heard of them? Writing lyrics has been a release for me, and I am enjoying putting those thoughts to music.

Slate: Have you seen my babies? Damn, woman, you got ovaries? If there are babies in the house, you need to see them! Love my little ones so fuckin' hard. Love makin' 'em more. Mmmm, yeah. My Ruby, she fucks like a–

Jase: The Foundation, definitely.

Slate: You did it again.

Jase, ignoring Slate's frown: When I'm not playing chauffeur to the tribe, I'm on the ice with the kiddos. Being able to bring hockey to kids who would never experience it otherwise means a lot to me. Some of the kids got skills, too. I see them going far, like Jonny and Kane. Tyler, too. Skills, man. They got 'em!

Gunny: Garage.

Tug: What is this 'down time' of which you speak? My life is the club, making the club better. I'm with Mason, there's no defining time without including the club's needs.

Erin: Where is the one place that you would like to take your woman for a getaway? You know sometimes we all need a little alone time, just to get away and focus on our relationships. I will even make this easy. I would go to The Keys. I am a big ocean lover. There is just something about that crystal clear water that makes my whole being relax.

cue babbling. Pull yourself together. This interview is not about you!

Mason, looking down, smiling: West coast, sittin' our asses in the hot sand, watching the waves roll in. Sea breeze bringing salt; lickable sweat coating her throat. Fuck yeah, there you go. Sand, sea, willing woman. Paradise.

Bear: Eddie and I have been talking about a cruise, but I dunno. It sounds like a lot of eating, and if we wanted to get busy we'd have to stay in the room, and then what's the point. I'll just keep her in my bedroom for a week, have the kids leave food on trays in the hallway. I can keep her busy that way, for sure.

Slate: Loved takin' my woman to that island Mason rented us. So fucking remote, we had to take a fucking boat to get there. Had to put my scoot in storage for a week. Fucking worth it, seeing her runnin' bare through the waves. Tackled her a couple times, gentle though, she was huge with our baby.

Jase: Babies, man, as in two of 'em.

Slate: Fuck you, I know how many kids I got.

Jase: But you didn't know. That's the point. She was preggers with twins and you were clueless.

Slate: She didn't tell me. All I wanted to know was if everything was okay, if they were healthy. And they were. So there. But, yeah, vacation, right? Critical lesson. On that beach, man, I found out fast sand and snatch don't mix. But the sun kissing her body brown, no tan lines anywhere? I could keep that woman naked all the time and be happy. Fucking Indiana and snow six months a fucking year.

Jase: Home. I'd take her home anytime. My home is wherever she is, so that makes it easy. Home in our house, home in the clubhouse, home in Canada or the USA. My special place is wherever DeeDee is. Don't tell her, though. I think she's got her heart set on Mexico. I don't speak the lingo, though. Hey, that rhymes. Lingo, though. Ha. So sounds like most of us like the sea and sand.

Gunny: Had enough fucking sand to last a lifetime. I bought a cabin on a lake over in Ohio, want to take Sharon there, find our quiet spot and just stay there for a while.

Slate: What the fuck, man. I didn't know you bought a cabin.

Gunny: Well, you don't know everything about me, fucker.

Slate: I should. I'm your chapter president. I should know everything about you, motherfucker.

Gunny: Did you know I'm about tired of your stupid shit, Slate? You want to push and pull at me all fucking day, you need to be ready to accept the beatdown that comes at the end of that fucking day.

Slate: Easy, Mountain Man. Bought a fucking cabin and didn't tell a brother. Fukerton, my ass.

Gunny: I ain't after your ass, brother.

Slate: Thank God.

Tug; Easy one for me. Vail when the snow files. I want to see Maggie there, in the mountains where the air is crisp and clean. Vail, or its like. Or Cabo. I could do sun and sea, too.

Erin: Now I am going to get serious for a few minutes.

Mason, you have had quite a few bad experiences in your life. I am interested to know how you think those experiences have defined your life and helped make you the man you are today.

Tug: Mason, be nice.

Mason: Brother, it feels like I'm fucking repeating myself.

Tug: No, this is different, man. She's asking about how you came to be, not what tenets you live by.

Mason: Yeah, so different. Sorry, again, Erin. To become a man, I think there's a recipe that can be followed. Good or bad, we all walk the same path at the beginning. Fear, loss, even rage, these are all emotions that all men feel. How you deal with them, that's what can define you. See the patch on Slate's vest, the one he pointed out earlier, L&R? Earned, freely given, loyalty and respect can go a long way to making a man who he needs to be. But, to find a space where that L&R can be tested, so you can find your mettle, be it strong or weak, that's a gift. Deacon—

Tug: Brother...

Mason: No, it's true. What Deacon did to me was a gift, because he showed me with every action, told me with every word, illustrated with every betrayal that what he was...wasn't what I wanted to be. Without that clear, brutal example, I might have drifted for years longer before finding my way. My lodestone. The club. A gift, because it wasn't anything I wanted. My daddy bein' what he was. Ma gone. Deacon was the clearest picture I could grab hold of. Then I found you, old man, showing me that lightness has a place, too. It's all good, Erin. Every single fucking thing that's happened to me, around me, because of me—has a reason. It's up to us to find out what that reason is.

Erin: Mason, where you see your club in 5 years, 10 years? And how do these men here with you today help you get there?

Mason: Tall order, asking me to tell the future, baby. But these men are the ones I trust to keep the club on the straight and narrow, to keep us moving the direction we need. I've been approached by international interests, taken a few trips across the pond, as they say. So far, I'm keeping us national. There's something to be said for America, and I'm proud to be a citizen of this nation. So in five years, or ten, I hope that the brotherhood we've built stands true and strong, continuing to support the brothers and their families in ways that matter. I hope that the brothers we have now will bring on other worthy brothers, enriching our family in ways we cannot even conceive of today.

I want to thank you from the bottom of my heart for agreeing to this interview. I was nervous coming in here today but you all made me feel right at home. You have the luckiest women in the world by your sides and I am so jealous! I can't wait to get back and get this posted to the blog! I am a devoted fan and hope this interview gets you quite a few more! *stands to shake hands with everyone and gets surprised with hugs instead! Holy hell these men smell good! They are like walking pheromones! And all that muscle to squeeze on! I am pretty sure I need a clean, dry pair of panties!*

Mason: None of that hand shakin', Erin. We're friends now, yeah? You stay safe, doll baby. You need us, you call us. I'll say it now, and these men are my witness. You need us, Rebels will roll. Yeah? Shiny side up, babe.

DALLAS

Why in the fuck did I get on the plane to chase some pussy? I had no clue, except when I saw Melissa snarling something at her motherfucking *husband* in the restaurant, I realised I wanted that for me. Her attitude. Her fucking tiny, stunning body, her shoulder-length hair where I could wrap my fist in it while I claimed her mouth. Just like I wanted to claim her body and mind.

How-fucking-ever, she was strong-minded enough to not be claimed anywhere but maybe the bedroom. I'd have to see if she'd heel for me behind closed doors.

The matter of her being married was an obstacle I could push over. Still, it was a pain in the fucking arse.

She hadn't worn her ring when she was back in Melbourne helping us find Nary, Vicious's woman, because I would have noticed something like that. So why had she hidden it? And why in the hell had she acted the way she did with me, like she wanted me inside her, when she was already taken?

None of it made sense, but I was going to get to the bottom of it.

Melissa was mine.

She'd decided to run when I told her not to. I'd fucking told her I'd claimed her as my woman. She had to have known I'd follow and find out she was playing some sort of game.

A game I was determined to win.

"Fuck," I clipped, and ran a hand over my face before picking up my whisky neat and taking a sip. Who would have thought I'd be chasing pussy? Not me in a goddamn million years. Yet, there I was. As soon as she turned up in Melbourne and gave me her attitude, I knew she was it. Even if I denied it so many fucking times, she'd gotten under my skin and once she was there, I couldn't stop thinking about her.

So whatever the shit was with her being married, I'd get it sorted and take her home with me.

A chair on each side of me pulled out. Glancing to Knife and then Beast, I lifted my chin and said, "Good to have you here, brothers."

Beast gave me a chin lift back. He never said a word. I wasn't sure if he couldn't talk at all or if there was a problem that kept him from speaking. Didn't matter though, he still got across whatever he had to say in one way or another.

"Glad to help out, brother," Knife answered. "What's the plan?"

Dodge, President of the Hawks MC Caroline Springs Charter, had sent Beast and Knife to Sydney as soon as I'd called him asking for some backup. It was good to have a family who would drop anything to do whatever you asked.

I had that in the army. Trevor Boon was a brother, but he didn't stick around once we'd helped Beth Cliff out of her shit in Ballarat with Stoke and Mally. Still, I understood Trevor had his own family shit to deal with, which was why I'd stuck with the Hawks back then. I wanted somewhere to belong, and I'd found it within the Hawks MC. I liked what I saw, the connection and safety they brought one another. I stayed, until I moved to Melbourne to help Dodge out with his shit. There'd been a few scum-suckers we had to clean out of the brotherhood, but now it was living free. I stayed in Melbourne. Guessed it was the best decision since I got to meet my tiny woman in the end.

Though, I'd soon see if chasing her was going to be the right move.

If whatever the shit she was playing was going to bring trouble breathing down the Hawks' neck, I'd cut her loose.

"We're staking out Melissa's place tonight. Want in there with you two at my back. I have to find out why she has a wedding ring on her fuckin' finger when she didn't wear one back in Melbourne."

"Done." Knife nodded and gestured to a waiter ordering him and Beast a beer. Once he'd done it, he slouched in his seat and asked, "She know you're here yet?"

I snorted. "Nope."

Knife smiled. "How'd you see her ring then?"

"I may be a big motherfucker, but I can be smoke when I want to be. Caught a glimpse when I followed her into the drug store the other day."

"This shit is weird. Anyone with eyes could tell she had a thing for you back in Melbourne."

Beast nodded in agreement.

"I guess we'll have answers one way or another tonight," I bit out as I watched my tiny woman hiss something else at her husband and storm out. I didn't miss the tears shining in her eyes either, no matter how far away I was. At the door, she paused.

Fuck, had she made us?

"Clear," I barked low.

My brothers moved in different directions while I slid out of my seat and under the fucking table. I wasn't ready for her to see me, not until I had answers. If me keeping low meant I had to make a fool out of myself by hiding in shit places, then I would.

There was a story behind Melissa's deceit, and I couldn't wait to find out about it.

When I saw the coast was clear, I sat back up and finished my drink. Knife and Beast appeared with fresh drinks, and Beast slid a spare one my way while Knife talked on his phone.

"He's here. We don't know anything yet. Okay." He sighed. "It's Julian."

Tipping my head back, I closed my eyes to the ceiling

and cursed under my breath. I did not want to have to deal with Julian, but I knew if I fucking didn't, he'd be on the phone to his girl, *my* woman, and she'd find out I was in town too early.

Taking the phone, I glared at Knife's smile and answered, "Yo?"

"What in the flaming hell is going on? You're in Sydney chasing my bestie and I hear she's married? As in *married*, married, with a ring on her finger and all? How could she not tell me? Do you need me to come there and slap some sense into her? I will. I'm ready to do some shaking and hair pulling to figure out what in the Jesus Christ is going on in her sweet little brain."

"Who told you?"

"Dallas." He sighed out my name; it sounded like he thought I was stupid. "You listen to me and listen well. I'm a part of the pussy posse. Nothing, and I mean *nothing,* doesn't find its way to my ears. I hear all when I have my girls at my back. Doesn't matter who told me, they're all protected by their hot males in their beds. What matters is if you need me to come take the wench out? What was she thinking? Why would she get married and not tell me shit? I mean really, what the fuck is up with that?"

"Stand down, Julian. If I can't work out what's going on, I'll call you in. But for now, know I *will* get to the bottom of this, and she'll be with me back in Melbourne soon."

"Good," he snapped. "I swear when she was here all I heard about was you. So to learn she's married does not jive well. Something is happening, and it's big. Take care with her, hero man, or you'll be dealing with me ringing you every day for the rest of your life."

Cringing at the thought, I then snorted and reminded him, "You were talking about knocking some sense into her not that long ago."

"That's different. You want to drag her back to your lair, bang her and claim her. All I want is to be her BFF for life. You'll be the one with her all the time, not me. You need to treat her with care if you want to keep in her panties. Hear me?"

"Fuckin' hell. Yeah, I get you and that kinda shits me."

"Aw, it's okay. Now you're going to be *doing* my BFF, you'll *get me* a lot more since I'll be traveling your way to see her."

"Do you want me to continue my play for Melissa or run for the fuckin' hills?"

"Play."

"Then do not threaten me."

"How is my time a threat?" he huffed.

"Forget it. I gotta get shit done, Julian."

"Okey dokey. Once you do, tell her I'm way pissed."

With a sigh, I closed my eyes and rubbed at my temple. "Done," I said before hanging up.

The first things I saw was Beast's shoulders shaking and knew he was silently laughing, while Knife threw his head back and just roared with it a few beats after I'd hung up.

"You wanna get a flight back now and leave her be?"

Clenching my jaw, I snapped my glare to Knife.

He whistled low, "Damn, she must'a got under your skin if you're willing to put up with Julian as her close friend."

I narrowed my eyes even more, but he just burst out laughing.

Flicking my gaze to Beast, I saw he was sitting there smiling.

Sighing aloud, I scrubbed a hand over my face. "What in the fuck am I thinkin'?"

Knife snorted. "Hoping she'll be your sunshine like the rest of the brothers have found."

"Maybe it'd be better to keep on as is," I said more to myself than my brothers. Then I thought of Melissa and how she'd sunk her claws in with her sass and smartarse mouth. She was embedded deep, and I couldn't seem to unhinge those fuckin' claws.

If her reason to why she lied wasn't good enough, I'd walk away and wash her from my mind.

If the reason for the lie was one I understood and could stand by, I'd get her out, make her safe, and fucking make her mine.

She wanted me. I wanted her.

It was time to make it happen.

Or at least see if it could happen.

"Nah, man. She's the one. You wouldn't do the chasing like you have otherwise," Knife said, and I saw Beast nod.

Rubbing a hand over my face, I said, "Let's head to the hotel. We'll get you two a room and then stake out her and his place. I'll go in if they're not there. If they are, we'll wait until they're asleep. Beast has my back in the house. Knife, need you on lookout. See anything fishy, text, and we'll get out."

Knife nodded. "Sounds like a plan."

Standing, I smirked and said, "By the way, the hotel we're stayin' at has some convention thing happenin'. You two have'ta share a room."

"What the fuck, brother?" Knife glared.

"Soon as Dodge said he was sending you two, I went and asked about a room. They had one left and it's a double bed one."

Knife groaned as he stood next to me. "Have you not seen our brother here? He's fucking huge, and you expect me to share a bed with the big motherfucker?"

"Well, I ain't sharin' mine." I laughed.

"Cold, brother. We're here to help, and you deal us this crap. If I'm looking thin in the morning, you'll know why. Beast would have squished me in my sleep."

Shoving him in the shoulder, I told him, "Stop being a pussy. Not like Beast here is complaining." My phone chimed.

Beast: **I'll go stay at another hotel.**

Shaking my head, I said, "No. Need you close."

ACKNOWLEDGEMENT

Thank you to everyone who has loved Nary and Saxon from the start, this book is for you. I hope you enjoy their story. Xx

Becky, thank you always for your belief in me. You kept me going when I struggled with such a hard story.

To everyone in the Hawks street team, thank you for your encouragement and help!

ALSO BY LILA ROSE

Hawks MC: Ballarat Charter

Holding Out (FREE) Zara and Talon

Climbing Out: Griz and Deanna

Finding Out (novella) Killer and Ivy

Black Out: Blue and Clarinda

No Way Out: Stoke and Malinda

Coming Out (novella) Mattie and Julia

Hawks MC: Caroline Springs Charter

The Secret's Out: Pick, Billy and Josie

Hiding Out: Dodge and Willow

Down and Out: Dive and Mena

Living Without: Vicious and Nary

Walkout (novella) Dallas and Melissa

Hear Me Out: Beast and Knife

Breakout (novella) Handle and Della

Fallout: Fang and Poppy

Standalones related to the Hawks MC

Out of the Blue (Lan, Easton, and Parker's story)

Out Gamed (novella) (Nancy and Gamer's story)

Outplayed (novella) (Violet and Travis's story)

Romantic comedies

Making Changes

Making Sense

Fumbled Love

Trinity Love Series

Left to Chance

Love of Liberty (novella)

Paranormal

Death (with Justine Littleton)

In The Dark

CONNECT WITH LILA ROSE

Webpage: www.lilarosebooks.com

Facebook: http://bit.ly/2du0taO

Instagram: www.instagram.com/lilarose78/

Goodreads:

www.goodreads.com/author/show/7236200.Lila_Rose